THE FIRST WITCH-MAGE

THE FIRST WITCH-MAGE
THE CHRONICLES OF THE WITCHBORN™ BOOK 1

ISABEL CAMPBELL
MICHAEL ANDERLE

DON'T MISS OUR NEW RELEASES

Join the LMBPN email list to be notified of new releases and special promotions (which happen often) by following this link:

http://lmbpn.com/email/

This book is a work of fiction. All of the characters, organizations, and events portrayed in this novel are either products of the author's imagination or are used fictitiously. Sometimes both.

Copyright © 2023 LMBPN Publishing
Cover Art by https://fantasybookdesign.com
Cover copyright © LMBPN Publishing
A Michael Anderle Production

LMBPN Publishing supports the right to free expression and the value of copyright. The purpose of copyright is to encourage writers and artists to produce the creative works that enrich our culture.

The distribution of this book without permission is a theft of the author's intellectual property. If you would like permission to use material from the book (other than for review purposes), please contact support@lmbpn.com. Thank you for your support of the author's rights.

LMBPN Publishing
2375 E. Tropicana Avenue, Suite 8-305
Las Vegas, Nevada 89119 USA

Version 1.00, November 2023
eBook ISBN: 979-8-88878-717-5
Print ISBN: 979-8-88878-718-2

THE FIRST WITCH-MAGE TEAM

Thanks to our Beta Readers:
Kelly O'Donnell, John Ashmore, Mary Morris

Thanks to the JIT Readers

Zacc Pelter
Jackey Hankard-Brodie
Wendy L Bonell
Deb Mader
Peter Manis
Jeff Goode

Editor
SkyFyre Editing Team

CHAPTER ONE

"Now that they've got it settled whose I be,
I'm going to tell them something they won't
* like:*
They've got it settled wrong, and I can
* prove it.*
Flattered I must be to have two towns
* fighting*
To make a present of me to each other.
They won't dispose me, either one of them,
To spare them any trouble. Double
* Trouble's*
Always the witch's motto anyway."

—*Robert Frost,* The Pauper Witch of Grafton

Brandon Cole had expected a call from Claire detailing his first mission for AID since being moved, but he had never expected *this*. "A witch liaison?" he repeated into the phone. "You're sure?"

"Yes," Claire replied, her tone clipped but still patient.

"And they want me to do it."

A pause.

"Ah," Brandon added. "I see. The simple tasks for the simple boys. I'm the new guy so I get the shitty job."

"It's not like that," Claire returned a second later. The noise behind her told Brandon she was calling from the New Orleans office of the Arcane Investigation Division. "This command isn't coming from me," she added, voice lowered a fraction. "It's come down from the Head. They want *you* to visit the local coven leadership and request another liaison."

Another. Because the first two had gone missing in the past few years thanks to a few highly dangerous missions chasing rogue mages across the states. Going to the coven leadership was always a pain in the ass, but it was worse now. There was no chance in hell they'd give up another witch. Claire, however, seemed to think Brandon, of all people, could do it.

"I feel like Jonah being sent to Nineveh," Brandon muttered into the phone.

"You're religious?" came Claire's light voice.

"No. I'm familiar with the story, is all."

"Well, don't get swallowed by a whale on your way. I'm sending directions over to you now."

Part of Brandon preferred to leap into the Gulf of Mexico rather than go out to the coven leadership.

The notification from Claire came through on Brandon's phone a moment later. From where he stood outside on the corner under bright sunlight, he squinted at his screen. "You're sure this is the place?"

"Of course." Claire sounded like she was beginning to lose her patience. "It would be best if you went today since we're tight on time." Brandon did not know why, and Claire sounded like she was in a hurry to get off the phone. She added one more thing before hanging up. "This is your big break, Brandon. It's what you've been waiting for. Don't blow it."

Brandon stared at his phone with the "call ended" message at the top under Claire's name and number. He blew through his nose and turned, half inclined to walk into the bar at the end of the street instead of going outside the French Quarter to find the coven leadership. Claire had been right about it being his big break, though.

The lead handler position for the witch liaison wouldn't have been a big deal a few years ago, but it was now. AID wanted to try a new team group, one with witches trained in martial arts. However, they couldn't have a team with witches if they couldn't get and keep one to begin with.

"Two," Brandon murmured as he set off down the street to his car. That was how many witches AID had lost in the past three years. He pocketed his phone and fished his keys out, remembering now that he had parked two blocks away the night before, thanks to the college kids taking up all the spots for a party.

Why AID had put him up in the middle of a college town when he was several years out from graduating, Brandon did not know. He didn't miss his higher education days, especially the all-night drinking. He'd awoken that morning after not getting much sleep to a message from Claire. It was as perfunctory as anyone could expect from her.

Call me.

At first, Brandon had been excited. It was time. *Finally.*

However, the moment the words "coven leadership" and "witch liaison" left her mouth, Brandon knew he was in for a bigger challenge than he had anticipated.

He reached his car, a sleek black sedan with no other remarkable qualities other than the fact that it was always sparkling and clean. Thoughts droned through his mind. *I'm the youngest guy ever to recruit a witch liaison for AID, so that's got to count for something.*

Usually, witch handlers were men in their fifties with plenty of experience working for AID or the army. A thirty-one-year-old like himself who'd only recently received a second chance in this field was not usually the type. *Besides,* he thought, *I hate the word they use. Handler.* It sounded like witches were heinous cats in need of wrangling. That's what AID described them as, but they were people like the rest of them.

Brandon unlocked his car and slipped inside. Immediately after turning the key in the ignition, he switched on the AC. The late spring weather in southern Louisiana always made him wonder if he should have accepted a job with AID at their New Orleans office when he could have kept pushing for a move to the Pennsylvania sector, his home state. AID's head told him it was New Orleans or nothing. Get screwed and never go anywhere in his field again.

So here he was, sweating his balls off on a street where the cars parked so closely together it was a miracle he didn't hit anyone getting out. *On my way to ask the coven if they'll give us another witch, though we've already gotten two killed,* he added as he snapped his seatbelt into place. He switched on the radio, hoping whatever rock station he had left it on would drown out his thoughts for a time.

As he pulled his car out, Brandon wondered if it was the humidity making him want to get out of his new task. Find a new witch to act as a go-between for the coven and AID and keep her alive. Brandon hadn't been around the last time a witch liaison went missing.

From what he had heard, it happened because the criminal mage they were chasing at the time tapped too much power and blew the poor girl up. The mage had simply been more powerful than the witch helping them. Though witch liaisons were go-betweens, they were also expected to provide magical assistance in combative operations.

Brandon sighed and promised himself a drink when the day was done, no matter how much success he had.

Michelle Folsom, Mother of the coven leadership, sank into the chair behind her desk and reached for the cup of tea beside a stack of folders, files, and loose papers. The tea smelled like relaxation, but there would be none for her for several hours. Not with that stack looking at her.

She eyed it with no small amount of distaste and sipped her tea. At least the drink would help ease the headache that had been raging all morning. Despite the bright sun outside, Michelle had drawn the curtains and lit several candles around the room. It relaxed her. The papers were reports and testimonials from the other coven members, various aides, agents, and the like who had gathered around the coven in the past several years to offer their assistance in troubling times.

Michelle Folsom was not afraid of hard work. Quite the opposite. She reveled in it. She enjoyed long hours in her office. However, they needed assistance from anyone outside the coven. The reports and testimonials would have been fine if it wasn't for who they were about.

She flipped open the folder on top of the pile. Though she had seen Theadora Blackwood's face several times in person throughout the years, she still glanced over the photograph paper-clipped inside. Theadora's keen green eyes seemed to stare out of the picture into Michelle's. Her untamed black curls reminded Michelle of the girl's mother. Anyone who looked at a photograph of each woman when they were the same age would have thought they were the same person. Michelle had to do a double-take.

In the picture, the girl looked ready to set something on fire. She'd always had a rebellious streak, as Michelle recalled. That streak had turned into a full-out wave in the last few years. Michelle couldn't exactly blame her, but she couldn't consider that now. She turned a few pages over, ignoring the photograph of the twenty-three-year-old standing with hands perched on her hips.

The next page listed several family members of Theadora's, mainly distant relatives she had probably never met in other parts of the world who didn't give a rat's ass about her. Another reason for her rebellion. Even so, the Blackwood family was one of the most famous witch families in the country, and Theadora was one of them, no matter how much she didn't want to be anymore.

Not only was she from a famous witch family, but she had also shown the potential to become an incredibly powerful witch. Or so said the pages and pages of reports. How members of the coven had garnered this much information, Michelle did not know.

As she perused the material, Michelle's brows lifted. "Theadora could become a coven mother one day when she's got a few more decades on her," she muttered. Provided she whittled that rebellious streak down. That would take work, and right now, Michelle was considering if it was worth it. Even for a Blackwood.

Headstrong, uncooperative, impulsive, and unpredictable were only a few of the words coven members used to describe Theadora in their reports. The testimonials were full of stories detailing how Theadora had offended them personally with all her "headstrong behavior." As she read these accounts, Michelle could not help but smile. *I was once like that,* she thought. Formerly described as "headstrong" as if that was something bad. Her eyes lingered on one specific testimonial of an elderly warlock.

Theadora Blackwood's obsession with trampling all over the traditions of the covens that both protect her and allow her to wield great power in the magical and the socio-political spheres is unacceptable! I propose her removal from...

Michelle didn't bother reading the rest. She had a good idea of what everyone thought. It wasn't only an obsession with "trampling all over the traditions of the covens" that concerned them. It was one thing to spit in the face of an organization that had existed for a long time. It was another to become obsessed with the idea of becoming a witch mage. A magic-wielding woman without a coven. On the loose doing whatever the hell she pleased. Michelle had felt that way once, though for different reasons.

I, for one, did not lose my famous and respected parents to a fire, she thought.

Michelle put aside the first file and reached for another but did not open it. It sat closed on her desk, and she sank deep into thought while holding her teacup, tapping its side with the long, almond-shaped nails she had filed to perfection. Few people who took one glance at her knew how lethal those nails could become.

She thought back to all the events that had occurred since Theadora lost her parents. The investigation into Theadora had not started until a few months ago when, after having missed far too many meetings with her Sabbat, Theadora's coterie had been questioned. They had confirmed that Theadora had purposefully neglected meeting with them. Strike one.

After this, the Sabbat's head, a venerable if hidebound witch by the name of Kirsten Fouche, had gone to confront the young woman. At first, Theadora had refused to meet, stating she was "too busy." Well, she might have been. Being a twenty-three-year-old with friends, university classes, and still grieving her parents and all that. Such things would keep a young woman busy. Plus, there was Theadora's preference for dance clubs and favorite bars.

When Fouche cornered the young woman and pressed the issue, Theadora had flown into a temper, disrespecting the elder witch "beyond acceptance." That was what the report said anyhow.

It was then Theadora Blackwood had claimed she would become a mage on her own so she could leave the coven. *For-ever!* Her words. Michelle could almost hear Theadora screaming those two syllables as she stormed away. Except she had not stormed away. If she had, she would have avoided the magical punishment Fouche retaliated with. Theadora had gotten the best of the elder witch and sent her packing. A testament to her power, Michelle knew, but also the reason for the stack of folders on her desk.

The coven Mother closed her eyes and rubbed her forehead, willing the headache to recede. In addition to the reports she had to get through, she also had to meet with Fouche and the other Sabbat head who had called for Theadora to be censured and undergo the Fleecing, a painful ritual that stripped a witch of their magic and connection to the coven.

If only Theadora had lost that little magical fighting match with Fouche, Michelle could have publicly reprimanded Fouche for inflicting a punishment on a lower coven member without seeking approval from higher-ups. Theadora hadn't only defied the coven with her goal to become a mage. She had trounced on a senior coven member. Punishment was warranted, but perhaps she could find a way to save the young witch from the Fleecing. Let the girl leave without inflicting the painful ritual.

Michelle sighed, more than willing to admit Fouche was well past her prime and too arrogant for her own good. *If I don't do something soon, the coven will descend into utter chaos,* she thought.

It wasn't only the inner turmoil between the witch hierarchies that would become a problem. It would be prime time for AID to use the coven's weakness and depose the current coven Mother, replacing her with another who would work better with them. *Plucked from the loudest and most obnoxious members of the hedge witch community,* Michelle thought with no small amount of distaste.

It had all started a few decades ago when enough catastrophic instances of magic across the country led the United States government to step in. AID became the organization in charge of tracking down and controlling people who crossed the line with their magic. That line had blurred in the years since. They had left the covens all over the country alone for the most part. They could only displace a coven Mother if they suspected her of criminal activity and could prove it.

Michelle didn't want the headache of an investigation. If they investigated one coven, AID offices across the country would be spurred to look into their local covens as well. The number of organized witch groups would go down. They didn't need that. They didn't need more magic users going rogue, whether because they wanted to or because circumstances forced it to happen.

She snapped the file she'd opened shut and put it back on the desk. Reading another report wouldn't help. None of them would tell her what the right next move was. Before Michelle could consider the matter any longer, a knock came at her office door, reminding her of an informal meeting she had today with one of her favorite agents.

"Come in," she called, standing. She gathered the materials on Theadora to one side of her desk as the door swung open on silent hinges. In slunk a wiry-looking man who was at least a head taller than her. Michelle herself was tall for a woman. Despite his height, the man's perpetual slouch made him look smaller. Probably for the best, Michelle always thought, because the man acted as a spy and doer of subtler deeds for the coven Mother.

"Good afternoon, Arthur."

His eyes, which most considered brown but looked red in the candlelight, met hers. He waited until she nodded her permission for him to sit. Arthur Adderget seemed to gather himself and coil into the chair as if sitting was not a normal position for him. Michelle was used to his mannerisms and did not give it a second thought. "What news do you have for me?" she asked, also sitting.

In a thin, whispery voice, he began. "The Arcane Investigation Division has contacted the coven. They are sending an agent today to speak with you about obtaining a new witch liaison to replace the one who died last year."

Michelle's hand tightened on the arms of her chair. "Of course they are." She released a deep sigh, doing nothing to hide her irritation. The nerve AID had in asking for another one of their coven members! Arthur recoiled at the spark in her eyes. For a fleeting moment, his were red, not brown. They blinked back to normal half a second later, and he waited for the coven Mother to calm.

Michelle pulled out a small flask containing dark amber liquid and poured it into her tea. As she drank, Arthur went on. "The man they want to send is a new team lead and the most recent addition to the AID New Orleans sector."

Michelle glanced at him over the rim of her teacup, then set it down slowly. "Oh?" They were sending someone inexperienced to ask the coven for a new liaison? What the hell were they thinking?

Arthur nodded. "They promise it won't be a death sentence like before."

Michelle rolled her eyes. "And how are we supposed to believe them?" She tapped her fingernails on the desk and thought for a long moment before loosing another sigh. "If we don't oblige, we'll be higher on their list."

If the coven descended into chaos as Michelle thought might happen, denying AID a liaison would only give them more reason to replace her. Or the whole damn coven. Arthur leaned forward, his words growing lower. "Maybe don't sssend anyone you can't afford to lose," he hissed.

Michelle almost reverted to her automatic answer, trained for political convenience. All members of the coven were of equal importance and value. She paused before this response could slip off her tongue and glanced at the stack of reports on Theadora. Slowly, a smile crossed her lips.

"Thought of something?" Arthur asked, slinking back into the chair, eyes glinting with anticipation.

Michelle met his eyes and did not falter when they turned red again. "I think I've found a way to handle my little headache."

CHAPTER TWO

"The origins of the Stairs of Sorcery are mostly unknown, except of their names, how many witches may belong to each one, and how they are to operate in relation to the source of power each coven may obtain. A coven may consist of thirteen witches divided into two Sabbats with three overseeing elders. These twelve make up the body of the coven, with one appointed coven Mother over them all. Together, the Thirteen bring about balance in the power they control, the gift the Lake of Power has granted to them."

—Orlena Gorbana, The History of Covens and Their Adjacent Societies

When Thea lifted her head and light streaming through her window, she cursed. "What fucking day is it?" she asked no one in particular since she was alone and had been for the past twenty-four hours, holed up in her apartment as she studied for one of her finals.

She checked her watch only to find out it wasn't on her wrist. Next, she looked at the wall where the calendar hung and discovered she had not turned the page when the month changed. She scrambled over her desk and found her phone. Dead. Of course. She cursed again and grappled with a desk drawer until she opened it and found a charger. A minute later, she had her phone turned on and the time in front of her. 11:00 a.m.

Thea blinked. Apparently, she had dozed off sometime in the night while eyeball-deep in dead languages and ancient texts. An assortment of open textbooks and reference materials were scattered on her desk, along with multiple high-resolution photographs of various artifacts and manuscripts that had been ancient when Columbus was thinking of sailing the ocean blue.

Thea rubbed her eyes and blinked again, glancing over the notes she had scribbled out the night before. They were a mess, hardly legible despite the morning light. Why hadn't she at least bothered to get up and shut the curtains? She had no way of telling when she had fallen asleep, but the exhaustion flowing through her told her it might not have been long. Thea stood with a start when she realized she had spilled something on the closest sheaf of papers.

"Shit." Her cup of tea was on its side, the dregs long since poured onto the papers. At least they had gotten onto her notes and not the reference material. Magic would fix the notes. After pushing a small amount of her power into the paper to dry them, she gave herself a satisfied smile. "Perfect." The sheets dried without much damage to what she'd written, only making them blurrier than before. It didn't matter since she could hardly read her notes anyway.

Thea glanced around her apartment, with the plush

green sofa and hand-sewn cushions she had bought off an old man down the street. A braided rug ran across the floor, covered in the laundry she had been in the middle of folding before she decided to study instead. Without looking into the kitchen, Thea knew the sink was full of dishes and the trash needed to be taken out.

She had been so *busy*. Busier than she had ever been in her life, and not only because she was trying to avoid the coven. Those sniveling old women would only put more on her plate. "No. Thank. You," she muttered.

After sighing deeply, Thea decided she was too tired to clean her entire apartment like a normal person. This was the sort of situation where magic came in handy. She fluttered her hand around with a wand and spoke a few spells, commanding different parts of her apartment to tend to themselves.

Books clomped off her desk and arranged themselves on a nearby shelf. The teacup she'd drank from the night before danced through the air into the kitchen. Thea lost focus, and it fell, shattering among the other dishes. She hissed. Maybe it was too soon after waking up to be using magic.

Papers gathered themselves into a neat stack on her desk, and her pens and highlighters fell into an open drawer. Her laptop, the screen dead hours ago, shut itself. By the time the apartment was mostly in order, except for the kitchen needing a lot of work, Thea had a splitting headache. That was the price of using magic when she didn't know what the hell she was doing most of the time.

As she entered the kitchen, hoping a cup of coffee would help, she found a bigger mess than she expected.

She'd anticipated the dirty dishes and full trash can, but not the random shit all over the counters. Instead of going to their appropriate closets and rooms, various items convened in her kitchen as if they were about to strike a mutiny against her. Most notable among these was her laundry.

Groaning loud enough to make the walls cringe, Thea jerked open the refrigerator door. At least she had leftover take-out and some cold-brew coffee she could pour into a cup. Upon discovering she was out of clean glasses, Thea settled for drinking it from the jug.

A knock sounded at her door as she raised the jug to her lips. "Someone coming to demand why I'm making such a racket," Thea muttered as she headed toward the door. Her books seemed to be fighting with one another for a prime spot on the bookshelf. Thumping sounds kept coming from that direction.

"Everything's fine!" she called in a peevish voice, not bothering to glance through the peephole to see who it might be. Probably Mrs. Farley from a floor above. That woman could be such a bitch about the smallest things. Then came a different voice than she was expecting. Instead of disdain, a warm, buttery tone floated through the door.

"Open up, Thea, and I'll give you a treat."

With a tinge of embarrassment, Thea remembered she had promised to go out for breakfast with her best friend Mia. Given the time and her late night, she had missed it. This must be Mia, coming to check on her like the good friend she was. Thea opened the door with the most apologetic expression she could muster.

Mia did not need her excuses. She could tell by the way Thea still wore yesterday's maroon crop top and black denim shorts that she had woken up not too long ago. Not only had she missed breakfast, but Thea intended to get materials from Mia. Not that she had told her friend what she needed them for.

After letting her best friend in, Thea rambled, "Sorry for being peevish with you. I just woke up, and I'm sorry for missing breakfast and..."

Mia smiled, her expression as warm as her voice. "I expected you might over-exert yourself studying again. I never went to the café. I stayed home, and when I didn't get a text from you this morning, I headed over here."

Thea wasn't sure if she should feel relieved or embarrassed. This whole "studying all night and forgetting plans with friends" thing was becoming too common. Last weekend, she had promised to go to an '80s dance night at her favorite club with a few of her university friends. While they had blacked out on too many vodka cranberries, Thea had fallen into a stupor caused by reading too many ancient texts in languages that required using magic to read.

Then there was Connor, the guy from her ancient languages class who had asked her out three times and been stood up twice, by accident on Thea's part. Well, maybe he'd get the hint that when she said she was busy, she fucking meant it. Her buzzing phone on the desk told Thea he might be calling her right now. She ignored it, turning her full attention to the person who mattered the most in her life. "Want coffee?"

Mia said she was fine without it but followed Thea into

the kitchen anyway. She leaned her arms on the counter. "You'd better tell everyone I'm the best friend you ever had. Not only did I come to check on you, but I also brought the materials you asked for." Her dark eyes glittered. "And another small treat."

Thea's expression was like a dog's before their owner gave them their favorite biscuit.

"Mia, you didn't have to!" Oh, but Thea was so glad she had.

Mia pulled a silver-wrapped chocolate bar from her purse. One of high quality and Thea's favorite kind. "I did have to, though. Lest my bestie Thea become akin to a rampaging monster."

Thea unwrapped the chocolate bar, already feeling more herself before biting into it. She gave Mia a sheepish look and squeaked, "I can't help it. I need chocolate like I need blood. You are the best person to have ever existed, Mia Delacroix." She devoured three-fourths of the bar, then savored the last few bites. As she did this, Mia assessed the mess in the apartment and frowned.

"Looks like you've been throwing around unnecessary magic. We've talked about this, Thea."

"I know, I know," Thea mumbled around a mouthful. "We aren't supposed to use magic on an empty stomach."

"And with little sleep," Mia added pointedly. The girl wandered to the desk Thea had pulled from her bedroom into the living room the night before. Mia bent over to parse through the various photos of artifacts left there. Thea watched her from the kitchen, noting how well put together Mia looked for the day.

Mia always looked great. Her rich dark brown skin

shone in the morning sunlight, her face framed by thick black curls. She wore her favorite jewelry today. Two dangling half-moon earrings with spiderweb studs next to them, a pendant necklace, and several handmade bracelets with small, dangling crystals. In her long skirts of different colors and patterns, she looked quite different from Thea.

Thea figured it wasn't only yesterday's clothes that made her look shabby but her unbrushed hair and smudged makeup. Oh, well. Mia had seen her in much worse states after long nights out.

She turned to the bag of goodies Mia had brought, quickly registering that she had everything she needed. She closed the bag and put it out of sight, hoping Mia would not ask about it until Thea had time to *experiment*.

Mia's voice carried from the living room. "I know this is all for your finals, Thea, but I worry you're trying to raise more demons than you can put down."

Thea rolled her eyes. "You sound like my grandmother."

Mia turned, brows furrowing. "You've never met your grandmother."

Thea shrugged. "Sounds like something a grandmother would say."

Mia crossed her arms. "Don't try to play this off like it's no big deal."

"Playing things off as no big deal is my special skill." Thea flashed her best smile.

It was, and Mia knew it. It was why she rolled her eyes but could not help smiling. "I'm no coven witch, but don't treat me like I'm stupid."

Thea noted the hint of amusement in her friend's voice but apologized anyway. "You're right, and I'm the luckiest girl in the world to have a best friend like you." She chucked the chocolate bar wrapper into the trash. "Who else is going to bring me my medicine?"

"Chocolate isn't medi—" Mia started, but Thea was already disappearing down the hall into her bedroom to change her clothes. The two girls had only met a few years ago in a local occult shop, but the moment their eyes had locked, they knew they were platonic soulmates. Years later, Thea could not imagine her life without Mia's thoughtful encouragement and good sense.

After changing into a dark red T-shirt dress suitable for humid late-April days in southern Louisiana, Thea emerged from her room. "I understand your concern, and it is good to have it, but I remember what I saw in my family's library. I'm not stopping until I find the truth. It's no coincidence the fire happened right after I saw what I did."

A flash of worry crossed Mia's face. "Thea, you haven't been to your family's estate since…" She trailed off, not wanting to say, "Since they died." Thea knew what she meant, though.

She shrugged. "I've been staying here because it's closer to school." That was part of the truth, but the deeper reason was Thea didn't want to be out at her estate. The coven controlled most of it anyway, and she was trying to avoid them. Some things made Thea want to go back, though. Like her family's library and the copious books that could yield truth to her. She wanted her parents' belongings kept safe.

She was not sure she could bear going back anytime

soon, though it had been three years since the fire that killed her parents. The grief was still a sharp pain whenever it came up, and seeing the estate again would only intensify that. *No, thank you,* Thea thought, remembering that everything keeping her busy had also kept her from spiraling into bottomless grief. Mia had been a lifeline through all of it.

Thea ducked into the bathroom and wiped her face clean before returning to the living room, where she found Mia again looking over the photographs of artifacts. Mia met her friend's gaze. "I don't want you working too hard to uncover something that can't be found. I don't mean to be unsupportive, but I don't want you burning yourself out. Literally."

Thea nodded and sank into a nearby chair. A momentary flash of memories flitted through her mind. A deciphered message in a hidden passage in her family's library. Glowing sigils on stone, opening her mind for a second to see the Lake of Power and the streams flowing from it. So many more streams than the coven had ever told her about. That moment years ago before everything had gone to shit where she had had utter clarity.

With the right will and skill, she could tap into the Lake. *All* of it. Her magic had felt almost dormant since then, only welling up in great bursts when she was extremely sad or angry. Like when Sabbat leader Fouche threatened to punish her for "trouncing on tradition."

Tradition, as she saw it, had gotten her parents killed. *So I don't give a fuck,* she thought.

Mia sat on the green sofa and regarded her friend with concern. "I know you disagree with how the coven operates, but tapping fully into the Lake might not work the way you want it to."

Mia had a point, but Thea couldn't help thinking the confines of the coven were too much. Being in the coven was like riding a bike with the training wheels still on. It was all to keep the less daring and dedicated from losing themselves. *I can master it,* she thought. *I know I can.*

The coven operated on a tiered system of witches called the Stairs of Sorcery. A coven was made up of thirteen witches, six of whom belonged to the Sabbat. Three of each Sabbat were the lowest, called a coterie. One appointed woman, the coven Mother, was the thirteenth. Or the first. Thea wasn't sure which, and it didn't matter.

Those without a coven were called hedge witches and usually were not in covens because their power was far lesser. The herbal, plant-based magic of the hedge witches made them capable of handling their magic without checks and balances. Mia was one such witch, and though she desired a community more than anything, she wasn't permitted.

Thea thought this was better.

Better to be free than tethered to the demands and traditions of the coven. She and Mia had disagreed on this for years but argued less often about it now. Without a coven, Thea wouldn't be a hedge witch, though. Her power was too great for that. She'd be a witch mage. Those were rare and disliked by most other witches. Oh, well. It wasn't like the local witches in New Orleans liked her much now, anyway.

Mia came to Thea's side and bent down. "I believe you.

You know that, right? What you saw in that passage, I believe you."

Thea gave her friend a tired smile. They were the words she had needed to hear. She remembered those weeks after the fire that killed her parents around the same time as her discovery of the passage and the book that had burned in the fire. She remembered telling the coven what she had seen and their brash disregard. They hadn't believed her. Hadn't thought anything she said was important.

Mia straightened again. "I know what that bag of ingredients is for. You're trying to avoid telling me, but I'm smarter than I look." Her dark eyes glittered as she thought of the magical reagents she'd brought from the shop she worked at.

"Oh, but Mia, you look and sound so smart. Don't say such things about yourself."

Mia only smiled. "Sometimes, safeguards are there for a reason, *mon ami*." Her French accent was perfect when she used the term of endearment.

At last, Thea stood and nodded. "I've got to use them, and I'm sorry for not being upfront about what I was doing. If there's a chance everything I saw was true, I have to try." Tapping into the Lake of Power. The one thing the coven forbade a witch from doing. It meant tapping into more power than most witches could handle. It was one of several reasons Thea was determined to leave the coven. So the rules could not apply to her anymore.

Thea returned to her desk, pondering the photographs. She murmured, "If only that book hadn't burned up, and I'd learned everything three years ago."

"Your obsession with an old man who hasn't been

around for two thousand years is amusing," Mia commented, having overheard Thea's words.

Thea turned to her with a wry grin. "I'm not obsessed with him. Ambrosius was the only mage ever to write books. You know, ones that can actually tell us things the coven refuses to acknowledge."

Mia tugged Thea away from her desk, having heard Thea's rambling about Ambrosius and his three non-existent legendary tomes a hundred times. "Come on. Let's get you out of this stuffy apartment. You need a break before you finish your finals."

CHAPTER THREE

"*Grand Archmagister Ambrosius is a man of legend, having existed at least two thousand years ago. He is the rumored writer of the Ancient Grimoire, a text containing three separate volumes for all mages everywhere to learn from. Ambrosius was a master of magic who spent his life studying the ancient arts and unlocking the secrets of the universe. Most mages do not believe Ambrosius ever wrote the Ancient Grimoire, and several deny his existence.*"
—*Orlena Gorbana*, On Mage Masters Throughout Time and History

Brandon knew not to expect drab office buildings for the coven leadership's point of convening, but he had not expected an old, stone manor house surrounded by a wrought iron fence and lush green gardens. He knew the coven leadership was located outside the city between plains, swamps, and rivers but didn't think he'd have to drive two hours to get there.

By this point, he was sick of being in the car and ready

to get the meeting over with. Then, another two-hour drive back to AID's New Orleans headquarters. He wondered if he would even make it home today.

Furthermore, all the way here, Brandon had been rehearsing what reasons he might give Michelle Folsom, the coven Mother. It had not helped that his companion, a colleague from AID, had ridden with him and talked the whole way, giving "advice" on how to work his way up through the Arcane Investigation Division without making too many waves. "Like a duck paddling across a pond," the former Marine had stated, smiling broadly.

Brandon did not feel like a duck paddling across a pond, and he didn't want to. He ignored his colleague on the way out of the car and to the house. Outside in the gardens, several people milled around, men and women in simple, light-colored robes. Other coven members, he presumed. Many glanced in their direction and, seeing the AID insignia on their clothes, made a point to look away.

Brandon got it. The coven leadership wasn't a fan of AID. Though he knew why, he didn't want to go over the history between the U.S. government and the magic users of the country again. The long, drawn-out saga had finally ended with the government appointing AID to investigate magic-involved criminal activity. Usually, they left covens out of it. Those groups were good at keeping to the rules.

The only time AID stepped in was when a coven Mother was suspected of foul play. In those cases, they investigated and appointed a new Mother from those already inside the coven. Brandon had heard of this happening only a few times since AID was established. Still, the threat hung over all coven Mothers.

Inside, he expected a receptionist but was greeted by a wry old man with wisps of gray hair and a thin but lithe body. Claire had warned him that Mother Folsom's favorite agent Arthur Adderget might meet him when he arrived.

Brandon cleared his throat. "Hello. I'm Agent Brandon Cole, and this is Agent Ajax Maddison. We're here to see Ms. Folsom."

"*Mother* Folsssom," Arthur corrected, drawing out the s enough for Brandon to notice. Brandon shared a look with his companion, whom Claire had insisted he bring along "just in case." Brandon wasn't afraid of Mother Folsom going full witch mode on him, but it helped to bring along someone more...intimidating.

Ajax Maddison, whom everyone at AID simply called Jax, was more than intimidating. The looming presence of the big, burly, dark-skinned former Marine was sure to give Mother Folsom a clear message. They came here to get what they wanted.

Arthur's gaze flitted over Jax, then narrowed slightly before sliding back to Brandon. "This way, Agent Cole."

The man led them into an office where pulled curtains revealed a row of glass windows overlooking the back garden. Thin wisps of smoke rose above several candles, indicating they had been blown out not long ago. Or someone had used magic to put them out. Standing behind a desk was Mother Folsom herself, wearing a two-piece tailored suit in a deep purple shade that set off her chestnut hair and bright eyes.

Brandon had never met Michelle Folsom, but he'd heard plenty about her. She could be reasoned with, unlike past coven Mothers, but she was still a challenge when it came to matters of persuasion. She was not a woman easily moved from her position. Once resolved on a matter, she remained there. Brandon could be a persuasive guy, but he had felt the need to bring along Jax for this conversation.

He dipped his head in greeting. "Thank you for meeting with us."

Mother Folsom simply motioned to the two leather chairs across from her desk, signaling both men to sit. She did not balk at their appearances. Not Brandon's youthful vigor and dark, side-swept hair or Jax's six-foot, five-inch form. She didn't look at Jax for more than a second.

She had a stack of papers and files in front of her, arranged neatly. She set her hands on top of them. *What the hell are those?* Brandon wondered. Were they files about him or someone else? Whatever they were, Mother Folsom seemed to think she needed them for this meeting.

"I already know why you're here," the woman began, locking eyes with Brandon. He couldn't quite make out if her eyes were simply a deep blue or purple. He had never seen eyes like hers before and would not soon forget them. Come to think of it, he amended, Arthur's eyes had been strange too.

He snapped back to the matter at hand, clearing his throat to make his case, but Mother Folsom spoke again before he could. "I'm afraid your wishes are untoward. The audacity AID has in requesting a *third* witch liaison after ensuring the death of two others. I've allowed you into my home simply so you can explain where this audacity comes from." Her words were firm, her expression tight.

This was going as badly as Brandon had expected. "AID is not requesting a liaison from your coven for the same reasons as before." He leaned forward, hoping his demeanor would make Mother Folsom think he intended a friendly arrangement, not a business proposal. If they could call this business.

"Oh?" Mother Folsom's right brow arched. "You mean, AID isn't requesting a witch liaison so they can send her off into whatever trouble they're facing alone with no plan of extraction, expecting her to expend all her power and thereby her life for the sake of those too cowardly to assist?"

Sharp words. Not all of what she'd said was wrong. Brandon shifted. "We want a new liaison to join a new team, mostly AID agents, but with a witch's assistance. It will be a sort of spy network, you see. Agents trained for the field will be on the team. The only thing AID is missing is someone with magic who can be trained in martial arts methods."

Mother Folsom's face went blank, and she replied dryly, "Witches are not raised to fight like humans. Our magic is our advantage."

"It doesn't hurt to learn other methods of defense and survival, does it?" Brandon countered, feeling whatever grip he had slipping. "My colleague here, Ajax Maddison, for instance, will be in charge of this new training and leading many of the operations."

Another thing Brandon had rehearsed in the car was when to bring Jax up. It wasn't only Jax's presence that he hoped to shake up the coven Mother with. He wanted Jax to recite his military experience and expertise. It also helped that Jax was a good two decades older than Brandon and actually knew what the hell he was doing.

Brandon expected a sharp snap to attention, then a parade ground belting out the requested information. Instead, Jax began in a low, slow voice. Brandon wondered if Jax planned to undercut him but soon realized this was not the case. "Agent Cole is right. I will be in charge of training any new witch liaisons. All missions will be under either my or Agent Cole's lead. As of now, neither of us are doing anything else for AID. This is our sole focus."

Brandon quickly saw the effect Jax's simple words had on Mother Folsom. Finally, the coven Mother placed her full attention on the former Marine, considering him with more interest than before. She tried not to act impressed as Jax continued, citing his experience and expertise as Brandon had hoped he would. Mother Folsom wasn't successful in feigning disinterest as Brandon caught her eyes lighting up as Jax spoke.

Mother Folsom leaned back in her seat, considering Jax's words after he finished. Brandon waited in tense silence, unable to think of anything else to add. Finally, her gaze drifted back to him. "And what is your part in this, Brandon Cole? You tell me you will be a team lead, but on what sort of missions?"

Brandon faltered. Actually, he did not know. After the recent debacle that brought him here, AID told him he would be on a need-to-know basis.

Mother Folsom went on. "My agent, Arthur, whom you met before coming in here, conducted thorough research on you before you arrived."

Brandon glanced again at the stack of papers and

files, wondering if they contained information about him. "Brandon Cole," Mother Folsom recited. "A thirty-one-year-old who has come up through the ranks of local law enforcement in his home state of Pennsylvania. A young man with aspirations of joining the FBI.

"However, a controversial case you were involved in led to political fallout, and you were assigned to the New Orleans AID office as a part of a cooling-off period. No doubt you have found your new position with AID challenging thus far." She leaned forward, her elbows perched on the desk and her fingers intertwined. "Tell me, Agent Cole. Are you here because you want what is best for AID or to prove yourself?"

Brandon shrugged. "Why can't it be both?"

He did not expect the smile on the coven Mother's lips. "At least you're an honest man." Everything she had said so far about him was true, but he hoped she wouldn't go on. Brandon didn't exactly want to relive all that had happened in the past few years. He'd come to AID to prove himself but also to redeem himself. Though the situation was more of a "wrong place at the wrong time" scenario than a flaw in his character and judgment, he had some making up to do.

Brandon hoped he had good judgment right now because it seemed Mother Folsom *might* be willing to consider giving them a liaison. He started to feel eager, but Mother Folsom caught the gleam in his eyes and frowned. "I have not made my mind up yet, Agent Cole. There is still the serious matter of two dead witches from my coven who have fallen under AID's watch. They were not women

I can easily replace, and my coven has suffered from their loss."

"I understand, Mother Folsom," Brandon replied and meant it.

Mother Folsom turned to Jax. "Even someone as impressive as you, Mr. Maddison, isn't going to make me forget that." She sat back, considering them both. "The things you have told me today are reassuring, but I'm not certain it will be enough. However, I do have a proposal for you."

Brandon stilled. He had not expected this. "We're not looking to barter—" he began, then bit back a yelp as Jax kicked him in the shin.

Mother Folsom's eyes grew cold. "You can hear me out, Agent Cole, or you can see yourself out."

Brandon fought the pain barking up his leg. He'd make Jax pay for that later when he played pop music on the way home instead of rock.

The coven Mother went on. "There is only one witch in my coven I am willing to permit to work for AID. She has some power but has not been properly trained for years due to extenuating circumstances. She will need more than martial arts training to cooperate, but I'm unable to give you anyone else."

Brandon's heart sank, but he made no objection as she continued.

"You must keep this witch alive for thirty-six months or until she leaves you of her own will. If you can do that, I will consider giving you another witch of higher power who is…easier to handle," she added.

Brandon wasn't sure what she was getting at. He was

not aware of any troubles or differences between the witches. "We'll take her. Thank you." He didn't see any other choice but to accept the coven Mother's proposal. He feared she'd withdraw it if he did not.

Mother Folsom seemed satisfied as she slid the stack of papers and folders across to Brandon. "This is everything you need to know about the girl. I'd suggest you do your research before you find her."

Brandon blinked. "She's not here with the other witches?" As far as he knew, the whole coven dwelled under one roof.

Mother Folsom chuckled. "No. She hasn't been here for several months, and we do not expect to see her again anytime soon." She fluttered a hand toward the papers. "She's all yours."

Brandon paused. He would have to convince this girl to join AID, it seemed. That had to be the first sign something wasn't right, correct? Even so, Brandon gathered the files and thanked the coven Mother again.

She waved a hand of dismissal. "Actually, you're doing me a great favor, Brandon Cole, by taking Theodora Blackwood off my hands."

CHAPTER FOUR

"Grand Archmagister Ambrosius' magnum opus, The Ancient Grimoire, contains three separate volumes, meant to be read in order. The first of these is called the Tome of Arcanum. It contains a wealth of information regarding the history of magic and the different levels of power a mage can attain.

"It is also within this book that we find the list of thirteen levels of mages, ranging from Acolyte to Grand Archmagister. Of the three volumes within The Ancient Grimoire, the Tome of the Arcanum is the only one that has been seen by magic users and historians within the past five hundred years. Still, many do not believe the Tome of Arcanum was written by Ambrosius himself but by his loyal followers throughout the years."

—Orlena Gorbana, On Mage Masters Throughout Time and History

"I didn't know when I was shipped out of Pennsylvania for AID that my first assignment would include so much... homework," Brandon muttered as he stared down the stack of folders Mother Folsom had given him regarding the new witch liaison. He'd taken last night off and slept soundly, but the instant he woke, all he could think about was that research. He waited until he was back in the office and had a cup of coffee in hand before he delved in.

He opened the first one to find a paper-clipped picture of a young woman with long black curls, keen green eyes, and a fierce overall look. Theadora Blackwood. That was the name at the top of the page. *Blackwood.* He'd heard that name before, but where?

After a few minutes of ruminating, Brandon figured it out. The Blackwoods were one of the most powerful witch families in the whole country. Five years ago—or maybe it was three, Brandon could not remember—the Blackwoods of southern Louisiana had died in a house fire. Well, not all of them, apparently, because Theadora had survived.

Brandon sat at his desk in the New Orleans AID headquarters office, an open folder in his hands. Theadora had lost both her parents in the fire. "Shit." He turned the page to find official paperwork regarding the fire and her parents' death, including the news headlines for that day and their obituaries. Photographs of her parents were clipped in as well, and Brandon could not help realizing Theadora and her mother looked almost exactly alike.

That poor girl.

The next page gave more basic information about her.

Theadora Anne Blackwood, born to Irene Anne Blackwood and Peter Jacob Blackwood on July 7, 2000.

She was twenty-three years old and had lost her parents when she was twenty.

Below this was the Blackwood family estate's address and several photographs of the place long before a fire had touched it. Brandon got onto his laptop and searched the address to find much of the house was still standing. All but the third floor of the east wing. Interesting. Did that mean Theadora still lived there?

He read another article stating the house was under the governing authority of the coven leadership of Louisiana, the coven to which both Irene and Peter had belonged for many years. Why was it called the Blackwood family estate if the Blackwoods didn't own it?

One thing the files did not contain was anything regarding interests the young woman might have, places she frequented, or circles of people she ran with. Whoever had put the information together must not have thought it was important.

Out of pure curiosity, Brandon typed in Theadora's full name to see what would come up. A few social media accounts linked to her name popped up, ones that actually belonged to her and ones that didn't. They were all private, though her considerable number of followers indicated she had not always had them privatized.

Brandon scrolled through the search results, finding several articles about the Blackwood estate fire. Finding nothing social media-wise to help him, he returned to the folder. His gaze landed on a slip of paper at the back. A background check had been performed to clear Theadora for handling artifacts through Tulane University. The date of the background check indicated she still went there.

At age twenty-three? Brandon deduced that if she was only going for a bachelor's degree, she might have taken a year to grieve her parents before returning to school.

Well, this could be what I need, he thought. He could

swing by the campus that day and talk to a few of her professors. Maybe meet her in person if she was around. Brandon gathered the folders, placed them inside his desk, and locked it, preparing to leave his office. Before he could move from his seat, someone walked through the door.

Brandon glanced up in surprise. "Claire, it's good to see you."

Claire Dubois smiled, her bright blue eyes meeting Brandon's. "I came to see how you're progressing. I figured you didn't get home until late last night, so I didn't bother to check in then."

Brandon appreciated this but remarked, "You knew it would be a long drive, didn't you?"

Her smile widened. "Why do you think that was the only thing I had you do yesterday?"

"You or the Head?"

Claire shrugged. "Command came from the Head. I ensured your schedule would not be overloaded."

Brandon saw he had yet another reason to thank Claire, the right-hand-woman of the Head of New Orleans' AID branch. "I'm heading out now," he told her. "To Tulane University, which I believe the new witch liaison attends."

Claire lifted a brow. "She's that young?"

Brandon nodded. "Twenty-three."

Claire's brows furrowed. "Strange. They don't usually send us someone that young. Oh well. It could work out better for us. Someone younger might be more willing to adjust to Ajax's training."

She had a point, but Brandon wasn't so sure. After reading those files, he could tell Theadora Blackwood didn't exactly have a great working relationship with the coven leadership. He explained to Claire what he had read, from the reports about the family's estate fire and Theadora becoming an orphan to what the coven itself had reported about her behavior.

"I see," Claire commented after a long moment. "The coven can't seem to keep one of their own in line."

"I'm not sure they consider her one of their own and vice versa." It made sense why they told Brandon they could have her. It also meant he had to find a way to convince Theadora to join AID. A headache formed behind his eyes. This wouldn't be easy.

When Brandon was told he'd have a cooling-off period working for AID, dealing with law enforcement regarding magicals, he thought he'd be bored out of his mind. It turned out a lot more drama and crime happened among magicals than he realized.

The common crimes of theft, vandalism, and bodily harm ran rampant among people who could more easily accomplish and get away with it via magic. Their magic also made them more difficult to trace. Brandon had seen a few instances where magicals disabled security cameras before entering a building to commit a crime.

These crimes were often carried out by magicals who did not belong to covens and were classified as rogue mages, working on their own and tapping into more power than they could handle. This often meant the criminals outed themselves by frying their own bodies with too much magic. Still, innocent people suffered in the process.

One of AID's many jobs was to keep those people in line where the covens could not. Of course, not all mages were the crime-committing type. Most agents within AID had a built-in bias against mages, but Brandon liked taking things case by case, person by person. Not everyone could be a greedy scumbag, right?

Claire must have seen the strain in Brandon's eyes because her face softened. "Take Jax with you. Maybe he can help."

Brandon bristled. "I don't need Jax's help. Or anyone's." As he spoke, he wasn't sure it was true. Jax's presence had certainly helped yesterday with Mother Folsom.

Claire gave him a steady look. "Take him anyway. I know it's not a tactical situation, per se, but Jax is on the team. He's still an agent and can perform in multiple ways. Besides, it would be a good chance for you to work together."

"We're already working together," Brandon reminded her.

Claire only gave him a slight smile and added, "It would be good for Jax. He's been staring at his computer screen all morning like it has somehow insulted his mother. He's probably been on one of those online forums about ex-military exploitation again." She eyed Brandon longer, then added "Don't be scared of Jax. He comes across like the kind of guy who could crush your head with a few punches, but he's a real softie deep down."

"He could be both," Brandon muttered.

"All the more reason to become friends with him," Claire replied before disappearing from Brandon's office.

Brandon blew out a hard breath before going in search of Ajax. Today would be much longer than he had anticipated.

THE FIRST WITCH-MAGE

If Thea didn't get chocolate soon, things would go downhill fast.

She had finished her finals and walked out of the main building on campus into bright sunlight. Squinting, she took out her phone to make sure she had not missed any calls from Mia while she was inside. Nothing. Good. She could call Mia later to make plans. With her finals finished, she could dedicate more time to the one person who had been by her side these past three years. When she wasn't scrounging for ancient artifacts or experimenting with the ingredients Mia brought her, that was.

Thea set off, deciding to head down the street to her favorite candy shop. The day was warm but not yet sweltering, so she did not worry about sweating on her walk.

Students poured past her out of the building and down the street into one of the main sectors featuring various shops and restaurants. Over the past few days, Thea had been immersed in studying, knowing she had to pass her final exams if she wanted to stay at Tulane and continue her research. If only all her searching would lead to the books she wanted, texts that had been lost for years. Texts she could have sworn were in her parents' library before it burned down.

So far, all she had learned were snippets from a book by Orlena Gorbana, indicating Ambrosius' books had vanished centuries ago, and one was even buried with him. If that were true. A lot of it was mere rumor, myth, or legend. Thea reviewed all she knew about the Grand Archmagister, the last of his kind to exist in the past few thousand years. Though plenty of other mages came after him, none had reached the rank of Grand Archmagister. You couldn't get any higher than that.

Unless I can tap into the Lake of Power, Thea thought. Even then, power was only one aspect she'd have to attain. She'd need knowledge, experience, and wisdom. There were no lakes for those things.

As for the Lake of Power, tapping into it was insane. A crazy idea. The worst thing she could do. *But I have to.*

Everyone who ever said anything about the Lake of Power in the coven had agreed on one thing. To draw from its power alone was insane. Others had tried with no success for centuries. The last person who had tried had met with horrific results. Combustion or something like that. Thea couldn't quite remember.

Frankly, she had pushed any warning the coven had given her from her mind. They had not seen what she saw that day three years ago in the passage. They did not know what she knew.

It didn't help that the coven wasn't only dealing with their own inner politics anymore. Not in the last ten years, anyway. The world had been post-veil for the past decade. Humans knew about the magic users. At least witches and mages didn't have to bother hiding their practices anymore, though plenty of people still did not approve of their existence, let alone their basic freedoms.

Four years ago, only a year before Thea's parents died, the Arcane Investigation Division was formed with the agreement of the international covens, confirming the North American covens would help. Now that witches were out of the closet, many decided the old ways could go straight into a ditch. Called rogue witches or mages, they were deemed a new type of criminal by covens and non-magic users alike.

Sure, some who had abandoned their covens were criminals. *But not all of us,* Thea thought. *Some of us don't want to belong to a band of liars and manipulators.* She had no evidence that her coven kept secrets or committed crimes. It was merely a deep-seated feeling she could not shake.

She turned the block and glimpsed her beloved candy shop that made her favorite chocolate in all the French Quarter. She quickened her pace. She wasn't sure if it was the sudden strong desire for chocolate as soon as possible or the thoughts swirling around her brain, but she was getting restless.

Someone on a bike zipped past her and wheeled in front, cutting her off.

"Hey, watch it!"

The young man laughed and biked ahead.

"Little fucker can't watch where he's going," Thea muttered. Her thinning patience was enough of a sign that she needed chocolate. And sleep. Lots of sleep after all the finals she had completed that day. Still, a need to learn more about the Lake of Power blared at the back of her mind. It had burned in her heart and soul for three years. Yet she was no closer to the truth.

Sighing deeply, Thea reached the sweets shop and went inside, thoughts still swirling. She was independently wealthy after her parents' death. Though her coven had taken over the Blackwood estate, they had no control over Thea's parents' money.

The estate had always belonged to the coven. Decades

ago, the first owner was one of Thea's distant family members and a coven Mother. Instead of passing the house down through her family, it went to the following coven Mothers. Each Mother had been generous enough to allow the Blackwood family to remain in the estate. Thea was the last Blackwood around. At least, as far as she knew. Her coven wasn't likely to give it to her.

Even with the coven controlling the estate, Thea would be fine. She could get the hell out of here if she wanted. Never have to see the coven again.

She shoved the thoughts aside and smiled for her favorite man in the world. "Hello, Mr. Benson."

"I've been waiting on you, Thea. Thought you might not stop in this week. The usual?"

The elderly man gave her a kind smile as she nodded vigorously and loaded a bag of her favorite chocolates. After she paid and bade him goodbye, Thea stepped out onto the street. She was not far from her apartment and could walk the rest of the way home instead of taking public transport.

Her phone buzzed. She smiled at the name appearing on her screen. Her favorite professor, Adaline Jones, was the one helping her find artifacts for her research. Her text read:

Hi, Thea. I've found something you might be interested in. If you have time, stop by my office to chat. I'll be here until 5 p.m.

Thea checked the time. It was only two. She could make it and get back home for a long night of watching reality

TV viewing and consuming chocolate. She took out one bar to eat on the way back to the school. As she headed there, a new excitement in her step, Thea wondered what Adaline had in store for her.

Jax seemed about as unhappy as Brandon about tagging along to Tulane.

"I don't see why you couldn't have called ahead and found out if she was there," Jax muttered as Brandon pulled out of the lot at the AID headquarters onto the main road.

"I plan to speak to her professors whether she's there or not," Brandon explained. "Besides, I've barely been out of the office this week."

Jax *hmphed* and did not say a word, only directed his gaze out the window at the clear blue sky and bright sunlight. Brandon switched on the radio to drown out his thoughts, going directly to his favorite rock station.

To his surprise, Jax's knee bounced with the beat of the music, and he went from humming to singing low in his throat.

"You like Black Sabbath?" Brandon asked.

Jax fixed him with a hard stare. "Of course I do. Anyone in their right mind would."

Brandon smiled. Maybe Ajax was cooler than he had previously given him credit for.

The two sang along to "Paranoid" for its two-minute, forty-three-second length. Ten minutes later, they pulled up to Gibson Hall. The main building of Tulane University was a Romanesque-style structure with stone overlaying brick. As a private research institution, Brandon wondered if Theadora Blackwood had a special reason for attending Tulane. Perhaps she had come here to research something regarding magic. He'd find out as soon as he began his search.

Brandon half expected Jax to stay in the car with the radio to keep him company, but the older man was out first, seemingly eager to get inside. Brandon followed him. Inside the building, they requested information from the receptionist about a student named Theadora Blackwood. "Anything you can give us," Brandon added. "Her classes and professors, namely."

"I'm sorry, but we are not permitted to hand out such information unless the student approves or the request is made by family members or for educational purposes," the receptionist replied. "Are you related to Miss Blackwood or here for educational reasons?"

For a fleeting moment, Brandon considered lying, telling the receptionist Theadora was his younger sister or cousin or something. Jax spoke first. "No relatives. We're a part of the Arcane Investigative Division." He flashed a badge. "We're here on a task involving Miss Blackwood."

The receptionist balked, and not only at what Jax said. His appearance alone made her skittish. "All right, I'll see what I can find." Moments later, she handed them a sheet of paper with a list of classes Theadora took that semester and the professors who taught them.

Brandon dipped his head. "Thank you." He and Jax grabbed a map from the reception desk and veered down a wide, white hallway, using the list to direct them to classrooms. In each one, they spoke with a different professor.

The professors all smiled and stated Thea was an exceptional student with good grades but not great attendance.

"She isn't very social," a professor of ancient studies told them. "Keeps to herself most of the time. Doesn't seem to have any friends in class. As far as I know, she leaves right after. Doesn't talk to anyone." He shrugged. "Not that it should matter much. She excels in her studies."

Maybe the girl was shy, Brandon thought. An antisocial girl with magic might not be the best choice, he considered further.

He thanked the man and led Jax down another hall to the last class on ancient artifacts taught by Ms. Adaline Jones. The woman was not there, but a janitor told them they might find her in her office. They headed in that direction, and Brandon noted that it was nearly two in the afternoon. If they gleaned anything from seeing Ms. Jones, they could grab lunch afterward.

Inside the office, a pretty woman in her late thirties sat behind a desk at a computer where she seemed to be entering information. She glanced up and stilled when she did not recognize the two men, especially Jax's hulking form. "Can I help you?" Her voice was light and sweet.

"Ms. Jones?" Brandon inquired. She nodded. "We are looking for Miss Theadora Blackwood and are wondering if you are her professor. If so, we would like to know more about her. Is she a good student? How long has she been in your class?"

Slowly, Ms. Jones laid down the pen she had been holding aloft. "What makes you ask about Thea?"

Thea. So the professor and the girl were on more personal terms, Brandon presumed.

Brandon glanced at Jax, then back at the professor. "We're part of a research team for AID, and Theadora Blackwood has become of special interest to us." It was vague but true.

"Thea is a wonderful student. Always has high marks."

"Is her attendance good?"

"For my class, yes. She's here every time. Hasn't missed a single class."

Brandon jotted this down on a notepad. Theadora had a special interest in artifacts. Interesting. "And does she socialize with others in the class?"

Ms. Jones chuckled. "Well, she's not exactly friends with the other students, but she is lively in conversation. She participates in all our discussions."

Brandon wrote this down, too. "That's all, Ms. Jones. Thank you."

She nodded. "I hope you find whatever it is you're looking for."

Brandon and Jax left the office. Brandon was about to suggest lunch when Jax stated, "That woman was a witch."

"How do you know?"

"I sensed it. Nothing wrong with that. However, it would explain why Miss Blackwood has a more vested interest in that class than others," Jax remarked.

Brandon figured this could be true.

"Say, do you have a picture of the girl?" Jax asked.

Brandon nodded and handed him the photograph. "That's her."

Jax examined it before handing it back. "How about lunch?"

Brandon was relieved to hear the suggestion. "What are

you thinking? Pizza, sandwiches, or..." He trailed off as Jax stopped short, eyes fixed on something down the hall. "What is it?" Then Brandon turned and knew. The picture matched the girl coming toward them. She did not seem to notice them. She was hurrying past them toward Ms. Jones' office.

Jax pointed and spoke loud enough for anyone coming down the hall to hear. "That's her! Miss Blackwood!"

Theadora froze and turned toward them, her eyes widening as she took in the two men.

"Theadora?" Brandon called, approaching her. "We'd like to have a word if you could—"

He didn't finish his sentence. The girl unfroze and bolted away.

CHAPTER FIVE

"*The second of the three texts comprising* The Ancient's Grimoire *by Grand Archmagister Ambrosius is called the* Codex Mystica. *It is a much more advanced text than its predecessor and delves deeper into both the mysteries of magic and the nature of reality itself. It contains powerful spells and incantations that can be used to manipulate the very fabric of the universe.*

Detailed instructions follow on different means by which one might ascend to higher levels of power. Or so say Ambrosius' followers throughout the centuries, many of whom are now dead. The Codex Mystica *has become a part of legend after not being seen for more than a thousand years. Many believe it was buried either with Ambrosius himself or one of his close followers.*"

—*Orlena Gorbana,* On Mage Masters Throughout Time and History

Brandon didn't waste a single second.

All his training kicked into full gear, and he set off after her. But damn, she was fast. Not only did Theadora dart through the hall, but she found a side exit and left the main building.

"I'll get the car," Jax told Brandon, heading off quickly toward where Brandon had parked. The latter sprinted after the girl across a lawn littered with students who turned curious eyes toward the darting pair, wondering what the hell was going on. Theadora headed for a grove of trees bordering a sector of buildings leading into the downtown area.

As they reached the woods, Brandon thought she might get winded and slow down. The opposite happened. Somehow, she became faster. *Magic,* he thought. She had to be using magic. Shit. He was in among the trees seconds later. She tore through the woods ahead of him, over protruding roots and vines as if they weren't there.

She turned her head once, and their eyes locked. Hers widened, not in fear but in fierce determination to get the hell away from him. Well, it wouldn't be the first time a woman tried to flee from him. Not like this, though. Not when she didn't have a damn clue what he wanted. *She must have seen we were from AID,* he thought. Otherwise, what had spooked her?

At that moment, Brandon realized she had something in her hand. A wand. Did witches still use wands these days? A spark of magic flew from the end. Before he could evade it, it hit him in the chest. He reeled back, stunned. A jolt of pain went through him, and he cursed. The pain seeped away a moment later, and he kept pursuing. What she'd done had slowed him down, though. Probably her point.

THE FIRST WITCH-MAGE

Brandon's phone rang. He answered while running. "We're headed through the wood east of campus," he yelled to Jax. He lowered his voice so she could not hear him to add, "Get the car by the street leading into downtown. She might go that way."

The girl turned again, waving her ridiculous wand. Magic zapped out, but Brandon had learned from the last blast. He ducked and increased his speed. Seeing he was onto her, the girl took off faster. She was bound to get winded sooner or later. Her magic had to run out. Or her focus. *Something, dammit!*

Brandon grew flustered. More than flustered. Recruiting a new witch liaison wasn't supposed to include sprinting through a college campus woods after a girl nine years younger than him. "We only want to talk, Theadora!" he shouted after her.

His words might have slowed her or given her a second of pause. She kept going but shouted back, "Get away from me! I don't want to talk to any of you scumbags!" She was definitely aware they had come from AID. Great. Whatever perception she had of them, it wouldn't help matters for Brandon.

"We don't want to hurt you!" he called, anger entering his voice. "We just. Want. To. Talk!"

And she didn't, apparently. She made that pretty fucking clear.

The edge of the woods came into sight. The girl dropped from a steep embankment into an alleyway between a stone wall and a brick building. Brandon followed, relieved to be in the shade after the sweltering sun and all the running. The end of the alley came into sight, but there was no way out except to climb over a dumpster and shimmy up a chain-linked fence. The girl faltered, then turned, not wasting a second to blast Brandon with her magic.

This time, he couldn't avoid it. The blast struck him in the chest again, and he fell flat onto the hard concrete. Brandon groaned. The next thing he knew, the girl was darting past him. He tried to snatch her ankle, but she avoided him with a hiss. "I didn't want to hurt you, but you need to stop chasing me!" she exclaimed.

She would have gotten away if not for the screeching of tires as a car arrived at the other end of the alley. Jax. *Thank God*, Brandon thought. Bringing the former Marine along had been one of Claire's best ideas. He'd thank her again and give her credit later. Slowly, he stood, shaking dust off his clothes and trying not to look like he'd had his ass beaten.

Before Theadora could blast Jax with her magic, the former Marine tased her. Then, he slapped Stygian shackles on her wrists. Brandon stood there, breathing hard. Good. At least one of them had thought to bring handcuffs treated with black metal that blocked magic. One of AID's first inventions when it came to facing criminal magic users.

Except this girl wasn't a criminal. Brandon understood why she had done what she had. Still, they needed the cuffs to make her stand still and not blast them again.

Theadora struggled against Jax. "Let me go! I haven't done a damn thing wrong!"

Brandon stilled, suddenly wondering if they'd been set up. Maybe Mother Folsom knew they would have to detain the girl, and that was why she'd offered Theadora. *Shit*, Brandon thought for about the twentieth time that day. He knew it would not be the last. Still flustered, Brandon directed his attention to Jax. "We'll take her back to AID headquarters and try to figure things out."

"Agent Cole," Jax replied with a warning tone. "I'm not sure that's a good idea. We could let her off with a warning not to attack us again."

Theadora snarled. "You were chasing me!"

"All we want to do was—" Brandon started.

"And I told you I didn't want to fucking talk." The girl showed teeth.

She had a mouth on her, that was for sure. Brandon recalled certain words he'd read on reports regarding Theadora. Headstrong. "Trouncing on tradition." Impulsive. The list went on. Other words came to his mind. Orphan. Misunderstood. Powerful. God, she was powerful. Mother Folsom said she wasn't well trained, but the girl had blasted Brandon hard enough to knock him off his feet. They would need her.

"We're taking her back," he repeated to Jax, heading for his car.

The former Marine mumbled something between a command and an apology to the girl before shoving her into the backseat.

How the hell had her day turned into this?

Thea wished she had the power to burn through her shackles. She knew what was in them the second the big, buff guy slapped them on her wrists. The instant they touched her skin, her magic evaporated. She'd heard before about devices AID had invented to keep down "uncooperative" magic users.

I'm not a criminal, she seethed inwardly. She shouted it next, hurling the words at the window she could not see through in the interrogation room. "I'm not a criminal!" That was what they had put her in, an interrogation room. Four gray walls with only two chairs and a table to occupy the space.

No one had come in to question her yet. The big guy had put her in here two minutes ago, muttering an apology for "all this nonsense." Then he left, not bothering to unshackle her. At least he hadn't taken her purse. She heard her phone buzzing inside it. It could have been Ms. Jones calling to see if she was coming, or Mia, or Connor asking for a date *again*. It didn't matter because she couldn't fucking get to it.

Thea scooted her chair forward, the bottom screeching against the ground loud enough to make her cringe. She didn't care if anyone else heard or who might be watching. She wanted her damn phone and her chocolate. Her wand was in there, too. It was a wonder they had not confiscated it. After seeing her use it...

Well, now they knew how untrained she was.

Most witches, at least experienced ones, no longer used wands. They were devices of a bygone age. Thea's wand had once belonged to her mother, and she had learned to use it for mundane spells when she was a child. She'd kept it more as a memory of her mother than anything else, but sometimes it came in handy. She wanted to hit Agent Cole in the chest again.

Why was this happening to her? She was halfway between raging and crying with no way to get the shackles off. Thea stared across the room at the double window despite seeing nothing but her reflection. Sweat slid down her brow from all the running, smearing the makeup she had spent so much time perfecting that morning. Fuck those guys for doing this to her.

"If you're out there, I need to know why," she seethed. "What the fuck am I doing here?"

No answer. Thea kicked the table, then hissed at the pain drilling up her foot into her calf. She sank back into her chair and released a low whine. Her phone had stopped buzzing. Whoever called had given up. If it was Mia, Thea hoped her friend would go to her apartment to check on her. At least someone would notice she'd gone missing, though Thea hoped she would not be at AID headquarters long enough to raise concern.

As much as Thea hated the coven over the past few years, she'd hated AID longer. They were a bunch of goody-two-shoes, government-appointed guys who thought they had business telling a magic user what to do with their magic. For some crimes, it worked, but they were known for overstepping their bounds time and time again. Plus, weren't these the people responsible for losing two coven members over the last few years?

The new fear made her direct her attention to the shackles. She willed them to shatter. Nothing happened. Thea was about to shout again when the door opened and, finally, someone entered.

Brandon was beginning to wonder if he had made a mistake as he watched Theadora through the two-way mirror and tried to figure out how the hell things had gotten out of hand so quickly. One second, he had spotted her. The next thing he knew, Jax was shoving her into the back seat of his car. Dammit, this wasn't how any of this was supposed to go. It certainly wasn't the way to begin a good-willed relationship with a new liaison.

She'd spooked like a wild animal. She hadn't stopped acting like one since they caught her. Brandon dragged a hand through his hair and considered his options. He could book her for magical assault on a federal agent, but his gut told him she was complicated trouble, and he didn't need that headache. It almost seemed better to let the whole thing go and tell Mother Folsom she needed to hand over a different liaison. *But she's not going to,* Brandon recalled. *No matter what we threaten.*

The only life Mother Folsom was willing to give up was Theadora's, which made Brandon keep her here. He wanted to know why. All his life, he'd been warned that his curiosity would overwhelm him. *Don't let it cloud your judgment,* he thought. Furthermore, his superiors would want him to make this work.

The door opened, and Brandon expected to see Jax, but it was Claire instead. Brandon had sent Jax to type up the paperwork on the incident. After the words came out of his mouth, he'd seen Jax's expression. Well, not so much his expression because the man was like a mountain, but definitely his eyes. Whatever goodwill classic rock had bought with Jax was gone.

Claire's face was solemn as her eyes met Brandon's. "I see you got the girl. She didn't come willingly, I guess."

Brandon shook his head, then explained how Theadora had assaulted him, leaving out the part where he had chased her across campus into the downtown area. It didn't look good. Not at all.

"I saw Jax a few minutes ago," Claire added. "He looked like he was about to punch his computer again. Whatever happened, he doesn't seem to approve. Tell me the full story, Agent Cole." Claire usually called him Brandon unless she was on the brink of reprimanding him. Addressing him as "Agent Cole" reminded him that they weren't buddies. She was his superior, and he had a job to do.

Brandon did as she commanded, starting with their search at Tulane University and what they had learned from Theadora's professors. Then he got to the part where Jax had spotted her and the chase began. Claire's eyes widened. "You *chased* the girl? We aren't an animal control group." She threw her hands up.

"She didn't want to talk!"

Claire shook her head. "Well, there's nothing in our protocol guidelines about that. Maybe there should be." No direct consequences from AID's higher-ups, then. Not yet, anyway.

"I made a mistake," Brandon admitted. "I shouldn't have given chase like that."

Claire cut him off before he could go on. "I recommend you go in there and talk to her. See if you can rectify the situation. You can also take those cuffs off her. The room she's in will stifle her magic." Right. Black metal in the walls and all that. "Whatever misunderstanding occurred, straighten it out," Claire insisted.

Brandon nodded. "Understood." He drew a steadying breath before heading in.

CHAPTER SIX

"The third and final text comprising The Ancient's Grimoire *by Grand Archmagister Ambrosius is known as the* Treatise of Enchantment. *A comprehensive guide to the various limitations and counters to various sorts of magic, it draws on ancient wisdom and knowledge passed down through the ages. It contains rituals, incantations, and sometimes mundane means of thwarting different kinds of magic.*

"Though perhaps the least dangerous and controversial among the three texts, it is the one that has not been seen for the longest time. Even before Ambrosius' death, it disappeared. Legend has it the text was stolen by a close follower turned traitor whose name remains at this time unknown."

—Orlena Gorbana, On Mage Masters Throughout Time and History

Thea watched Agent Cole enter and narrowed her eyes. He looked younger than any AID agent she'd seen before. Granted, she hadn't seen many. He must have been either late twenties or early thirties, slightly older than her. And somewhat hot, if she was admitting the truth. She'd always been fond of tall men with dark, slightly curly hair and light eyes. Plus, he obviously packed it on at the gym. Yet everything she'd gone through with him today made her want to punch him in the face, not ask for his number.

He stopped short, staring at her, then cleared his throat. "Miss Blackwood, I apologize for keeping you waiting."

She huffed. He had a lot more to be sorry about than the ten minutes he'd left her in here alone. "Tell me what the hell is going on *right now*."

Agent Cole remained calm and sat on the other side of the table, placing several folders in front of him in a neat stack. Thea frowned. What the hell was inside those? Were they about her? She sighed. "Can you at least get these damn things off me?" She put her shackled wrists onto the table. "I promise not to blow a hole through the door." *Yet*, she added silently.

Agent Cole nodded and came over, unshackling her before sitting down again. "The doors aren't locked if that makes you more comfortable." Thea rubbed her wrists without a word and felt her magic coming back slowly but surely. However, in this room, it was muted more than normal. There must have been something in the walls. That was why the man across from her felt comfortable removing her cuffs.

"Like I said, we only want to talk."

"About what, Agent Cole?" Thea hissed.

"You can call me Brandon."

Brandon. What a boring name. "And you can call me nothing at all."

He blinked, surprised at the bite in her voice. He didn't

let it faze him for long and opened one of the files. He searched through a few papers with dark brows drawn together. Meanwhile, Thea wondered what sort of guy she was looking at.

As a coven witch, she'd grown up with inbuilt biases about AID. Mostly, she knew they were unnecessary in the modern age, where normal people knew about the magical world. Knew but didn't always understand. Thea needed to know what type of AID guy this Brandon fellow was.

Some were magical wannabes who had gotten into AID because they couldn't do magic but wanted to be close to it out of adoration or bitterness. Some were by-the-book fellas looking to cash in on the better pension and insurance the newer agency offered.

A third type of AID agent existed, too. Those looking for any chance to bring down magic users because they hated or feared them. The witch hunter sorts who wore suits instead of cloaks and wide-brimmed caps.

"What are you?" Thea drawled. "A magical wannabe who couldn't wait to get close to someone like me, a guy looking for good insurance, or a witch hunter? Going by that little chase, I gather you might be the third."

Brandon blinked again as the girl leaned forward, resting her forearms on the table. He cleared his throat. "I'm none of those things."

Thea lifted a brow. "Interesting."

He didn't seem to like how her eyes penetrated him to pick up on every thought he had. His face was blanker than he might have figured. Thea had to give him credit for that. She couldn't read a damn thing about him. Unlike him, who seemed to have a whole file about her in front of him.

She leaned back, sighing. "You know, there are witches who've started calling the whole country New Salem." It had started in 1994 when the Paranormal Enforcement Office took things too far. They launched a raid on a coven estate in New England that left the entire coven dead, along with several of their family members. Even the non-magical staff working at the estate had been butchered. Killed in the nastiest, most gruesome way possible.

Thea reminded Brandon of this bit of history. "Is that what you hot-shot guys plan to do to me? Wouldn't matter anyway. I'm sure my file has already told you my family is dead. Why not get rid of me too?"

His cheeks flushed. "We don't want to kill anyone. We don't want to hurt anyone. The event you're talking about was indeed a tragedy. There's nothing to justify the raid. But the PEO was dismantled in disgrace. AID was formed from its ruins, but it's not the same. Not at all."

He spoke with enough conviction that Thea shut her mouth to listen.

"AID has worked hard to weed out any witch hunters within its ranks. If there are witch hunters in the organization, I don't know about them, and I'm certainly not one of them. As for the chase and forcing you to come here, I'm sorry." Real sincerity filled his eyes.

Thea looked away, crossing her arms.

"If it makes you feel better, my partner Jax will probably beat my ass over this later."

Thea liked that idea, but she did not indicate this. "Still, the AID record over the past twenty years or so hasn't exactly been spotless."

He sat back, giving her a look of interest. "You know your stuff."

"Duh. If that file tells you anything about me, it should say I'm an occult history studies major. That includes knowing what's happening with people who aren't friendly to my kind."

"Some of us are trying to help your kind. I didn't know Tulane offered that kind of class."

"I requested that they create the major for me."

He blinked again. "How'd you manage that?"

She shrugged. "I had to make the money from my parents' estate count for something. I'm doing valuable research."

Brandon very much wanted to know what she meant but didn't ask. Thea wasn't inclined to elaborate further and was growing impatient for answers. "You want to know why I chased you, Miss Blackwood, but I'm interested to know why you ran," he commented instead.

"Because I've seen pricks like you before. I want nothing to do with AID." Her voice might have been fire before, but it was ice now.

"Understandable," Brandon returned. "Maybe you need more trust to tell me. I get that. Really, I do. I'm not any of the things you think I might be. Actually, I was sent here against my will. I had a...fallout with my last job. They thought working for AID would cool me off."

"You don't seem hot-headed to me."

Brandon chuckled. "You don't have to have a short temper to fail."

Thea shifted. She was both curious about this man's

past and inclined to get the hell out of here as soon as possible. "Sooo you're here temporarily?"

Brandon shrugged. "We'll have to find out. This is my first mission, and so far, it's not going well."

"*I'm* your first mission? Why?"

Brandon tapped his stack of papers. "Your files here are from the coven leadership. They have nominated you as our new witch liaison."

It was Thea's turn to be surprised. "*What?*"

"That's right."

"Why the hell would I want to be your messenger?"

"Clearly, you don't, but we hope to change your mind. First, with an apology. I hope you can accept it. Also, you should know being a liaison doesn't make you merely a go-between. Actually, you'll be dealing with your coven very little."

Thea rubbed her wrists, her mind racing with new questions. Not having to deal with her coven seemed nice, but at what cost? Working for AID. *No. Thank. You,* she thought.

"I'm surprised no one in the coven leadership told you beforehand. We figured you might have gotten word before we showed up," Brandon added.

I don't talk to the coven anymore, Thea almost stated, but she didn't know this guy. She wouldn't give him any close information. Not until she knew more.

Brandon continued. "Maybe you had a reason to run, but don't you want to know more about what being a witch liaison would mean, Theadora?"

Her head snapped up, eyes blazing. "It's Thea. I haven't gone by Theadora in a long time. And to you, it's Miss Blackwood. Thea is what my friends call me."

He put his hands up. "I'm sorry." She could tell he meant it. Furthermore, his face seemed to show as much nervousness as she felt.

Maybe I've put him through the wringer enough, she thought. This didn't mean she had to like him, but she could be less cruel. He clearly intended to let her go when this discussion was over, if they could call it that.

"This witch liaison thing must be a big joke," she commented at last.

"I'm not joking," Brandon returned.

"Not from you, dummy. From the coven. That old hag Fouche probably did this to get rid of me."

"Fouche?" Brandon queried.

"Never mind. She doesn't matter. Point is, whoever nominated me probably thought I wouldn't actually join. They don't intend to give you a liaison at all."

"Don't you have to do what the coven tells you?"

Thea laughed bitterly. "That's funny, Brandon."

He cringed at the way she said his name.

A slow smile crept across her lips. "The coven is trying to get rid of me. They might be hoping AID will get me killed like the last two liaisons. Like how the coven got my parents killed."

This revelation was new to Brandon. She could tell by the shock in his eyes. He gathered himself a second later. "I read about that. I'm sorry."

He meant it. No one but Mia had meant that in the last three years. Only Mia gave a damn that she was a sad orphan, refusing to go back to her family home or accept support from the other people who had helped raise her. She had her money and school and one good friend. That was enough. Thea had to remind herself this Brandon guy had chased her down and forced her to come here against her will before she started to like him.

Brandon leaned forward. "Wouldn't joining us and staying alive piss the coven off, then?"

Thea hadn't thought of that. "Go on."

Brandon explained to her what they were looking for. It wasn't only a messenger. Actually, she'd have very little going between to do. She would train with Jax and be part of a mission task team. She'd be the one with magic and a valuable asset.

"To do what?" Thea demanded. "Hunt down other mages for their so-called crimes? No, thank you."

"Other mages? You're in a coven."

"Not for long."

Brandon paused. "Interesting."

She grinned. "If I joined, I would not be your liaison for long. I'd be a mage aid or something. How would your higher-ups feel about that?"

"I don't know. I wasn't expecting this." Brandon was honest, at least. He wasn't trying to look smarter than he was.

"I'd like to at least get you through onboarding and processing," Brandon admitted. "We could do a trial period. One month. Then, if you still hate us and the training, you can leave. No questions asked."

Thea arched a brow. "And your bosses are okay with this?"

"I haven't run it by them, but I feel it is only fair to you."

This made Thea pause again. *Why the hell am I actually considering this?* She thought of Fouche. That bitch. The idea of working with AID to piss off the coven sounded... well, fun. "I'm a pretty busy girl," she told Brandon. "I would need time to do my own things."

"Ah, yes, your research."

"It's important to me. By the way, you interrupted a meeting with my professor today."

"I'm sorry," he stated again. "I will find a way to make it up to you."

Having a favor to ask of an actual AID agent might come in handy one day. "I can't start with AID until I can talk to the coven and confirm they actually nominated me."

Brandon opened his mouth to argue. "I spoke with the coven Mother yesterday. We can call her now if you'd like."

Thea shook her head. "I will see my coven Mother face to face." She stood. "I'll be in touch. Don't look for me again. If I want to work for you, I'll come back here."

"Or call me," Brandon insisted, also standing. He drew out a card and handed it to her. His number was typed at the bottom.

Thea could not believe this was what her day had turned into. At the back of her mind, she considered something else. Maybe getting connections and training with AID would help her when she finally figured out how to tap into the Lake of Power. She didn't need to tell Brandon that. Or anyone else.

Thea gave Brandon a curt nod. "Show me how to get out of here and call me an Uber while you're at it. I'm sure we're miles away from my home." Brandon agreed without objection. When Thea was standing outside once more in the bright sunlight, she could only think, *What the hell have I been thrown into?*

She checked her phone at last. Boy, did she have a story for Mia later.

CHAPTER SEVEN

FIRE AT BLACKWOOD ESTATE KILLS TWO, LEAVES ONE INJURED.

Yesterday, May 21, 2020, a fire broke out on the third floor of the Blackwood family estate north of Lake Maurepas. Though firefighters arrived in time to keep most of the house intact, two of its occupants, Irene Anne Blackwood and Peter Jacob Blackwood, were killed, leaving their daughter Theadora Anne Blackwood an orphan. The young woman is twenty years old and does not require a new guardian.

The fire left one woman, a servant employed by the Blackwoods, injured on the premises, as well as several men who also worked at the house. She is recovering at the East Jefferson General Hospital. The source of the fire has not yet been confirmed by officials. No official word as to who the estate will pass to has come out.

—May 2020 news clipping regarding the Blackwood Estate fire

Thea considered her options.

Go back home and chill the fuck out or face the coven leadership right now. She knew sitting at home would only piss her off more, no matter how much chocolate she indulged in. So, at sunset, Thea drove to the estate two hours outside the French Quarter.

She hadn't bothered to call ahead and inform anyone she was coming. Even if it was night and many of the witches would already be retiring from the day. Not that they had hard work to do. The day of a coven witch at the estate was milling around, waiting for the spirits to speak or news of a disaster elsewhere in the country.

Thea parked at the front of the building and marched up the long stone stairs, not bothering to knock on the huge oak double doors. She let herself in by speaking the magical password over the pentagram etched into the door's surface. The same pentagram shape tattooed on the back of her neck glowed along with the door.

Inside, she found the front hall empty. At hearing the front door open, two witches from the Sabbat Thea was not in came into the hall. Both stopped short in surprise. "Theadora."

She breezed past them, up a spiral set of stairs, and directly to the office at the back of the house where she hoped to find the coven Mother. She didn't care if Mother Folsom was busy. She'd make the woman have time for her.

Thea didn't bother knocking on that door either. As soon as she stepped in, a figure who was not Mother Folsom confronted her. "Arthur, pleasure to see you as always," Thea announced in a voice that didn't sound pleased in the least.

The old man had always creeped her out. She wasn't

sure if it was the long, knobby fingers with rings weighing them down or the piercing nature of his gaze. Maybe it was that he could come up behind someone so quietly they didn't notice until he hissed in their ear.

The wiry man's eyes narrowed to slits. "Missss Blackwood. Itsss a ssssurprise to ssssee you."

She'd forgotten about his hissing tone of voice. Another voice reached her. "Arthur, you can leave Theadora and me alone for a moment." Mother Folsom stood at the window, not behind her desk as usual. Arthur glowered at Thea before dipping his head. "As you wish, Mother." He slunk out of the room, leaving the two witches alone.

Mother Folsom turned, her face unreadable as always. "I didn't think AID would work so fast to find you. I guess you being here means they've already contacted you."

Thea snorted. "'Contacted' isn't quite the right word." She didn't bother to tell her coven Mother about the chase and the shackles or being in an interrogation room with Agent Cole.

"It was Fouche, wasn't it? That bitch wants me out and handed me over to AID. I figured I'd come and make sure you knew." Secretly, Thea harbored hopes she would see Fouche and give her a piece of her mind. Again.

Mother Folsom did not show surprise, which knocked Thea off kilter. Instead, the coven Mother motioned for the younger woman to sit in one of the leather chairs on the other side of her desk. Thea plopped down as Mother Folsom took the seat behind the desk. "Fouche has had nothing to do with this. She doesn't know about it yet."

Thea blanched. "Then how the hell did—" She stopped short, the sinking feeling of betrayal filling her. "You did it.

You offered me up." Thea always had reservations about the coven Mother, but not like this. She had never expected this sort of action from Michelle. As far as she knew, Mother Folsom was the only person in the whole damn coven who actually cared about Thea.

"I'm sorry, Thea. I am. I didn't have any other choice." Mother Folsom had deep sincerity in her eyes. Maybe not as much as Brandon had shown, but it was there.

Thea clenched the arms of her chair. "There is *always* another choice, especially when I'm the youngest person in the whole damn coven! Why me and not an old fart with more *experience*?" Her voice and expression were pleading, and pity flickered across Mother Folsom's dark purple eyes.

"The coven is on the edge about things with you, Thea." The "Theadora" was gone. Was Mother Folsom calling her Thea to calm her down or because she wanted to show she cared?

Once, Mother Folsom had lived with Thea and her family. The Blackwood estate had been prime land for witches to work from, with the ley line of powerful magic running beneath it. Thea had grown up with the coven Mother right down the hall. Things had changed in the past few years. Mother Folsom had always said the coven came first, and Thea…well, she wasn't second.

Thea clenched the arms of her chair again. "So Fouche does have something to do with this. I knew it. She told you I beat her ass. Well, it was her fault to begin with. She attacked me first!"

Mother Folsom nodded. "I understand, Thea, but I can't overrule the coven's general consensus about you."

"Why not?" Thea bit back.

Mother Folsom gave her a pointed look. "You know very well why, Thea." Past coven Mothers had been mutinied against for decisions they'd made that the coven found unfavorable. Her place of power was only that—a place. She could be moved.

Thea did not give up her pleading. "I didn't have to become part of the coven until all that shit happened three years ago." Her parents' death, the fire, and the vision in the library. Someone had to take her mother's spot, and at the time, Mother Folsom thought Thea would be the right fit. Oh, how wrong she had been.

Mother Folsom continued. "If it was only you, Thea, I could listen. But I have eleven other members to adhere to. All who are older than you."

"Yeah, yeah. Let the young ones rot, I get it."

More pity entered Mother Folsom's eyes.

"I also have centuries of carefully cultivated tradition, debts, and privileges to consider," Mother Folsom reminded her. "It comes down to this. You can join AID or be subject to a Tribunal that Fouche and others have called for. Myself and the two Sabbat leaders will interrogate you before the coven." Fouche would be a bitch to her, and the other Sabbat leader, Douglas Hendriks, was a wild card. "Your fate would be put to a vote, Thea. If you join AID, at least you have some control of your destiny."

Ha. Destiny was a funny word. So was control. Thea had not been in control of her destiny in years, if ever. That day in the passage three years ago had only been to tease her, tug her toward an impossible future. Now, she had to choose between two organizations. Which one disliked her least?

"It is possible the coven would assign a variety of punishments if they find you guilty," Mother Folsom stated. "Or they may agree to only one."

Thea didn't need her coven Mother to say the words for her to know. The Fleecing. The last person who had undergone the Fleecing had been away from the coven for over fifty years. Where that poor woman was now, none of them knew.

Thea had a lot to think over. Did she want to run the risk of the Fleecing? Being cut off from the coven wasn't what worried her. It was the painful ritual, the stripping of her magic. Without it, she wouldn't have a chance in hell to access the Lake of Power. Not that Mother Folsom needed to know that. Any hint of what she was trying to do would be reason enough for the Fleecing immediately.

"I guess the writing is on the wall then," she grumbled. It was AID or nothing. AID or hide from the coven for the rest of her life. AID or lose her magic, the only thing she had left that felt tied her to her beloved parents. "How long do I have to…serve?" she asked.

"Three years."

Thea lurched forward in her seat. "Years?" She remembered Brandon's proposal of a one-month trial but did not tell Mother Folsom about it. A sinking feeling filled her when she also recalled the last two liaisons who had died. No one in the coven had told her what happened. It was "confidential" information, or so they said. Thea had a feeling everyone knew but her.

Mother Folsom attempted a reassuring smile. "Cheer

up, Thea. I met Ajax Maddison. He seems like a formidable man. He will teach you some valuable lessons, I'm sure."

"And did Agent Cole come and speak to you, too?"

Mother Folsom nodded. "He's not too bad on the eyes, is he?"

Thea rolled her eyes. "Don't try to convince me to join AID by pointing out a hot guy."

"So you *do* find him attractive?"

Thea stood. "I'm done talking about this."

Mother Folsom put up her hands in defense. "All I'm saying is there's more to Brandon Cole than meets the eye."

Well, at least Thea could agree with that. She stuck her hand in her pocket and traced the edge of the card he had given her. Maybe she would call. "I can sweeten the deal," Mother Folsom added, leaning forward with her hands folded together.

"You're not going to betroth me to anyone, are you?"

She chuckled. "I'm glad you still have a sense of humor, Thea." It was one of the things that had not died with her parents, a survival mechanism so she didn't spiral right into the bottom of her well of grief. "After three years, you will be free to return to the coven as you are. You can become a Sabbat leader then if you want. You could replace Fouche."

Thea narrowed her eyes. That sounded too good to be true. Was Mother Folsom trying to tempt her? What unforeseen conditions were involved?

"Or, you will be free to go your own way without any prejudice from your coven," Mother Folsom offered.

Even more tempting. Thea played with the card in her pocket. "I'll think about it." She let herself out of Mother

Folsom's office, the house, and into the clear, starry night. At least out here, she felt like she could breathe normally.

Michelle Folsom watched Thea leave from the windows in her office, which overlooked the front portion of the coven's estate. The large, circular gravel drive and the hedges trimmed to perfection stared back at her. The sky had turned dark, casting the grounds in soft, purple shadows.

Lights glimmered from the floors below where, no doubt, the other coven members gathered, speculating on why Theadora Blackwood had come, then marched out again. Michelle watched Theadora pull out, the beam of her headlights panning over the windows she stood at. *I'll have to prepare what to say to the others soon,* Michelle thought.

Of course, she didn't quite know what that would be since the girl had not yet made up her mind. Michelle had a feeling Theadora would play it safe for once in her life and take the offer from AID. *And maybe my headache will go away,* she thought.

She returned to her desk and dialed downstairs to her secretary, who answered. "Please send up Arthur, Helena. Right away."

"Will do," Helena answered.

A few moments later, as Michelle was drawing the curtains in her office and lighting several candles with a quick flicker of magic, a knock came at the door. "Come in."

Arthur slunk in as always, dipping his head. "How did it go?"

"As expected. She came sooner than I thought but said all the things I figured she would. I believe things are going in the right direction."

"And her obsession with this mage pursuit?" Arthur prodded.

"Still a problem." Michelle pressed her lips together into a thin, grim line. "We'll need to keep an eye on her regardless of what she chooses, though I do hope if she joins AID, she'll forget about the whole thing."

"Do you want me to follow her, Mother?" Arthur remained standing by the closed door, hands behind his back.

Mother Folsom shook her head. "Hold off on that for now, though it's not such a bad idea." The time might come for that. At the back of her mind, Michelle acknowledged Arthur was a skilled and loyal agent. Sometimes, he was too skilled and was known to take matters into his hands, if he thought the fate of the coven or Folsom's position was threatened.

"You may go now, Arthur." Michelle turned back to her desk. But the man remained.

"There is one thing, Mother. I meant to report earlier, but the Blackwood girl showed up."

"Go on."

"There are bodiesss to be dissspossssed of jussst round back. But you needn't worry about it if you have other pressing matterss. The threat hasss been taken care of."

Michelle was surprised to hear this but did what she could to hide this from her agent. Nevertheless, Arthur read it in her silence. "A few rogue magesss trying to come onto the property. They showed sssigns of misssconduct. They have already been dealt with."

Michelle wondered what this meant but decided not to ask. She could find out from one of the witches. She nodded. "Good, Arthur. Thank you." Again, at the back of her mind, Michelle hoped Arthur would not begin to see Thea as a threat and kill her for one transgression or another.

Inwardly, she considered the alternative. Either Arthur killed a young, talented witch Folsom was fond of, or less likely but still possible, Theadora killed one of her most skilled operatives. Having Arthur follow Thea around was a disaster waiting to happen. One of them would go down, and if it was Arthur, Thea would follow it back to her. Michelle did not need Thea feeling more betrayed than she already was.

"Keep your distance from the girl for now, Arthur. The girl needs room to breathe without all of us looking over her shoulder. However, you can supply me with internal reports of the AID operations concerning Theadora. They will send me reports, of course, but that's out of courtesy. They'll keep anything out they want to."

Arthur dipped his head. "Of courssse, Mother."

Michelle sat down as a new thought came to mind. "While you're at it, you may as well dig up fresh dirt on Fouche. The cranky old bat won't be happy when she finds out we're not crucifying Isadore. I'd like to have something ready to shut her up so she can't do anything but nod along with my plan." Plus, the job would keep Arthur occupied and away from Thea.

I'm cooking up the best plans, aren't I? Michelle thought, feeling pleased with herself.

Arthur nodded again and gave the coven Mother a snake-like smile. "Of courssse. I'd be happy to do it." He disappeared through the door, and Michelle was left to greet the coming night and hope everything didn't go to hell when the sun rose again.

CHAPTER EIGHT

"Irene Anne Blackwood was born on October 13, 1980, to Edward and Louisa Brownston, both of whom have passed. She passed away on May 21, 2020, due to a fire at the Blackwood family estate. She married Peter Jacob Blackwood, also a victim of the fire, on December 6, 1995. She is survived by several distant family members and one daughter, Theadora Anne Blackwood.

Irene was known in her community as one of the local coven witches but was overall well-regarded by both magic and non-magic users. She was charitable to several local organizations, including hospitals, food pantries, and housing for the homeless."

—From the newspaper printed obituary of Irene Anne Blackwood

When Thea got home to her apartment later that night, she stopped short on the threshold. Something was different. It smelled *nice* in here. As if someone had lit a candle and blown it out before they left. Other than Thea, only one person had a key to her place.

"Oh gods, Mia, you're the best person on the entire planet." Thea was near tears as she entered the kitchen and found it spotless, with every dish washed, dried, and put away. On the counter was a bar of silver-wrapped chocolate and a note in Mia's beautiful handwriting.

> *I know you've been having a tough time. Enjoy a clean apartment tonight and your chocolate. Plus, I need you caught up on* Love is Blind *episodes so I have someone to talk about it with.*
> *XO, M*

Mia didn't know the half of it regarding the "tough time," but she always sensed when Thea was going through something. Thea plopped onto her sofa with the chocolate, the warm message from Mia wiping away all the unpleasantness she'd been through that day. She opened her laptop, remembering Mia's birthday was coming up, and searched for presents. She had to find the best gift in existence. Maybe concert tickets to Mia's favorite indie-folk band. Mia's favorite imported yarn, to be enchanted for maximum crocheting, of course.

Later, Thea would track down Mia's favorite tea from a teashop in the French Quarter. New crystals would never hurt, and Mia had been complaining about how worn her boots were for weeks now. *I'll bake her favorite cake too,* Thea thought as she purchased Mia's favorite yarn from Germany and selected the fastest shipping available. One of the good things about the money her family had left her was being able to buy the best presents for her friends.

Thea started to feel better. Focusing on things that mattered got AID and the coven off her mind for a time. As she finished her online shopping, an email popped onto her screen from Adaline Jones.

I'm sorry we didn't get a chance to meet today, Thea. Do come by my office in the morning if you'd like to talk. Maybe your no-show had something to do with the two hot-shot guys who waltzed into my office asking about you this afternoon. I hope everything is all right.
Best,
Adaline.

Thea responded that everything was all right because at least she was unharmed and no longer in an interrogation room. She said she would do her very best to show up tomorrow. After closing her laptop, Thea decided on a long, hot shower and bed. Tomorrow, she would not think about AID and the coven until she had to.

Thea arrived at the main building at Tulane University the next morning before any other students showed up, hoping she would be the first to visit Adaline during her office hours. Adaline Jones wasn't only Thea's professor but a friend who had seen in Thea a desire beyond finding old, magical artifacts. As a hedge witch herself, Adaline understood the desire to know more despite having no knowledge of Thea's vision and the reason behind her parents' death.

Thea walked into Adaline's office with a bright smile and offered her a box of her favorite chocolate donuts. "I couldn't get one for myself and not you."

Adaline smiled. "It's a good trade because what I'm about to give to you will make you forget all about chocolate donuts."

Thea sat down. "That's a hard thing to do. I'm intrigued."

Adaline reached into one of her desk drawers and took out a file of papers. It was the first file Thea had seen in the past couple of days that didn't make her wary. "I recently came across some research from a former artifacts professor at another university across the country. Denver, to be exact. Mr. Lawrence Carlson. Ever heard of him?"

Thea shook her head.

"I hadn't either until I found this." She slid over a photograph showing three old-as-shit books, all bound in leather with faded writing on the spines. Thea leaned forward, eyes widening. "This can't be…"

Adaline nodded. "But it might." The lost texts of *The Ancient's Grimoire* by the long-dead Grand Archmagister Ambrosius. "Of course, the writing is in another language. A dead one at that, and I can't use magic on the photographs to tell what it says. You would need the books themselves."

"Does this tell us where they are?" Thea's voice was hopeful.

Adaline shook her head. "It does tell us Professor Carlson saw them at some point. This photo matches one of his cameras. Perhaps he once owned them. We can't know for certain."

But they were real. Someone else had seen them. That was a start. Excited, Thea asked, "Have you talked to Professor Carlson?"

Adaline's expression sobered. "He's dead. Has been for nearly fifty years."

Thea's heart sank.

The professor went on. "He published his research about fifty years ago, but he went missing shortly after. His findings were stripped from most records both online and off."

"Then how did you find it?"

Adaline gave her a knowing smile. "By consorting with spirits." A sparkle came into her eye. Adaline was more of the academic sort of hedge witch, not one to mess with plants and herbs. She was well in tune with the spirits and was a master with tarot, or so Thea had heard. She'd never asked her professor for a reading, not wanting to know anything about her future. She was afraid, too. What if all she saw was failure? What if Adaline saw her plans to reach into the Lake of Power and warned her against it like everybody else?

"This led me to another old coven manor house out of state," Adaline told her. "Up north in the Appalachian region. I found his full printed research there. It was hidden and took literal digging, but I got it back here anyway."

Thea showed surprise. "How did you find time for that?"

Adaline shrugged. "I think the time found me." She took papers from her folder and handed them to Thea. "I made you a copy of his research. It's yours to keep. Don't let anyone else know you have it. Someone made the poor man vanish and destroyed his publications for a reason."

Thea hesitated only a second before taking the papers. "Thank you. You have no idea how much this means to me." Thea could finally learn more about the lost books of Ambrosius and perhaps find out how he had tapped into the Lake of Power.

Adaline smiled briefly, then became somber once more. "You must promise me you'll be careful, Thea. I can't lose my favorite student over some old man's clues."

Thea stood. "I will be."

"And keep in touch over the summer."

"I will. We'll get together from time to time."

Adaline smiled. "I hope so. Have a good day, Thea."

Thea said goodbye. On her way out, her thoughts swirled back to the coven and AID. This research could help her find out how to access the Lake, and working with AID could give her a better standing with the coven. *I have to keep what I'm really doing on the DL,* she thought. She made the sudden decision to swing by AID's offices that evening before returning home.

The parking lot at AID was nearly empty when Thea arrived. She stood at the door until a guard came and opened it for her, frowning at the young woman in ripped black jeans and a maroon tank top. He took in the pendant necklace with its white crystal, the black painted nails, the assortment of bracelets, and the half-moon tattoo on her right wrist. If he couldn't tell she was a witch by sensing it, he could by looking at her. Thea had never shied away from the aesthetic side of coven life, though most of her fellow coven mates preferred long robes or cloaks to jeans and T-shirts.

Thea flashed a smile at the guard. "I'm here to see Brandon." She felt like a college girl showing up late to a party after everyone had gone home, hoping the party-thrower was still around. She looked like it, too, coming here after dark. Brandon might not be here, but she could leave a message.

The guard's frown deepened, but he let her in with a grunt and told her she could find "Agent Cole" on the second floor. Thea followed his directions and wove up the stairs and through hallways, past open but vacant offices and cubicles, until she heard rummaging in a room at the back of the building. There, she found Brandon bent over a laptop, his brows furrowing in deep concentration. She checked her watch again. It was almost 8 p.m.

"A little late for all this, huh?"

Her voice startled him. When he looked up, he didn't hide his surprise. He stood quickly, almost knocking over a glass of water. "Theadora. I-I mean, Miss Blackwood. What are you doing here?"

She smiled, crossing her arms as she leaned against the door frame. "Your story checked out, Agent Cole. Mother Folsom said you'd contacted her."

"And? Are you here to give me good news or bad?"

"I would have ghosted you if it was bad news." She'd considered burning the card with his number on it and watching it melt into her trash can. Instead, she'd stuck it on her fridge with a magnet. Here she was. *I can't believe I'm about to get a job with AID, of all places.* She didn't need the money, but her research had shown that though the last two witch liaisons had died, they'd been well-paid beforehand. Perhaps she'd be paid more due to the extra risks.

Brandon looked relieved.

"Don't get too excited yet. I'm agreeing to a one-month trial. Basically, I'm thinking about working for you. Nothing else." He motioned for her to step into his office and take the chair opposite his desk. "Well, this is nicer than the interrogation room, isn't it?"

"Again, I'm sorry about that," Brandon replied.

"You still owe me one."

"Yes, I do." He sat as well, trying not to look flustered. Thea thought it was cute.

"So what's this onboarding process going to be like?" she asked after surveying the bland furnishings in his office. The only thing of note was a small, framed photo of a dog on his desk. Perhaps a childhood pet.

"There will be training, of course," Brandon told her. "Headed up by Jax. You met him."

Thea examined Brandon's face for any signs that Jax had beaten his ass. There weren't any.

He continued. "Before that, there will be legal and magically binding paperwork. You will have to treat this job as confidential, and you can't use your magic against members of AID except in cases where your life might be in danger."

Thea snorted. "Did the last two liaisons have that option?"

Brandon hesitated. "I don't know. I wasn't around then."

Right, he was almost as much of a newbie as she was. Too bad she didn't have FBI training in her back pocket.

"There have been cases though," he stated. "AID members being possessed by a dimensional being or controlled through dangerous magic by higher beings."

Thea arched a brow. "That's happened?"

"Unfortunately."

"Tragic." She didn't put any care into her tone. "I'm not signing anything that binds me. Forget it."

Brandon, to his credit, did not back down. "You're not the only one who needs to feel like you can trust someone. It goes both ways. Us non-magic users are practically blind compared to your natural awareness and abilities. Blind but not harmless, I should add. We already have to trust you a lot more than you have to trust us. You could take advantage of us."

Thea shifted. Wasn't that what she was already doing? Using AID to increase her power and standing so she could tap into the Lake when it was time? She hoped Brandon didn't sense her ulterior motive. Besides, it wasn't like she planned on hurting anyone. She sighed. "Fine, I'll sign your contract. We can do a month-long one, and if things are going well after that, a new one."

"Fine. I'll draw up the paperwork tomorrow and send it over."

This was all starting to sound more serious and adulty than Thea liked. *Welcome to the real world,* she thought. A strange, weird, real world.

Brandon went on. "You will need training in the

various protocols of AID. Investigation procedures, evidence gathering, suspect apprehension, artifact acquisition and disposal. Those sorts of things."

She almost groaned. Here she was, finishing school and having to dive headfirst into new lessons. Thea felt like teasing. "The artifacts thing will be a piece of cake. Will you teach suspect apprehension, Agent Cole? You certainly know how to give good chase."

His cheeks colored. "Are you going to give me hell for that forever?"

Thea shrugged. "Until I'm bored and find something else to tease you about."

Brandon ignored this remark. "You will have basic training in tactical restraint."

"With magic or everything else?"

"Both."

"Is there someone who knows magic that can train me?"

"We're working on that."

"So that's a no."

"For now."

What an invigorating conversation, Thea thought. "I can handle myself," she told him.

"It's all non-negotiable," Brandon replied. "Non-skippable, that is. It's for your own good."

She'd heard that phrase far too many times in her twenty-three years. Thea scrutinized the agent. "I was right about you being a by-the-book sort of guy."

Brandon shrugged. "Sometimes I go with the RAI instead of the RAW."

"Huh?"

"Rules as Intended over the Rules as Written. But generally, yes, I try to follow the rules."

Thea chuckled. "You must be a D&D nerd. Who else uses terms like RAW and RAI? Table-top gamers, I guess." She tilted her head, examining him again. "Though I suppose you're better looking than most I've met." Dammit, the words flew out of her mouth. This time, both of them flushed. Thea was better at playing it off. *Better not flirt with your new boss,* she told herself. *Especially one nine years older than you.*

Brandon became flustered, and Thea wasn't sure if it was because she'd outed him as a geek or because she'd stated he was attractive. He cleared his throat and redirected the conversation. "Here's the initial paperwork to sign. It outlines what training you'll have and that you have agreed to do it." He handed her a pen, but Thea waved it off, preferring the purple glittery gel pen from her purse.

She bent over the papers and scribbled her signature. A sparkling purple *Theadora Blackwood*. She clicked the pen shut. "Perfect. Now what?"

"I'll get the rest of the paperwork for you tomorrow." Brandon stood and offered her a smile. "Thank you for doing this, Thea. I'm looking forward to working together."

She smiled back, also standing. "And I'm looking forward to Jax beating your ass in training. That is if you find the time to join us." She didn't wait for a response but let herself out with a sway of her hips. She didn't bother to glance behind her to see if Brandon was still watching.

Outside, she sucked in a big gulp of cool evening air.

Things were about to get a lot more interesting. Thea knew she'd be stretched thin on time with her new job and secret plans to learn more about the Lake. Breakfast dates with Mia would be much harder to schedule.

CHAPTER NINE

Peter Jacob Blackwood was born on January 2nd, 1978, to Richard and Etta Blackwood, both of whom have passed. Peter passed away on May 21, 2020, due to a fire at the Blackwood family estate. He married Irene Anne Brownston Blackwood, also a victim of the fire, on December 6, 1995. He is survived by a few distant family members and one daughter, Theadora Anne Blackwood. Peter was known in his community as a philanthropist and user of magic, though he did not belong to a coven like his wife Irene, who was a part of the local coven of New Orleans, Louisiana. Peter donated much of his estate earnings to local theatres and up-and-coming performers.
—*From the newspaper printed obituary of Peter Blackwood*

Thea wasn't sure how much time she would have after she got through the paperwork for AID, so she decided to start her experimentation with the materials Mia had brought to her. Screw *Love is Blind* catch-ups and sleep. She'd find time for those things later.

She arrived home to her apartment to find it as she had

left it, still clean and empty. She called Mia immediately. "I know it's getting late, but how do you feel about getting up to some witchy shit tonight?"

"Well, my date from Tinder ghosted me, so my plans are out the window anyway," Mia replied, sounding more relieved than disappointed. From what Thea heard earlier that week, the guy was a bit of a creep anyway. "I'll be over in ten."

As Thea waited for her friend to arrive, she dug the bag of ingredients from her cupboard where she had hidden it. She hoped the landlord Mrs. Farley had not gone through her things if she decided to make a surprise check while Thea was gone.

Yes, she knew this wasn't quite a legal thing for the landlord to do, but it was a matter of choosing her battles. She could have a screaming match with Mrs. Farley about what was on the lease and wake up half the building or avoid her. The pouch of ingredients was still there, so Thea didn't have to bother thinking about the old woman anymore.

After Mia arrived, Thea pushed aside the sofa and coffee table to clear space on the living room floor. Mia entered, brow raised. "I guess we're starting with that bag of experiments I brought you the other day."

Thea smiled. "We sure are. I'm going to try a potent scrying ritual so I can get a look at the Lake of Power." Mia's expression changed from wariness to outright concern, so Thea added, "Don't worry. I've been reading tons on how to do it, and I'm only going to look. Nothing else."

She had been asking Adaline Jones loads of questions

and practicing smaller scrying rituals. Thea had seen a few places, including her neighbors next door. That had been a big mistake, as Mr. Benson was wrinkly as a raisin and took the longest baths known to man. She hadn't meant to scry into his fucking bathroom, but sometimes the magic did whatever the hell it wanted.

Thea shook the memory from her mind as Mia joined her on the floor. "Are you sure this is okay, Thea?"

Thea nodded. "I need to see if the Lake is how I remember it when I saw it in a vision three years ago." Her glimpses of the Lake back then had been fleeting fragments. Ever since, she'd had a burning desire—no, a *compulsion* to see it again. As if the Lake itself was demanding her attention. She didn't tell Mia this. Instead, she peered at the little box in Mia's hands. "What's that? More chocolate?"

"No, unfortunately."

Thea did her best to hide her disappointment. A pity since, with everything she'd had going on, she'd had to restock from a cheap vending machine earlier in the day. The horror! The box Mia held was old, and the wood was scraped and chipped. Yet Mia cradled it as if it was precious. "Is that a jewelry box, then?" Thea asked.

"Not quite." Then Thea noticed a subtle sigil carved on the top. As Mia turned it around, she spotted a big freaking padlock on the front. She gave Mia a questioning look. "It's a binding box," Mia explained at last. "It will bind and secure anything that might try to come through the scrying portal."

"But you didn't know I was going to scry."

Mia fixed her with a stare. "I'm the one who brought

the ingredients, Iz. I knew right away what you were trying to do."

Thea grinned. "You know me so well."

"I know the ingredients for a scrying ritual." Mia laughed. "This box belonged to my grandmother. I saw her use it once or twice. I figured it might be useful to bring along in case…well, I'm not sure what's going to happen."

Thea didn't know either, but she didn't reveal this to Mia. "If we do it right, we won't need it."

"Emphasis on 'if.'" Still, Mia was willing to help. She sighed. "I hope the feel of this trap on this side of your portal will lead most things to retreat. Generally, entities in various dimensions don't want to leave their home plane, though an occasional few are more than happy to grab onto someone and be dragged to the other side."

As a hedge witch, Mia knew a lot about plants, herbs, spirits, and energies. She was more connected to the earth and its raw, magical properties than anyone Thea knew. She'd also learned a lot about creatures and beings that lived in other places. Beyond. Other realms.

Thea shivered at the thought of what she might encounter. *You've already begun. Don't back out now. This is more important than ever,* she reminded herself as she drew the various components from her pouch. They included special stones with sigils carved in the top, containers of herbs, and other enchanted ingredients. As she opened each vial, sweet smells rose into her room. Mia closed the open window in case anyone on the street below wondered what was going on and came to investigate.

Thea started laying the stones out in a circle, directing the points toward the center so, when she drew her magic up to connect the stones together, none of it would flare outside the circle. Mia held her padlocked box close, watching as Thea worked. "Does your coven know about this, Iz?"

Thea tensed but kept her voice light as she replied, "Not exactly."

"You know they wouldn't like this."

Thea set down a fifth stone, sighing. At that point, she decided to spill everything. She couldn't tell Mia the coven threatened to make her undergo the Fleecing without telling her why or what was getting her out of it. She also couldn't explain why she was joining AID if it wasn't for wanting more access to the Lake of Power. She began with the debacle concerning Fouche and the old hag's proposal to have Thea undergo interrogation in a coven court and possible Fleecing.

Mia's eyes went wide. "Isn't that super painful?"

"And it strips me of my magic," Thea answered. "I don't want to be part of the coven anymore, but if they make me Fleece, I won't have my magic to become a mage." Or look into the Lake of Power. If she had a destiny, it would be stripped away from her.

Then she told Mia about AID. How she had been approached by Agents Brandon Cole and Ajax Maddison to become their new witch liaison. She did not include the bits about being chased and put into an interrogation room or that Brandon was somewhat cute, knowing how Mia felt about AID. Like many other witches, especially hedges without the protection of a coven, Mia wanted nothing to do with them.

"Weren't they responsible for the last few liaisons going

missing?" Mia asked, brows drawing close together. A thin line formed between them.

Thea nodded. "But I'm not letting that happen to me. I gave them my own conditions. I've got a month before I decide if I'm sticking with them." Thirty days would feel long, or it might fly by. Thea wasn't sure yet. "Besides, it's all so I can do this better." She gestured at the stones she had already laid out.

Then Thea told her friend of her recent meeting with her professor and what she had gleaned about Ambrosius' books. "I know you think I'm crazy for my obsession with the guy, but I think those books are real and could tell me a lot. Plus, he was a Grand Archmagister. That's what I'm trying to be."

Mia shook her head but could not help smiling. "You've always been so ambitious, Thea. I don't know how you stay so motivated all the time."

Grief was part of it. Staying distracted was another part. Thea didn't know how to slow down anymore. "Now that I'm thinking about it, maybe joining AID for a time will be a good thing," Mia added.

Thea was surprised. "You, of all people, would be against it. Why the change in heart?"

Mia shrugged. "You could help people. Steer AID away from the witch-hunting shit and all that."

Thea related to Mia what Brandon had said about doing away with the witch-hunting types among their ranks. "Even if he's wrong, at least I know someone in AID who would help me fight against witch hunters down the line. That's never a bad thing."

Mia nodded. "Right, and any chance to use your magic

to help others is a good thing." Spoken like a true hedge witch. They had always been the more helpful sort of magic users, implementing their knowledge of herbs and plants to heal, protect, and save lives. It was a hell of a lot more than the covens did sometimes, even if the hedge witches had less power.

Thea put an arm around her friend. "I'm glad I have you with me on this. We'll find a way forward together. Even if we're in a shit-sandwich situation."

"*You* are in a shit-sandwich," Mia replied with a laugh. "Stuck between the coven and AID. I'm here to pull you out if you need it."

For a moment, Thea felt only warm gratitude. Then, another feeling flooded in, a slight sensation of guilt. Mia had her own troubles. Hedge witches weren't regarded kindly by most non-magical people or those who belonged to covens. The coven witches consider the hedge witches lesser than magicals. Sometimes lesser than non-magic users since they had the power capacity but not the ability to access it like the covens could.

It didn't help that organizations like AID didn't treat hedge witches well either. If anyone was in a life-long shit sandwich, it was Mia. Looking into her friend's warm, brown eyes, Thea realized Mia saw hope in doing this. Not only for Thea and herself but for all hedge witches and mages everywhere. The outcasts among magicals.

Determination renewed, Thea fetched a flat disk filled with specially prepared water. She set each stone into the water one at a time and tapped them with her magic, letting small tendrils of light pour from her wand into it.

At her side, Mia used a brass key to open the padlock

on the small box. Using her magic, Mia primed the box to snap shut should anything leap out of the scrying bowl during the ritual.

The light from the stones connected, and the bowl became milky and bright. Usually, with scrying, she did not need stones, but this was a special ritual. It was not usual for a witch to seek the Lake of Power.

"Here goes." Thea drew a deep breath.

Mia gave her one final nod, then Thea plunged her face into the water. Time and space stretched before her. Rather than staring into a bowl of water, she felt like she was peering into a well of deep, vast darkness. Gradually, she saw beyond that darkness into the vista of the Lake of Power itself.

A glowing pool of silver seemed to stretch in every direction. Something that looked like a combination of a waterfall cascading into the lake and a large, gnarled tree sprouted up to fill its center. The waterfall parted around the tree, filling the place with a roaring sound. Thea looked down to find herself standing there, ankle-deep in the Lake, though she could not feel the water itself against her skin.

The sky past the lake was a hazy gray, showing nothing of what might lay beyond the water. Thea stood there for a long moment, mesmerized. Like a moth drawn to a flame, she wandered toward the waterfall and the tree as if it called to her, but a distant voice came from somewhere behind her.

Thea could not quite make out Mia's words because they were so watery and distorted, but the familiar voice alone was enough to make her focus. Thea turned. There would be no point staying in the lake if she could not find the tributaries with which to draw from it. She wandered toward the water's edge, looking for the shore where the tributaries should be.

The first time Thea heard of the Lake of Power, she was five years old. Her father Peter had explained it in enough detail to tell her he had once seen it with his own eyes. Those who belonged to a coven could draw from the Lake of Power, like dipping a ladle or bucket into the water.

Most of them didn't characterize it precisely as a Lake but more as a well. Growing up, Thea had heard both used. The Lake of Power and the Well of Power. She liked Lake better. The Well was more like the magic inside her body, needing her to draw it up to use it.

Thea reached the bank and pulled herself up to find the tributaries. Each of the small streams flowed out from the Lake in all directions, effectively irrigating the magic user who would form the path and connection from the streams to their own body. The coven's rules had always been to draw from one of the streams, not directly from the Lake itself. Drawing from the larger body of water would inundate the user with too much magic at one time. Witches and mages had lost their lives doing it.

I have to be careful, Thea reminded herself. She sank into the soft sand at the Lake's edge. Filled with anticipation, she dug at the edge with her magic, intent on carving out the thinnest ribbons of magical power. *Start small*, she told herself. She had never done this alone before. She could take her time.

The ribbons of water she pulled out with her magic were pathetic compared to the size of the Lake itself, but the cooling sensation of the magic over her own made her forget all about this. Thea released a deep, satisfied sigh and dug deeper. The magic poured into her faster and faster, with more force and warmth than before. It was like drinking directly from a firehose.

Slow down, she told herself, releasing a few of the ribbons to trickle back into the Lake. If she didn't learn to control herself and the magic pouring into her, she'd be deep in that Lake and never come back out.

With a shiver, she wondered how many lost lives were at the bottom of that water. Thea did not have another moment to consider this, for an urging voice reached her from far away. Mia. Again, she could not tell what her friend was saying, but the tone of her voice told Thea she was urging her to come back. Mia had seen something happening to Thea or a flash of something in the scrying water that made her think Thea shouldn't be here any longer.

One more second, Thea thought. If she could fill herself with slightly more power, she could return ready to do whatever the hell AID wanted. She could find out more about what this Lake of Power did. What she could do with it.

Then, from the corner of her eye, Thea caught a flicker of something moving. Shit. She'd caught something's attention. Fearing the worst, she began to withdraw from the water. It wasn't a quick and easy thing to do. She had to pull the ribbons off her one by one like unsticking leaches from her skin, except the water gave her power instead of taking away from her.

The thing, whatever it was, came toward her. A mass of

shadows leaped from the lake, tearing the water apart as if it was nothing. Thea couldn't quite make out the shape of the being, only that it was a mass of darkness heading directly for her. *Shit, shit, shit!*

Thea could not turn to confront the thing and wasn't sure she could use magic in this place. The Lake did not want to be disturbed, or so her father had told her many years ago. She had to get the hell out. From the other side, Mia could do nothing but urge her on. Thea had to get herself out.

The shadows grasped her, hot and tight. Thea cried out, but the sound died in a gurgle of water. The thing pressed into her, and a maddening surge of fractal colors spun in her head. The thing was going to overtake it. Fucking hell. Thea felt it filling every part of her. Then, like skin being torn off her, she felt the thing being dragged away. A screech filled her ears, then the sound of something snapping shut. The box. Thank God for Mia and her quick thinking.

Thea pulled her head from the water bowl and gasped in the air. She turned wide eyes to Mia, who had finished padlocking the box. Mia returned Thea's stare. "That was a close one."

CHAPTER TEN

"While Hedge Witches are known for their deep connection with their natural surroundings and the energies of magic, they are often considered 'other' by those who practice magic inside covens. The difference between a Hedge Witch and a Mage is that a Hedge Witch is, by nature, always outside a coven. They are, from a young age, not permitted to join a coven due to their lesser power. Covens consider something that cannot be used for immediate defense or destruction a lesser power. Hedge Witch magic is used primarily to heal. A Mage, on the other hand, might belong to a coven for a time but break away. Usually, a witch who does this is held in contempt by the coven they left."

—Orlena Gorbana, The History of Covens and Their Adjacent Societies

Brandon had not intended to stop at a bar before going home, but he couldn't help himself. He'd had a long day. Not only had he been putting together the paperwork for Theadora's contract, but he'd been inundated with reports for his team specifically. His team that wasn't quite yet a team. Not when there was only himself, Jax, and Thea, and they hadn't started training with Thea yet. The training window would have to be smaller than he anticipated if they were ever going to use her as a consultant on the incoming cases.

Brandon finished one Old Fashioned before his phone buzzed. Jax's message blinked across his screen.

Be there in ten.

After entering the bar, Brandon decided it was as good a time as any to set things right with Jax and get a head start on their training plan for Thea. It helped that Jax lived near this particular bar and would be more than happy to have Brandon buy a drink for him. When Jax arrived, Brandon already had his scotch ordered.

"Don't tell me you plan to get me inebriated before we discuss things," the former Marine remarked. "Otherwise, you might get me to agree to anything you want."

Brandon offered an apologetic smile. "Consider this an olive branch."

Jax sat, and his teasing smile told Brandon he did not mind the drink. "Claire tells me you somehow convinced the Blackwood girl to join us. How'd you manage that?"

Brandon still wasn't sure, but he told Jax how Thea had come to AID headquarters after dark, told him his story checked out, and agreed to a one-month trial. Jax frowned. "And do Claire and the others know the girl has only agreed to one month?"

Brandon shook his head. "I'm hoping to convince Thea to stay longer."

"What an optimist you are." Jax sipped. "And you're already calling her Thea? You two are getting friendly fast."

Brandon flushed. "She nearly blew my head off when I called her Theadora. She told me to call her Miss Blackwood."

"Noted."

"We have to make sure she trains for combat readiness," Brandon remarked. According to the terms he'd drawn up for Thea's liaison contract, she would be under no obligation to participate in any tactical situations as her role was only as a consultant. The reality was that if she was only a consultant, things could turn on their head at any moment during an investigation. Having the liaison prepared should things get dicey was imperative, no matter who they were.

"I plan to cover all the basics in a week with you observing, of course," Brandon added after ordering another drink. "I'm sure you'll have valuable input, and I'm not only saying that to butter you up."

"Oh, I know," Jax returned. "You'd be in much deeper shit if I hadn't agreed to be on your team. Plus," he winked, "I think the girl will end up liking me better anyway."

Brandon gave him a look as if to say, *We'll see about that.* He had a hard time picturing Thea liking a guy with an authoritative air. Someone like Jax. But Thea had already surprised him, and he'd only been around her twice. "We'll see," he conceded aloud before lifting his glass back to his lips. "After she has the basics down, you can run her through a more intensive course to try to maximize her areas of specialty or reinforce areas of weakness."

Jax merely nodded along as if he'd already thought

through the details. Brandon went on anyway. "I wonder if we should try team-building tactical exercises where she can use her magic. We have to get familiar with how it works and build morale, especially since things haven't been super smooth in the way we came together as an investigative team."

Jax was silent for a long moment, leaving Brandon to the roar of his thoughts and the din of the bar around him. The clinking of glasses, the drone of the TVs, and general chatter and ambiance. Finally, Jax spoke up again. "If I've read the girl right, she'll show competence with the basic training. From what I've seen of how she holds herself, she'll adapt better than most women her age. As far as the team building…" He trailed off, shaking his head. "I'm not so sure about that."

Brandon had been worried about that as well, but it would have to work. He leaned back, sighing, then told Jax he had several cases stacking up already. They would need their attention sooner or later. Training could not last long. "I'm sure she can handle herself, but AID doesn't need a third dead witch," he admitted.

On this point, Jax could fully agree. In a voice Brandon found surprisingly gentle, Jax added, "You were the one on your ass when you chased the girl down."

Brandon's face reddened with embarrassment, and his eyes moved everywhere but to Jax. Seeing he was taking it hard, the former Marine tried to be consoling. "You're better than me, kid. You know how to get back on your feet and shake shit off. It's harder for me to get my big butt up again." Jax chuckled as if he'd cracked the best joke of the day.

Though Brandon didn't find it funny, he appreciated his colleague's efforts and smiled. The sting was out of the barb somewhat, but Brandon resolved inwardly to prove himself capable of leading the team. He didn't have magic or years of experience in the military, but he had a few things going for him, right? Youthful vigor, natural charm, and an ability to read others' strengths and weaknesses and position them appropriately. His resume stated all these things, anyway.

Brandon stood after finishing his second drink, claiming he needed a piss. Though this was true, he also sought a moment alone to gather himself. The next week would be a challenge. Jax said he should be going and bid him goodbye. Brandon stayed at the bar a little longer, then finally sought solace at home. He sent a text to Thea before heading to bed.

Training starts tomorrow. Be at AID first thing. I'll have coffee.

Her reply came a few minutes later.

Mocha, please. If the coffee doesn't have chocolate in it, I'll simply die.

Brandon grinned. Though the girl had her dramatic flares, she wasn't exaggerating this one.

Brandon was surprised to see Thea already there when he arrived the next morning. She'd made herself quite at home behind his desk. She had her feet propped up and was holding a paper cup. "Oh, thank God," she exclaimed when he walked in with a drink carrier. "The coffee you AID guys have here is total shit."

Well, he could agree with her on that. "Please get away from my desk."

Thea hummed as he handed her the requested mocha Frappuccino. She took one sip, then gave him a nod of approval. "Don't get used to it," he told her. "There won't be special treats every day of training."

She grinned. "I see. This was an incentive to get me in here for the first time. Are you planning to lock me up again? Don't worry, Agent Cole. I signed the papers. If there's anything I'm good at, it's keeping my word."

"Let's go, then," he invited after setting his things down. He led her down a level to the locker rooms on either side of the gym where AID agents could work out or train. He handed her a set of clothes. "Here, wear these."

Thea gave the clothing a rueful look. "How do you know they're my size?"

"You provided your measurements in the paperwork as asked."

"Oh. Right."

She disappeared into the women's locker room and appeared several minutes later. By this time, Brandon had also changed, and Jax had arrived. Thea paused at the sight of the former Marine she had not seen since he stuffed her into the backseat of Brandon's car a few days ago. "He's here to watch and give pointers when necessary," Brandon assured her. No taking her away in stygian cuffs. Thea, to her credit, didn't look nervous. Maybe she should have, Brandon thought. Training wouldn't be a walk in the park.

"We'll start with positioning and distance." He guided her to the center of the gym floor. Other than Jax, they were alone. The other AID agents had been told to clear the gym that morning. "After that, we can test you to qualify for a firearm. If you pass, you can carry one on the job. You'll learn to judge when to draw one and how to keep distance from a target."

Thea said nothing, merely nodded. Brandon wasn't sure how much of the information she was taking in.

They started by getting into position for basic grappling. To Brandon's surprise, Thea's positioning and stance were almost perfect. He only had to angle her hips slightly. "There. Now you're ready."

They grappled for about half an hour. She was good at that, too, only needed a few reminders and pointers. When Brandon called for a brief water break, he asked, "You've had training before. Where?"

"My father taught me the basics in kickboxing and jujitsu," Thea replied, her expression as serious as when they entered the gym an hour ago. The usual dramatic energy she brought to the room had fizzled out in the exertion. "Obviously, it's been years since I've done it, so I'm a little rusty."

When she wasn't rusty anymore, she'd be a force to reckon with. Not like Jax or another long-time member of AID, but a valuable asset to the team, nonetheless.

They trained for another hour with Jax looking on. The former Marine said nothing, simply sat there with his arms crossed and dark eyes taking in everything Thea did. She followed Brandon's directions to a T, never arguing with him but not making it any more fun either. She kept quiet, the perfect student.

When she left, claiming she had plans that evening, Brandon stared after her, wondering what was wrong. He turned to Jax when he could no longer see her. "I don't get it. She's good. Great, even. I'm not sure what's bothering me about that session."

"She made herself unreadable," Jax replied, approaching Brandon. "I know I've only met her once before, but I could see every damn thought she was having. She turned it off to train."

Brandon hoped Thea would loosen up as they kept training.

In the soft, warm glow of her kitchen that evening, Thea put the finishing touches on Mia's birthday gift, writing a quick but kind note in a card before slipping it into the bag. She gave herself a satisfied smile. "There. All perfect." The gift wrapping and card writing had been a momentary distraction. Since training that morning, she'd been in an off mood. It had been a long time since she had done anything like that, and the last time…

Well, Thea had been much happier back then.

Almost four years ago. That's how long it had been since she stood on the grounds at her family's estate behind the house across from her father. His eyes sparkled as he taught her to ground herself, plant her feet apart, and swivel her body just so. He'd beaten her ass that day. Thea chuckled at the thought as a tear slipped down her cheek. God, she missed them.

She turned to the other side of her kitchen counter, where a small, framed picture of her parents sat. In it, Irene and Peter held one another with their new home, the Blackwood family estate, looming in the background. Though her parents had lived there and other Blackwoods long before, it did not now belong to her or anyone else in her family. The original Blackwood had passed it down to coven Mothers.

Their family hadn't returned until Michelle Folsom allowed Peter, a member of her Sabbat, to live in and maintain the house. Now that Thea's parents were dead, the coven had taken the house back. What the hell they were doing with it, Thea did not know.

Another tradition I'm trouncing on by not going back, I suppose, Thea thought.

She had no intention of returning to the estate, even taking in the smiling faces of her parents in the photograph. Too many bad memories. Too many good memories. The whole damn place haunted her. *I'll stay in this apartment forever or move in with Mia into a cottage. Or live far, far away from here.*

She had to leave the coven first. Untether herself. Walk free. That came with time at AID first. Thirty-six months if Mother Folsom had her way. The dinging of her phone interrupted Thea's thoughts. A text message from her and Mia's friend Caroline popped up.

We're on our way to the bar for the party. See you soon.

Thea typed in her reply.

Leaving now. See you soon.

Thea gathered her things, including Mia's gift, and headed to the apartment door. A night out would clear her mind. At the door, Thea glanced back. Her gaze fell on the binding box Mia had left on her mantle, the entity from the other side of the portal still trapped inside. Each time Thea passed it, she could sense an *other* presence inside, though the box never moved. There was no sign of the being inside getting out anytime soon.

She and Mia had not yet had time to investigate it further, but Thea hoped to soon. Maybe after a little more training, when she felt more prepared.

Thea locked her apartment door behind her, hoping her nosy landlord wouldn't sneak in later to "check on things." After descending a flight of stairs and leaving the building, Thea stalled outside at the sight of a peevish old man who could often be found smoking cigarettes at this spot.

"Evening, Mr. Clarke," Thea greeted him.

He nodded and grunted. Thea headed to the bus stop, aware driving would not be an option if she planned to enjoy the night in full like a real twenty-three-year-old. One who didn't have to get up again tomorrow for training with AID.

"Someone's been comin' 'round here sniffin' for ya, girl," a surly voice remarked. Thea turned. Come to think of it, she'd never heard Mr. Clarke's voice before.

"Oh?"

"Tall, wiry sort of fella. When he talks, he sounds like

he's lost his voice. He's all whispery. Said he was looking for an Theadora Blackwood. Figured that might be you, Thea." Everyone in the apartment building, which only had six units, knew Thea, whether they liked her or not. She was the only resident under the age of forty.

She paused. The description Mr. Clarke gave was familiar. "Arthur."

"What's that?"

"Never mind. Thank you, Mr. Clarke. I'm sure it was nothing. A damn solicitor or something."

"Right," he drawled, lifting the butt of a cigarette to his lips for one last puff. Thea turned down the street, suddenly puzzled and a little put off at what Mr. Clarke had told her. Why was Arthur Adderget sniffing around for her? What the hell did he want? Had Mother Folsom sent him to keep an eye on her, or was he hunting around of his own accord? In addition to training again tomorrow with Brandon, she would call Mother Folsom and demand to know what was going on.

CHAPTER ELEVEN

"Thirteen offices comprise the U.S. Arcane Investigation Division. Each office is headed by a Senior AID Agent who oversees a team of agents, analysts, and support staff. Agents are trained in a variety of fields, including magic, forensics, and combat, and work closely with local law enforcement agencies to investigate and neutralize supernatural threats.

"The New Orleans office also operates a training facility where agents from all over the country are trained in combat and investigative techniques. Though some offices across the country also train in magic, the New Orleans office does not yet have the magical staff needed for this training. The facility features a range of specialized equipment, including wards, magical barriers, and containment cells, as well as a library of books and artifacts related to the supernatural."

—From an online article detailing the offices of AID across the United States by journalist Brock Stanton

Thea was late the following day. So late that Brandon almost drank the mocha he'd bought for her. He said he wouldn't keep bringing them, but maybe one every day for the first week wouldn't be too bad. He regretted this as soon as he saw her rolling in an hour and a half after they were supposed to start. He handed her the drink. "We've lost time. Let's go."

Thea looked tired. More than tired. "Are you hungover?" he demanded as he led her to the locker room.

"What if I am?"

"Last night was Wednesday."

"And it was my best friend's birthday. I'm not hungover, though. I got to bed late." Something else flashed in her eyes. Not fatigue from sleep deprivation but a weariness of a different sort. That of someone who has suffered a lot of grief. Thea turned and went into the locker room, giving Brandon no apology for her tardiness.

He waited for her only five minutes. At least she changed quickly. When she emerged, he saw she'd drank more than half her coffee. In a gentler tone, he invited, "Let's get started. We'll cover striking and grappling more specifically today."

Thea glanced around the gym. "Where's the big guy?"

"You mean Jax? He walked out after an hour of waiting for you. He might come back, but you might be better off today if he doesn't."

Thea shrugged. Again, no apology.

Brandon pushed his exasperation down. No need to lose his cool. They got into positions across from one another. Thea went at him, kicking above his hip level. He caught her leg and sent her sprawling to the ground. Thea groaned. "Guess you're not going easy on me anymore, huh?" She got to her feet.

Brandon remained serious. "Some of your tricks work for sport, Thea, but they're discouraged or downright dangerous for tactical situations. Don't kick above hip level, for instance. Don't get put on the ground without first determining if there are other targets around who could stomp on your head while you're still wriggling around. What I mean to say is—"

"Yeah, yeah. Offense over defense. I get it." Thea didn't sound annoyed, only bored. "Let me try again." The second time, she stayed on her feet much longer, though Brandon still beat her in the end. Sweating and breathing hard, she called for a third round. This time, she managed to pin Brandon for about three seconds before he launched her off.

A brief water break, and they were at it again. By this point, Jax had returned and watched them from the other side of the room. From time to time, he would come closer, circling them with a hardened expression and arms banded across his chest. Brandon ignored him, and Thea seemed to be doing a good job of that, too.

Their lighter sparring picked up in intensity and pace. Soon, they both moved quickly enough that Brandon went into full instinct mode, not giving much thought to his movements. Thea struggled between her line of thought and her instincts. Finally, before either could win, Brandon stopped. "I think that's enough for now. We can't have you burning out."

Thea nodded and glanced at Jax, who stared back, offering no comments. "Can I go now?" she asked.

Brandon nodded. "Be back in the morning, and don't be late." He watched her go for a second time, wondering where her sparky snark had gone and what about the training had made her seem so dismal. "I don't get it," he again expressed to Jax.

The former Marine eyed him. "The training is bringing back memories. She said yesterday that her dad trained her first. It's been a little over three years since her parents died."

Right, Brandon thought. Why Thea didn't live at the Blackwood estate since the fire had damaged only part of it, he did not know. He'd learned from her paperwork that her address was an apartment complex in the French Quarter. Upon further investigation, Brandon realized her place was only a few blocks away from his. He changed his clothes, hoping tomorrow's training would be better and that, somehow, he would find a way to lift Thea's spirits.

"Answer the fucking phone already!" Thea hissed as the call went to voicemail for the fourth time that day. She kept trying to contact the coven leadership, but no one answered, not even Mother Folsom's secretary. She ground her teeth, realizing she would have to go to the coven estate herself to find out why Arthur had been looking for her. She wasn't keen on driving that far again, especially after feeling sore every morning when she woke up.

This training was doing her in. She came home each night tired to the bone, barely able to stay up long enough to shower and eat a decent meal. Tonight, she would reward herself with her favorite chocolate and a bit of red wine.

Thea fell asleep on her sofa, trying to catch up on *Love is Blind* episodes for Mia's sake. She awoke the next morning as the sun peeked through her curtains. She heard a humming from the kitchen, accompanied by the sound of something sizzling in a pan. The scent of bacon rose in the air. Thea had not heard Mia come in, but she smiled. A visit from her best friend was never unwanted. She padded into the kitchen, still wearing the bathrobe she had slipped on after her shower the night before.

"Good morning, Bright Eyes," Mia greeted her. She'd been calling Thea "Bright Eyes" in the mornings for years now after initially joking that Thea looked asleep for at least an hour after she woke up. Years of assignments and finals had done that.

"I thought you were road-tripping with Caroline this weekend. What changed?" Thea went to the fridge and opened a jug of orange juice. She drank straight from it as Mia replied.

"Figured I'd have more fun staying here with you. That's all."

"Liar." Thea grinned. "You would have a lot more fun in Miami at whatever festival you two planned to go to. Tell me why you're staying behind."

Mia flipped the bacon. "We have to do something about that box, Iz. We can't leave an other-dimensional entity sitting on your mantle."

"I know." Thea rubbed her eyes. "As soon as I finish this week's training, we'll figure it out, okay?"

"Speaking of training." Mia waggled her eyebrows. "You still need to tell me about your new gym partner."

"He's not my gym partner." Thea capped the juice and

put it back in the fridge before leaning against the door with her arms crossed. "He's an AID agent in charge of whipping me into shape."

"But he's not bad-looking," Mia added. "I'll admit I snooped online. He's the sort of guy who has all his social media private, but his mom doesn't."

"Oh God, Mia. Please tell me you didn't stalk his mother online."

"Nice lady, or so she seems. Brandon's cute, especially his baby pictures." Thea rolled her eyes but couldn't help the grin that came to her face. Mia giggled. "Even if he's as basic as all the other white guys."

"Well, 'basic' is not my type," Thea reminded her as they sat at the kitchen table and devoured the bacon. She got three pieces down before she bothered to check the time, then leaped to her feet. "Shit, I'm going to be late again." She hurried into more suitable clothes.

Before she fled through the door, Mia tossed her a muffin. "Food for the road. Good luck today!"

Thea flashed her friend a grateful smile. "I don't know what I'd do without you, Mia."

"Starve, probably," Mia added, still grinning. "Show that Brandon guy what my best friend is made of today!"

"We'll spend about half our time warming up today with what we've already been doing," Brandon explained when Thea arrived. This time, she was only a few minutes late. He didn't comment on it. He also hadn't bought her any coffee. "The rest of the day, we'll run through scenario training."

Thea arched a brow. "Scenario?"

"Target practice." He gave her a grin. "It's time to get you into better tactical shape. That means tightening you up where you're still loose."

Thea gave him a look. Jax coughed from a few feet away. Brandon went red but moved on. "Let's spar." The next few hours passed quickly. Thea remained focused, shutting out any intruding thoughts about Arthur or the coven. The training was actually *fun* when she thought about it. The soreness wasn't her favorite, but she could deal with it. Training gave her more of an excuse to take luxurious baths when she got home.

They took a break at lunchtime. Claire called Brandon away to report on their progress, so Thea was left with Jax in the gym break room. "You're not doing too bad," the former Marine commented as he sat beside her, offering her a sandwich from his pack. Thea hadn't had the time to pack herself food that morning. "But you're not acting very resourceful."

Thea glowered. "What's that supposed to mean?"

"Well, for one, you don't prep well. You don't stretch beforehand, you barely drink any water, and who the hell knows what you're having for breakfast, if anything."

Thea became silent.

Jax chuckled. "You're going to burn out if you don't take care of yourself." He set another sandwich on the table. "Eat this. We're shooting this afternoon."

Thea cast an interested eye toward him. "Why don't you talk any during training?"

His eyes twinkled. "Don't worry. I'll talk plenty when the training gets to a level only I can instruct."

Thea swallowed. Uh-oh. She watched him leave the room and wondered what new hell she was in for. An hour later, Brandon informed her they would be heading to AID's outdoor range a few miles north. It was then Thea learned AID had a lot more land than the lot the headquarters building stood on. Several hundred acres around headquarters belonged to them, secure the whole way around.

At the range, Brandon handed her a pistol. "This is what you'll start out with. It has regular bullets right now. Eventually, you will use bullets that slow down a person's magic. They're quite effective."

Thea stiffened. She'd almost forgotten that AID tracked down criminal witches and mages and made them pay. A bullet hurt, but one that slowed magic was worse. It made healing a lot harder, sometimes impossible. She kept these facts to herself as she raised the pistol and aimed at a target several yards away. Thea steadied herself, aimed, then fired. The bullet went slightly to the left, but not too far, only missing the target by an inch. The kickback of the firearm did little to her.

"Try again," Brandon instructed. This time, she hit the target. The *pinging* of bullets against it satisfied her. She shot a few more rounds before Brandon commented, "You're doing well. We'll make the targets move now. The sort of things you'll be firing at in a tactical situation won't be standing still for you."

Thea kept silent as she fired at the moving targets, hitting about half of them and totally missing the others.

When she had to reload, she did so quickly, as if she had learned to do this years ago. "Did your father teach you to shoot, too?" Brandon asked.

Thea paused. She didn't want to talk about her father or affirm the well of emotions rising within her. She nodded anyway. "He started me young. Target stuff with a static pistol and shotgun skeet shooting. We did it out at my family estate."

"Ah." Brandon nodded. "I see how you got down the solid fundamentals." He let her shoot at the targets for a few more minutes before stepping in to show her tips on stance and habits to get into. "This will all help you maintain a more mobile position in a tactical situation as opposed to static like most of your experience."

Thea didn't reply but thought, *I hope I won't need any of this. Magic should be enough.*

After shooting wrapped up, Brandon told her she could go. "Tomorrow will be the last day for the week." He grinned. "We're combining everything we've been doing this week. Get ready."

Thea nodded, then went back to the locker room to change. It was rude being quiet around Brandon all the time, but it was better than snapping at him every time a command sounded like something her father would say. Sighing deeply, she decided a lavender-scented bath was the thing to ease her mind for the night.

Brandon read the surprise on Thea's face the next morning when she arrived and realized today's training would not only be her and him with Jax watching. "Thea, this is the tactical team here at AID. Some of their recruits will be running an obstacle course with us today." Thea eyed the six individuals in gear with guns at the ready. They were all younger, though not as young as Thea, and gave her only passing glances. Brandon did not bother sharing with them that Thea was the new witch liaison in training.

Brandon handed her a shotgun. "Use this today. We've had the rock salt inside altered out of state, so it won't do any damage if you hit someone today. They're altered by magic."

Thea lifted a brow. "How?"

"Our last liaison helped us develop them for training purposes before she…left."

Died was the better word, but Brandon hadn't been there, so he didn't say this.

Thea hefted the firearm up. "So, no gym time today? Straight into whatever this obstacle course is?"

Brandon explained they would be using a range belonging to the New Orleans SWAT department, a tactical obstacle course to simulate having to move through different settings. "It will help you become ready to fire upon targets while being mindful of possible civilians. The other trainees will be in there with you as well as simulants, both targets and innocent civilians."

Thea took in his words without much reaction. "And will you be in there too?"

"I'll be watching on screens from the outside to gauge your progress. You won't be in any real danger in there."

Thea agreed to the test, and they were on their way. When they arrived at the range, they found Jax waiting in the screening room, where he would watch with Brandon. After seeing Thea off, Brandon joined Jax. "You think she's ready for this?" Jax asked.

Brandon sure hoped so. "Claire and the others are breathing down my neck about hurrying training along. The cases are piling up."

Jax frowned. "It won't do any good to rush her." Brandon knew this but hoped Thea's base experience with shooting and hand-to-hand combat would speed up training. At least they weren't in the gym for the fifth day in a row. After today, he would give her the weekend to rest and recoup. Next week, she would be all Jax's. That would let Brandon assign tactical operatives to cases that required less magical consultation, buying them as much time as possible to get Thea into shape.

The recruits got into position in front of the doors leading into the range. A horn blared, and the doors opened. Brandon watched as the team entered and fanned out. Thea did not stay close to the others but veered to the right into a simulation set of several tall buildings meant to appear like New Orleans. Territory she was familiar with. The key was figuring out which simulations were targets and which were civilians. A number blinked above him. One. It turned red. One of the recruits had accidentally shot a civilian simulation.

Jax jotted something on a notepad.

A number on the other side of the screen flashed up, turning blue. The one turned to a two. Brandon's gaze returned to Thea's figure as she darted along a simulated alleyway, taking out two more targets. The blue number went up to four, then six, as the recruits on the other side took down two more. "They're not doing too bad," Jax commented. "Though if Thea doesn't join the team, she'll find herself in a pickle before long."

Brandon had been thinking the same thing. The recruits made their way through the obstacle course on one side of the map while Thea was on the other side, fighting on her own. Soon, she got trapped between two holographic buildings with three targets coming from her at both ends. She shot down one, then two. A third behind her. Three more launched forward. They couldn't harm her, but her time was running out. She had to take all the targets down to receive good marks.

Brandon watched her take down the other three, going slower with each fight. Then she darted out of the alleyway into a building, moving too quickly into a room full of targets holding two civilians hostage. Brandon hissed as the civilian number went up two more. "She got impatient. She should have waited for backup." He remembered what he and Thea discussed regarding being offensive versus defensive. It looks like they'd have to work on defense more.

Jax might have agreed with Brandon, but if he did, he didn't say so. He kept taking notes. Finally, the tactical team lead in charge of training the recruits called that all the targets were down, but so were several civilians. The time was nearly ten minutes. "Some of them have a good handle on what they're doing. This has shown us who needs work." The tall man nodded toward Thea on the screen. "That one needs to know how to work with a team."

Thea had gone rogue the whole time. While she had

done well then, they couldn't have her running off alone on a real mission. Not when they were supposed to be a team.

Brandon and Jax met Thea back in the gym. She seemed pleased with herself. Brandon opened his mouth to rebuke her for going off alone, but Jax put a hand on his shoulder, stopping him.

"Miss Blackwood, what you did in there was uncalled for."

Thea blinked. "What?"

"You put yourself and several civilians at great risk by going off alone. You should have stayed with the team."

Thea stood from the bench where she had been sitting. "It wasn't real."

Jax fixed her with a hard stare. "If you can't handle the simulation, there's no way in hell you're going out in the real world on a real mission, understand?"

Thea was silent for a second, then nodded. "I'm sorry."

It was Brandon's turn to blink. He had not expected Thea to take Jax's correction so well. He couldn't help feeling irritated with her for it when she reacted badly to his own corrections. Jax turned away from the girl, winking at Brandon. The former Marine had done it so Brandon didn't have to look like the bad guy.

He turned to face Thea. She had fire in her eyes, but it wasn't anger. Determination. She wanted to prove herself. "Monday morning, we're going through that again. You, me, and Jax." He turned away without a goodbye, but he could sense Thea smiling behind him.

CHAPTER TWELVE

"In addition to its investigative and training activities, the New Orleans AID office also has close ties to both the coven of New Orleans and the local Hedge Witch community, which it works with to track and contain supernatural activity. The office also maintains close relationships with the local government and law enforcement agencies, ensuring it has the support it needs to carry out its mission effectively."

—*From an online article detailing the offices of AID across the United States by journalist Brock Stanton*

Thea finally got a message through to the coven leadership. On Monday morning, when she called for what felt like the fiftieth time, Mother Folsom's secretary answered in a clipped tone. "Coven leadership. How can I help you?"

"It's Thea. Theadora. I need to speak to Mother Folsom now."

The secretary sighed. "Mother Folsom is not available at the moment."

Thea considered taking drastic measures, then relented.

"Fine. Tell her to stop sending Arthur sniffing after me. It's not cool. If she wants to know what I'm up to, she can ask. No need to stalk me." She hung up before the secretary could reply.

Thea decided a day of training might do her good. If nothing else, it would get her away from her apartment and distracted.

Brandon and Jax were waiting when she arrived, but not in the gym. They were at the front entrance. Brandon tossed Jax a ring of keys as he grinned at Thea. "Ready for round two of obstacle course training? This time, it's only the three of us."

Thea had prepared mentally for this and smiled. "No coffee today, Agent Cole?"

"We'll see how you fare in the course today, Miss Blackwood."

Thea wondered if they would get back to calling one another by first name anytime soon. Jax watched the two with narrowed eyes, then grunted, his sign that they'd better get a move on. When they arrived at the range, Thea found the simulation already set up for them. It wasn't the same as before. Instead of a sprawling city of targets and civilians, a vast, dark forest spread out before them. "We're hunting today," Brandon told her as he handed her a shotgun. "This is Jax's favorite course. He designed it himself. No one has beaten his record yet."

"And will he be in there with us?" Thea queried.

Brandon shook his head. "Only you and me, sweetheart." He didn't say this gently, and a spark of mischief entered his eyes. "Jax will be watching to make sure you don't go rogue and screw me over."

Thea did not share in his mischief. "What sort of targets can I expect in there?"

"You'll have to wait and find out." When she gave him an open-mouthed look, Brandon added with a chuckle, "On most missions, you won't have a damn clue what you're going to be up against. You have to be prepared for anything. You're free to use your magic this time if you'd like."

Thea shook her head. Brandon looked surprised, but she didn't bother telling him why. He didn't need to know she'd reached the Lake of Power and had tapped in more than she could handle. She'd felt her magic burning through her all week and had released it little by little. If she let it flow freely now, she might not be able to contain it. The last thing she needed in her second week at AID was to show them she couldn't control her magic.

"We'll try a few speed runs first," Brandon explained. "You against me. I'll take the left side of the course, and you can take the right. Whoever's out first wins."

Thea arched a brow. "Wins what?"

Brandon grinned. "The loser brings the other coffee the rest of the week."

At this, Thea frowned. "You're familiar with this course, aren't you?"

"That's the thing. What makes this course tough is the fact that it changes every time. You never run the same route twice."

Thea stuck out her hand to shake his. "Deal."

Jax counted them down, then the doors into the course opened. Thea set off at an even pace, soon losing sight of Brandon as she dived in among the tall, dark trees. She could have sworn the forest was real, not a simulation, by how cool it felt under their shade. The ordinary sounds of a forest gathered around her, too. A swift wind, birds chirping, and the occasional crack of a twig as a small animal darted past.

Thea focused on what lay ahead, wondering if it would stay this easy. Keep going. She had to find her way out eventually. The farther she got, the more the forest seemed to change. The trees grew somehow taller and closer together until she wove through a labyrinth of them on a path so narrow she felt the trees might close in around her. The forest changed as she did the course.

So much for a real mission, she thought, knowing she would probably never end up in a forest that changed on its own. Jax had other ideas in making this course for them, it seemed.

Before she could figure out where the hell she was going, a crashing sound filled the simulation and a beast bounded directly at her from ahead. He was wolf-like in appearance but much larger. Thea's eyes went wide. What the hell? He was milky in substance, translucent enough for her to know it wasn't real. Only part of the course. She fired her gun, using the bullets muted against real people to hit the hologram. It entered the wolf, and the screen spasmed. The figure fell away. Breathing hard, Thea realized though the conjured wolf couldn't hurt her, it had slowed her down.

She picked up her pace and, in a few minutes, saw the end of the tree line and bright sunlight in the range itself. As soon as she broke through the trees, Thea skidded to a halt. Brandon stood there, smiling. "Took you long enough.

I thought you might beat me after how you fled the day I met you."

Thea glowered. "I had a wolf to get through. You didn't!"

"You're right. I had two bears." Thea was tempted to wipe the smug look off his face, especially as he added, "Looks like you'll be bringing me coffee this week, Miss Blackwood. You're lucky I'm simple. Black coffee, one cream. That's it. No ice."

Thea rolled her eyes. "All you white agenty men are the same. Soooo basic. Besides, you haven't won yet. I'd like to see you try to beat Jax."

She could have sworn Brandon paled a fraction. A low laugh came over the speakers. "The girl is right. I think I want in on this because I know someone will be bringing me coffee the rest of the week." Jax appeared a moment later. "Ready, Cole?"

Brandon braced himself. Thea grinned. Brandon cast her a glare. "Don't think this gets you out of training today."

She maintained her winning smile and counted them down.

Jax tore into the forest like the wind, moving with speed, precision, and utter ruthlessness. He ripped past trees and cut through beasts that rose from nothing, forming out of the ground and lurching forward. Brandon lagged behind. Though he was also fast and could more than stand his ground, Jax was a force to reckon with. Thea whistled, glad Brandon had been in charge of her training so far.

Jax emerged first, followed by Brandon a few minutes

later. "Impressive," Thea drawled. "Wait until I get in there with my magic, though."

Brandon eyed her, sweat dripping from his forehead. Whatever he thought of Thea's statement, he didn't get the chance to comment. Jax checked his watch and muttered, "Great. That wasn't even in my top five times on this course."

Thea was beginning to think her training might get easier, even if she had to get up extra early every morning to bring Brandon and Jax coffee. She also made a concerted effort to stretch beforehand and have a proper breakfast. She was surprised when she walked in on the second day of her second week to find Brandon nowhere to be seen. Only Jax, grinning at her like a wolf sizing up his prey.

"Congratulations, Miss Blackwood. You have passed your first stage of training. The second stage will be with me and me only."

Thea's heart sank, but she tried not to show it. "What are we doing today?" She expected them to return to the range, but Jax told her they would be staying in the gym and practicing their grappling and striking. "But I've already done all that," she protested.

Jax's amusement faded. "You've done it with Agent Cole, not me."

That didn't sound good. Thea scanned him. "I thought we were trying not to waste time. More of this doesn't sound like it will teach me anything."

Jax observed her, then replied, "Your issues with

authority and team cohesion are Brandon's problem, but I'm going to help him out. What we will do will help you too. It's high time you were pushed far enough to feel you might break apart. You have to learn your limits and see the benefit of where a team can make up for your shortcomings."

Thea stiffened. Apparently, the stunt she had pulled the other day still had ongoing consequences. Jax wouldn't let her forget about it anytime soon. She steeled herself. *Better make the best of it.*

She got into position opposite from Jax and went into the light sparring techniques Brandon had helped her polish. For a while, she felt good and quickened her movements, proceeding at a steadier pace. Jax matched her move for move, so she was unable to strike him. At least she wasn't on the floor yet.

This didn't last long. Jax stopped for a second after about twenty minutes. "Good. Your endurance seems to be better. We'll work on measuring resistance now."

Thea raised a brow. "What?"

"You heard me." The big man did not give her any further explanation, instead launching directly into another match. His movements were a lot more aggressive this time. Jax used his greater size and strength to get the best of her. Before she knew it, he had laid her flat. She groaned as the air whooshed from her lungs. *Fucking hell.*

Jax stood over her. "You never know what kind of guy you'll have to defend yourself against out there. They could be smaller than you or larger."

Thea groaned. "At least give me a hand up."

Jax shook his head. "Do you think a real opponent will offer you a helping hand? Get on your feet yourself."

Thea managed it, but not without giving Jax a disdainful look. He was starting to piss her off. He smiled, showing that was exactly what he wanted. She noted as soon as she stood what parts of her body would bruise later and what bumps she would have to tend to. Sore muscles would be a minor concern.

They went at it again, and Jax somehow put her on her back for the second and third time faster than before. The man moved like the wind. Thea should have known it would be like this after watching him race through the course he designed. "You're not paying attention," Jax growled when Thea got to her feet again. Frustration burned within her. Jax said something, probably some correction, but she didn't hear him. She was too busy trying to stay on her feet.

A fourth and fifth time, she was on the floor again, this time with him pinning her down with his knee on her back. Thea did what she had to in order to reverse on the big man. It seemed to work for a second, then Jax rolled with it, dropping her into a rear naked choke. Thea felt his huge arms slowly tightening around her. Fuck's sake, she only had seconds of consciousness left, and she had no doubt he'd let her go there to teach a lesson.

"You're doing good, but you need to do better," his gruff voice announced in her ear.

Thea struggled against him, the weight of failure sinking in her chest. Panic took hold. She didn't know what else to do. She scrambled for an ounce of her magic. That could get him off her. As she was about to dip into the well of power within her, he let go. She turned to find him shaking his head, disappointed. "You can always tap out, Thea. Otherwise, your pride is going to get you hurt." Had he sensed her reaching for her magic? Was it okay for her to rely on it?

They tried once more. This seventh time, Thea didn't want to get up again. Let him have it. Let him win. She didn't care. Jax stared down at her, shaking his head. "You're going to give up? We've barely started."

Thea whimpered.

"Get up," he commanded.

She did so slowly. "I'm done for today."

"What was that?"

"I said I'm done for the day." The conviction in her voice was strong despite her body not feeling the same.

Jax chuckled. "You didn't last long, Thea."

All of a sudden, she hated hearing her preferred name. She fixed him with a burning stare. "I did everything I was taught. Why did I still fail?"

Jax shrugged. "It isn't so much about what you did wrong but what to do when you fail. You will meet plenty of people on missions who match your power level, probably with magic, too."

Thea's mind went to the Lake of Power. *We'll see about that.*

"Fine," she stated. "Let's go one more time."

This time, she did everything right. She moved exactly as Jax had commanded. Instead of flattening her, he pinned her to the floor with his knee on her back. Thea noticed he didn't use his full weight, but still, it wasn't comfortable.

"You're still getting used to all this," he reminded her,

his voice suddenly gentle as he kept her pinned. "After it becomes natural to you, you'll be damn near perfect. I want you to be ready for when you fail, though, because you will." He took his knee off her and extended a hand to help her up.

"Thanks for the vote of confidence."

"We all fail."

"You don't seem to."

Jax chuckled. "Agent Cole could tell you a few stories."

For the first time since coming into training that day, Thea smiled. "Next time I feel down, I'll call Brandon and ask him to tell me one."

Jax's expression became serious. "You can go in a minute. I have something for you first. Follow me." Thea trailed him out of the gym into a common space that was, for the time being, empty. "Brandon told me to give this to you after training today. You still have a lot to work on, but he seems to think you'll do better if you feel like you're officially part of the team."

"What do you mean? I already signed all the paperwork."

Jax slid a box across the table. Thea opened it, eyes going wide. Inside was a navy blue jumpsuit designed for missions. Tailored exactly to her size. She could tell without putting it on that it would hug every curve and aid her in any movement she made. On the top left above the breast was a silver nametag.

Thea Blackwood
Witch Liaison
AID

She smiled. It was nice seeing "Thea" instead of

"Theadora" on an official nametag. One making her an AID agent at that. The coven had never let her go by Thea, especially in official matters. Maybe this AID thing would work out for her. *After I load up on ibuprofen and ice packs,* she thought, knowing she was in for a long week of training with Jax.

Seeing the suit and nametag made something click inside her. She would keep up with the training. She would try to listen to Jax. She would learn what she needed to. She turned to him. "Thank you."

Jax grinned. "Thank Brandon. He sees a lot of potential in you." He turned to leave the room but lingered at the door. "I do, too."

CHAPTER THIRTEEN

*"'Tis said, she first was changed into a
vapour,
And then into a cloud, such clouds as flit,
Like splendour-wingèd moths about a
taper,
Round the red west when the sun dies in it:
And then into a meteor, such as caper
On hill-tops when the moon is in a fit:
Then, into one of those mysterious stars
Which hide themselves between the Earth
and Mars."*

—*Percy Shelly,* The Witch of Atlas

By the end of her second week of training, Thea was feeling pretty good about herself. For the most part. She arrived home sore every night and had bought more ice packs, Epsom salt for baths, raspberry leaf tea, and chocolate than she ever had in one week in her life.

On Friday night, she waited in her bedroom for a text from Mia. Her best friend should be on her way any minute now. They planned a night in with plenty of reality TV and, if they got the courage up, opening the damn binding box still sitting on Thea's mantle.

Twenty minutes after the agreed-upon time, Thea heard a knock at the door. Strange, since Mia always let herself in with the spare key instead of knocking. Thea peeked through the peephole to see her upstairs neighbor, a middle-aged woman named Pamela Henderson. She opened the door, wondering what the hell their landlady had unleashed to send the women down a floor to call for Thea's aid.

Thea's neighbors often called upon her for various tasks. She was taller than the old ladies who summoned her to reach things off high shelves. She was thinner than Mr. Clarke, who asked her to pull small things out from behind his stove from time to time.

Pamela looked nervous when Thea opened the door. More nervous than a simple task such as getting something off a shelf required.

"Thea? Oh, you're here. Good. I'm worried about Mr. Clarke."

Thea rolled her eyes. "Did he leave one of his cigarettes lit when he fell asleep again and burn a curtain?"

"If only," Pamela replied. "He's not there. He hasn't been home for three days."

Thea's brows furrowed. That wasn't good. Mr. Clarke didn't work anymore and only left his apartment to smoke outside. Normally, he smoked inside, but when Mrs. Farley was around, he avoided her wrath by going out. He'd also befriended the neighborhood pigeons and fed them scraps of bread. Thea often saw him on her way in after training. Come to think of it, she had not seen him all week.

"I spoke with him on Monday," Pamela explained. "He had an awful cold. I told him it was from all that damn smoking he does. I insisted he see a doctor, and he said he might."

Another surprise since Mr. Clarke had strong opinions about those "greedy medicine men."

"Maybe he's gone to see one and is staying in a hospital," Thea offered.

Pamela shook her head. "I've called every hospital in the area. None of them have a Mr. Clarke as their patient."

Thea picked at her lower lip. "Well, if he doesn't turn up by tomorrow, we should call the police. Have you told Mrs. Farley?"

"I was about to. I came to check if you'd seen him recently."

Thea shook her head. "I haven't, sorry."

Pamela left, and Thea closed the door, leaning against it as she dove deep into thought. For Mr. Clarke to be missing was strange indeed. Where could he have gone? As far as she knew, he had no family. Not even a car to drive anywhere.

Thea was pulled from her thoughts when her phone buzzed with a text message from Mia.

Sorry, Iz. Can't make it tonight. Have to stay at the shop late.

Thea felt disappointed. She'd wanted to tell Mia all

about her week, but she understood. It was good for Mia to be busy for once.

She returned to her living room, glanced at the binding box on the mantle, and considered dealing with it tonight. *No, that's stupid. Mia would kill me if she found out I opened it on my own.*

Another text saved her from further consideration. Thea's brows furrowed as Brandon's message flickered across her screen.

If you don't have plans tonight, let's meet up for a talk.

He sent her a link to a local bar. It was Thea's favorite, one she and Mia frequented most Friday nights. Still, she hesitated. Talk about what? She had not seen Brandon all week. She had trained with Jax while Brandon dealt with an influx of cases. They hadn't asked her to help with any yet. Better that way, she thought, since she hadn't a damn clue yet what her "consulting" would look like.

Thea sighed. On the one hand, she wanted to get work off her mind. On the other, her Friday night had been blown wide open. "Fine. Why not?" She typed in her reply.

Be there in ten. Our deal about me bringing coffee does not extend to alcohol, I hope you know.

Brandon did not send a reply as Thea got ready, spending a tad bit more time on her hair and makeup than she would have if she were going out for drinks with Mia. When she stepped out into the warm night, smiling, Thea thought, *I'll have more to tell Mia when I see her again.*

THE FIRST WITCH-MAGE

Brandon sent Thea the address to the bar he frequented the most, though normally not on weekends. He spent an hour after work here sometimes or hung out when games were on that he didn't want to watch in his stuffy apartment. It was the same bar he'd met Jax in two weeks ago before Thea started her training. It was much busier than he was used to, being a Friday night and all. A younger crowd had surged in, and the din was louder than usual. He could barely hear the TV.

It didn't matter anyway. He hadn't come here to watch basketball. At first, he'd come to relax and get a drink so he could be out of his apartment. He could not stop thinking about Thea's training and how high the pile of cases requiring his attention was getting.

Brandon checked his phone to see Thea's reply and smiled. He fully planned to buy her a drink or two. Not because, after a week of training, he'd begun to think she was a little cute. Only a smidge. *Don't go there*, he thought. *You're her boss.* Because his thoughts had started to drift in that direction, Brandon texted Jax to come and join them. They were all a team anyway. Jax's reply came soon after.

I'm in the middle of something. I'll come after.

Then, a voice he recognized reached him. "It's funny seeing you in a place like this and dressed like *that*."

Brandon glanced up to see Thea in low-waist jeans and a black top that showed part of her midriff. Her hair was down and wavy, her make-up done. He hadn't seen her like this, not when they were training, and she'd never bothered getting dolled up before. He liked this version of her and wondered how many nights she spent out on weekends, especially now that she was in training.

"What? I look funny because I'm not in a suit or tactical gear?"

Thea's eyes twinkled as she slipped onto the bar stool beside him. "I'm saying it's weird to see you in street clothes, that's all. You don't look like you're about to get your ass beat by a twenty-three-year-old." Before he could protest, Thea called for a drink.

The bartender recognized her and came over. The two chatted for a minute as the man made her drink. "Come here often?" Thea asked Brandon, turning back to him. The amusement in her eyes had faded as if she had already grown bored with him.

Brandon shoved away the feeling that she might not like being around him. "Sometimes. On weeknights."

Thea raised a brow as she sipped from her straw. "Don't party much?"

"Don't have the time." She seemed to forget he was older than her sometimes. He often forgot how young she was. She'd developed a maturity not many at her age had. All thanks to her parents dying in a fire and being forced into a coven she didn't want to join, Brandon surmised. He recalled a few things from his own past, but he shoved away any thoughts of what had happened when he was her age. He'd grown and moved on.

"I assume I won't either when missions start. That's what you called me here for, isn't it? Couldn't it have waited until Monday?" Thea asked.

"The mission starts Monday if we can work it out that way. I wanted to get you up to speed before then. By the way, things at AID don't always work like a nine-to-five. We'll be called onto mission whenever it's needed."

"So why not start now?" she quipped.

"Because you don't know what's going on, and you need to prepare yourself."

Thea appeared not to like the sound of that but didn't say anything. She only sipped her drink. Sometimes, her silence unnerved him.

Brandon tried not to let it get to him. "Jax told me about your training this week. He says you're as up to snuff as you're going to get while being off the field. It's time we brought you in on your first case." He slid a file over to her. "A string of disappearances in the area have drawn more attention than normal because they've been happening in portions of the population where it isn't usually difficult to measure."

"Meaning?" Thea asked, opening the file to find several names, photographs, and information about missing persons.

"Meaning local law enforcement has done all they can to figure out what the hell is going on and can't come up with anything. They've called AID in to help because there's a good chance magic is at play with the disappearances."

Thea flipped through the photos, noting that the missing persons ranged in age, gender, ethnicity, and background. None of them seemed to have a common thread. No mention of any of them being magical or not, which she actually found relieving. At least the government hadn't started making magicals register so they could track who was practicing and who wasn't, though she knew some sectors were fighting for that to happen.

Brandon watched Thea for a long moment before saying, "I'm surprised you haven't brought up the socioeconomic implications of this. AID jumping on the case."

Thea closed the file and met his gaze. "I'm too much of a shut-in to be an activist if that's what you're getting at. My family once owned a large country estate outside New Orleans as part of an organization, however unwillingly, that has held the stranglehold over magical power and authority for the past few hundred years. I think I'm the last one supposed to be lecturing anyone about injustices past or present."

Brandon's brows furrowed. He forgot sometimes that she wanted nothing to do with the coven she belonged to. She wanted to be a witch mage. "All right, then. As you can see by the file, some of the missing include a few students at your college."

"Now that I'm thinking about it, I did see something posted around campus. Being busy with training and all that has left me out of the loop on current events, including local ones." Thea could see now that Brandon wasn't looking for her to be an activist, only for her to care about her peers being missing. Feeling a touch of embarrassment, she asked, "Have any bodies been found?"

At that moment, a third figure approached through the crowd and joined them, almost unnoticed due to all the activity. Jax nodded at the file. "I see Agent Cole has been bringing you up to speed, Miss Blackwood."

She smiled at him, and Brandon noted how comfortable the two seemed around each other with their easy smiles and words. A week of intensive, military-style training would have accomplished that, he supposed. "Just getting started, Mr. Maddison."

Jax grunted. "Never call me that again. It's Jax. That's it."

Brandon brought Thea back to the topic at hand. "No bodies have been found. As far as we know, the first disappearance happened three weeks ago. Someone missing for that long raises serious questions as to whether they'll ever be found again."

Thea looked uncomfortable. "Do you know how all these people are connected?"

"We don't know for certain," Brandon admitted. "All of them share small commonalities. Not as people, but regarding their disappearances. They've all gone missing, or been taken, at dusk or dawn, often when they were moving in or around the Garden District near Lafayette Cemetery."

"Weird," Thea remarked.

"It gets weirder. With every case, each person was seen by someone else only an hour or two before they disappeared. They'd also recently recovered from an illness. It didn't seem strange the first time when a Tulane student's mother said her son had recovered from a bad cold and was going for a walk while the sun set. It got weirder when we started hearing similar stories from everyone else."

Thea's brows pulled together. She thought back to what Pamela had told her about Mr. Clarke less than an hour ago. She flipped through the file again, looking for him, but didn't find him. Shit. Perhaps he had gone missing like the others, and since no one had reported it yet, Brandon didn't have Mr. Clarke's case on file. "Lafayette Cemetery, you say?"

Brandon nodded. "What are you thinking?"

"That place is known for having disquieted spirits. It's no wonder local law enforcement kicked the case over to AID. The problem is to get answers, we need to talk to them. The spirits, that is."

"Like…ghosts?" Brandon queried.

Thea nodded. "Some scrying magic on the place and a witch is all you need. Looks like hiring me to be your liaison will work out after all." She considered the fact that the necromantic arts weren't exactly her forte. Not so much in that she couldn't do it but she didn't like it. Directly communing with the dead typically required at least a coterie to engage without risk. A Sabbat was better. Thea was only one person and was not inclined to call upon the coven for help, especially because the person who wanted her out the most led her Sabbat. *This is the perfect chance for me to test tapping the Lake of Power,* she thought.

Thea would have to ask Mia for notes on binding circles for ghosts, but she didn't tell Brandon and Jax that. "I'll need a few days to prepare."

"Fine," Brandon replied. "We'll meet at dusk at the cemetery in three days."

Thea shook her head. "The spirits won't be easy to contact then. We're better off going closer to midnight. They're chattier during the witching hour, you see. Also, if we end up dealing with a supernatural predator or evil spirit, it won't be a bad idea to show up while it's hunting."

Brandon and Jax shared a glance, seeming surprised at Thea's wealth of information on the subject. "We don't have to deal with that, though," Jax countered. "If we catch the damn thing hunting us earlier in the day, we can turn around and hunt it."

Again, Thea shook her head. "I'd rather get the info, then go hunting. An evil spirit interrupting my chat with a ghost means we risk losing what we need to find out. Dawn won't be too far off from that time anyway."

Jax looked at Brandon for the final say. Brandon patted Thea on the back. "We'll go with your plan, Blackwood."

Brandon wasn't done with meetings. Not by a longshot.

On Monday morning, as he began preparing everything he would need for a midnight mission in a graveyard, someone knocked on his open office door. He turned to see Claire's assistant standing there. "Ms. DuBois wants you in her office in ten minutes."

"I'll be right there."

When Brandon entered her office, Claire smiled and motioned for him to sit opposite her on the other side of the wide mahogany desk. It had been a few weeks since he'd seen Claire, and he had no doubt she wanted a report on Thea's training.

Claire didn't waste any time. "How is Miss Blackwood coming along?"

Brandon described Thea's training for the first week, including the hiccup of her going rogue in the simulated obstacle course. He added that Jax had corrected her, following up with a week of intensive training.

"Good," Claire replied when Brandon finished. "I heard

you were going on your first mission with her. Are you certain she's ready?"

"She's young, and she holds her cards close to her chest," Brandon admitted. "But she's proven herself a quick learner, and the information she's already given us regarding our mission is invaluable." He dragged a hand through his hair. "I'm not sure she likes me all that much."

Thea's smiles and teasing had extended to him, of course, but she seemed to be like that with everyone. She was always more relaxed with Jax.

"Of course, she doesn't *have* to like me," he added. "I've noticed that Jax has bonded with Thea during their training. I feel like Thea sees me as the guy who chased her across Tulane's campus. Funny, since it was Jax in the end who tased her while I was trying to get her to talk."

She'd done plenty of talking since then, making it clear what she thought of both AID and the coven. The girl liked to work alone, and for good reason, but her being a loner didn't make her trustworthy. Trust on this mission or any other was vital, and if Thea couldn't like him, how was she supposed to trust him? Trust would keep them all alive.

Claire listened intently through all this. When Brandon finally finished, she nodded.

"Part of it may be that Jax is older. Miss Blackwood won't look at him like someone she has to compete with physically or socially. There's also the fact that, though Jax is older, both he and Miss Blackwood are under your authority." She shrugged. "Like it or not, Brandon, some people struggle with authority figures." Jax could respect an authority figure, but it wasn't always easy when that figure was twenty years younger.

Brandon's heart sank. None of this was helping him. He felt like a third wheel on his team. He was supposed to lead, not trail Thea and Jax all over New Orleans. Claire read the concern in his eyes and added, "Continue modeling good leadership. Listen to the girl when it comes to her matters of expertise. If she feels like a valued member of the team, she'll get better. You will have to trust her judgment."

"What if I don't trust it?" Brandon asked, leaning forward.

Claire shrugged again. "Then pretend you do. That is unless there's a case of something egregious."

Brandon was not good at pretending. It was his blessing and curse. Every thought and feeling he had registered on his face. He wasn't like Jax, where he could mask himself, making his expression unreadable. Thea was better than he was, too.

"Thank you, Claire. I'll do my best." He stood to leave but thought of something else. "Have you ever had to do that? Trust my judgment even when you don't trust me?"

Claire laughed, shaking her head. "No comment."

Brandon nodded. "Well, that's all the answer I needed." It seemed everyone was better at pretending than he was.

CHAPTER FOURTEEN

*"I think I was enchanted
When first a sombre Girl—
I read that Foreign Lady—
The Dark—felt beautiful—
And whether it was noon at night—
Or only Heaven—at Noon—
For very Lunacy of Light
I had not power to tell."*

—*Emily Dickenson*, I Think I Was
   Enchanted

Thea stared at the binding box on her mantle as if it was about to explode. "It's about time I dealt with you." She hadn't a damn clue what was inside it, but she doubted the thing would be friendly. Plus, it had been inside the box for a week and a half. It wouldn't be happy about the confinement.

Thea texted Mia, asking if they could trade a night out

for "dealing with the demon." They had started referring to the entity as a demon because it was how most hedge witches referred to extra-dimensional entities. The shadowy substance Thea had seen by the lake was dark enough to be categorized as demonic, right? She had described it many times to Mia, each time earning a look of puzzlement from her friend.

"All you keep saying is that a big black blob came running at you," Mia had commented.

"It's more about how it *felt*, not what it looked like!" Thea had replied. Dark, mysterious. Dangerous. *But not necessarily evil,* she'd thought many times since. She had been afraid of it more because of its sudden appearance and because she hadn't a damn clue what it was. Then the whole possession thing had happened, not helping things.

With her first AID mission looming, Thea was determined to get into the box and see if the being inside could help her. If she was going to go up against whatever was snatching people, Thea wanted to find a better way to access the Lake of Power. Seeing how this being had come from *inside* the Lake, it seemed like her best bet.

Thea did not tell Mia any of this until she arrived. When Mia walked in the door and found Thea holding the box like a child about to open a Christmas present, she frowned. "I'm not sure this is a good idea. Why can't your new pals at AID help you with this?"

"Any and all extra-dimensional beings are supposed to be banished with all means of calling them back disposed of as a matter of course without explicit sponsorship from a coven." Thea sighed. "What are the chances my coven is going to allow that?"

Mia gave Thea a look as if to say, *That was gibberish.*

Thea shrugged. "I'm reciting section 10A of the AID recruit handbook. Did you know they have a whole separate booklet for witch liaisons?"

"I didn't," Mia replied, setting her things on Thea's sofa and sitting down. "How would I?"

"I guess you're right." Thea told Mia all that had occurred since she'd last seen her, including her intense week of training with Jax, finding out that her neighbor Mr. Clarke had gone missing, and her conversation with Brandon and Jax at the bar. The longer she spoke, the bigger Mia's eyes grew.

Mia considered her words, then remarked, "Extra-dimensional entities are banished because they can be very dangerous, Iz. What happens when your coven or AID finds out what you've done?" Hedge witches seldom agreed with covens or AID, but on the matter of extra-dimensional entities, everyone seemed to be in agreement.

"They won't find out," Thea promised. "Besides, I need to do this. I need a way to tap into the Lake of Power without scrying all the time. Otherwise, I won't be able to prove myself the way I want to at AID. It's all on the path to becoming a mage and getting out of the damn coven."

"And finding out what truly happened three years ago, I suppose," Mia added, sounding more understanding. She considered Thea, wheels turning in her mind for an objection, but she soon realized her friend would not be dissuaded. "Fine. I'll help. The least I can do is make sure my best friend doesn't get devoured whole by a demon."

Thea grinned. "If we keep calling it that, it might not be willing to befriend us."

"We're going to try to *survive* the thing," Mia replied. "We can't consider friendship with it!"

Still, Thea's eyes twinkled. "Not with that attitude." She often put on a front of amusement when she doubted herself. Mia knew this well enough. Thea added in a chirpy voice, "After this, I need you to show me how to make containment circles for ghosts."

"One thing at a time, Iz." Mia started her preparations, using ritual stones to form several circles at different points in Thea's living room, in which she could bind the entity if she needed to. The binding circles would help banish the creature if necessary. She hoped it wouldn't come to that. Maybe being inside the binding box for over a week had weakened the thing.

Mia used her wand to direct her magic into each stone, linking them so the circles formed a path across the living room like stepping stones over water. Her attention to detail, patience, and artistic ability made her ritual magic, which was all about preparation and precision over power, some of the best work Thea had ever seen.

She watched her friend move, admiring all the steps Mia took. Mia was far more methodical than Thea, needing to draw her magic a little at a time to have the most effect.

In magical combat, Mia's sensitivity and slower approach to magic meant she couldn't be useful. However, Mia was hard to beat when she had time to prepare and proceed carefully. At least Thea had never met anyone better. Combat was another story. Mia was good for healing spells afterward, and Thea had learned that herbal magic should never be discounted.

When Mia finished, looking like she was about to collapse with exhaustion after using so much magic, Thea wrapped an arm around her. "You're magnificent. This is why you're my best friend. What I can't do, you are marvelous at."

Mia gave her a tired smile. They both looked at the binding box on the coffee table with its huge padlock dangling down. Neither was certain what would happen, and a fresh tension filled the air. "Ready?" Mia asked.

"As ready as I'll ever be. How do I open it?"

Mia fished the key from her shirt where it hung on a chain around her neck. She handed it to Thea without a word.

Thea inserted the key and turned. A soft click followed, then slowly, she raised the lid. At first, nothing happened. The box appeared empty. Thea would have been convinced there was nothing in there if she had not felt the being's potent presence fill the room. It was the exact same thing she'd felt while at the Lake of Power. Something dark, mysterious, and dangerous. *But not evil.* "Well, where the hell is it?"

Before Mia could respond, an explosion of blue, green, and purple cinders came from the box in a thick cloud. Thea coughed and grabbed Mia. "What the hell?" she demanded between coughs.

Mia's magic from the circles flared up, creating a shield around the entity so it could not get to them or escape the living room. The cloud was the same shape as what Thea had seen on the other side of the portal, except this time, it was no mass of dark shadows. Thea jumped back, pulling Mia with her as she watched the colors butt up against the incorporeal boundary of the ritual circles. The barrier held. Thea saw the strain it was causing Mia. She'd have to calm down the entity so Mia could let the shield go.

A realization came to her, and she laughed. "It's nothing but pure magical energy." It wasn't a demon or anything close to horrific. It wasn't the residue of life echoes and memories empowered by magic, like a ghost or a wraith, but pure energy with a will of its own and independent direction. It was…

"Beautiful," Mia murmured.

Thea had to agree. The entity swirled inside the barrier. At first, Thea thought it was testing the boundaries, but as she let her magical awareness open up, she realized it wasn't testing so much as exploring. *She's trying to understand what is going on,* Thea thought. Smiling, she commented to Mia, "She's curious."

"How you know—wait! *She?*"

Thea had not realized it until Mia pointed it out, but yes, *she.* Somehow, as the entity moved across her magical senses, hints of information slipped through, almost subconsciously. "Yeah. Don't ask me how something without a body has a gender, but definitely a she."

"Can you…talk to it?" Mia asked. She had always been the one more familiar with communicating with spirits, but in this case, she was lost.

"I can try." Thea reached out with her magic, caressing the barrier with its warmth, hoping to draw the entity closer. The cloud indicated that it recognized her attempts but did not seem capable of communicating. "I think I'll have to reach through the barrier and touch it."

Mia looked alarmed but made no protest. "Do it fast. I can't hold this thing much longer."

Thea put her hand against the barrier. It sang with magic and warmth, everything good and steady that was Mia. She slipped her hand through, then a leg. She put her whole body past it when nothing happened. It was harder than she expected with Mia's wards so tightly woven. Thea parsed through the threads of magic until she was inside the barrier.

A new sensation met her on the other side. The tickling, prickling feel of the entity making contact with her magic. Then, before Thea knew it was happening, the being collided with her body. It was not like being hit with a wave. More like having a sheet thrown over her. The being surged through Thea's body, bright and powerful.

Thea had a fleeting moment of panic. "Shit! It's trying to possess me!"

"Hold on!" Mia called from beyond the barrier, sounding farther away than she actually was. "You can push it out!"

Thea's magic rose in a furious pulse, driving the entity out of her body. It bounced against the other side of the barrier. Thea staggered back at the feeling of Mia reaching through to grab her. She stepped outside the shield a second later. "Shit, that was close," Mia breathed. She had begun sweating from the strain of keeping the barrier up. Seeing her friend almost taken over by the wavering creature beyond had only added to her stress.

Thea barely paid attention to this because something else was happening beyond Mia's shield. A wavering voice spoke from the cloud of colorful sparks. "I'm sorry! I didn't mean to! I'm sorry. I wanted to speak to you."

Thea and Mia shared a look of amazement, both concluding that mere seconds the being had been inside Thea made her capable of communicating like humans. "I didn't mean to invade you like that!" came the silky, girlish voice again. "I'm still learning the rules of this dimension."

At least Thea had been right about one thing. The being was curious, merely exploring. It had been fine until it tried to explore *her*. Thea decided she could forgive the being and stepped closer to the barrier, hoping her voice would carry through to the creature. "Who are you? I guess a better question is *what* are you?"

"You humans don't ask everyone new you meet that, do you?" the creature returned lightly.

Thea and Mia shared another look. "Well, no," Thea replied. "We usually ask names, but I'm not sure if you have one."

"A name, hmm." The being seemed to consider this, then understood what it meant. "I do have a name, yes. It's Kirathazbegaul."

"A bit of a long one, yeah?" Thea returned, uncertain if she could repeat it.

"I don't know what that means."

It was clear the entity had caught onto parts of speech and had instincts but could not yet grapple with most whole concepts. Whether they were instincts garnered innately or copied from Thea, neither of the witches knew. "My name is Thea, and this is my friend Mia."

"Friend?"

Thea hoped the longer this creature was in their

dimension, the more she would understand. "How did it feel hitching a ride with Thea while she was taking a peek at the Lake of Power?" Mia tried, hoping the more questions they asked, the more understanding the creature would gather.

It was as though Kirathazbegaul was waking up for the first time and realizing the world around her. Thea wondered if she had ever been to a dimension similar to this one before.

"Oh, I'm one of those spirits who move around and through the Lake of Power, if that's what you call it. A bit of a silly name. I've heard better ones before." How this was possible, Thea did not know, but she let the being continue.

"They call us Guardians of the Deep. That's the Lake. The deepness from which all magic flows. Guardians keep watch to see what comes to draw from its power. When I sensed you, I knew something was different. I'd never seen anything like you before." The creature did not have a face, but Thea felt it was looking at her.

Thea could think of a few reasons why she might have been perceived as different. For one, she had come to the Lake alone. For another, she had tried taking as much power as she could hold instead of selecting the designated amount by a coven. Maybe there was something else, too, but Thea didn't know what it was.

"So you decided to investigate by rushing her?" Mia demanded.

"Investigate." The creature pondered the word. "I only wanted to know what she was." It was clear the creature could tell the difference between Thea and Mia talking to her. "I ended up getting caught in her wake when she started to retreat." She turned back to Thea. "Your potential for power is exceptional. It snagged onto me and wouldn't let me go until you came through."

Thea stood there in shocked silence. Not only had this creature not tried to overtake her, but Thea had made her come through the portal. *Should I apologize?* she wondered.

The entity's voice lowered to a soft whimper. "Then you shoved me into that tiny binding box. I was hurt at first. It was so small and dark in there! After a while, I realized it was the best thing for me. Without it, I would have been in real trouble. I can't keep my magical energy from dissipating in this dimension where things work so differently until I get used to it. The box gave me the time and space to practice without fearing I'd suddenly disperse!"

"Have you been watching me?" Thea queried.

"I have. You aren't around much."

Thea chuckled. "I've been busy."

"Busy." The entity pondered that word.

"So what do you want now?" Mia asked, still gauging whether or not the creature was friend or foe.

"I want to stay, of course! I want to learn everything there is to know about this new place. If you want to dip into the Deep again, you'll need my help. My power, since it is linked to the Lake, will help you draw power directly."

Thea smiled. "Perfect." This was the exact thing she'd been hoping for when she opened the box. Things were going far better than she thought, and she was glad to be holding a friendly conversation with the creature instead of battling it in her living room. "We can test it out, but this means removing the barrier. I hope I'm being clear when I say I don't approve any more of this possessing stuff."

"It wasn't fun for me either," the creature replied in an almost squeaky tone. "I only do that when I'm desperate."

Thea nodded at Mia to take the barrier down. Though she was still wary of what the creature might do, Mia was relieved to finish using her magic. The cloud emerged and rushed around the room with the general excitement of a curious little kid. "What's this?" she asked about the TV. "And this?" hovering over the sofa.

She went to a window, but Mia called her away. "Don't touch anything! You might burn it." However, they quickly realized the sparks did nothing.

"What's this?" she asked about a record player. She hovered next to a wall where several framed pictures hung. "Who are these people?"

Thea and Mia giggled, not moving as they watched their new companion flit around. "I think I might actually like her," Mia murmured to Thea. "I didn't think I'd be coming over tonight to make friends with the demon."

"We are not calling her that anymore."

"Well, we're not calling her Kirathaz-whatever either." Mia turned to the entity. "We're going to call you Kira if that's all right. It's called a nickname. We humans do it for people whose names are longer."

"For instance, Thea is a nickname for Theadora," Thea spoke up.

"All right. Call me Kira if you must."

"Do you…always look like that?" Mia asked.

The cloud flared with light. Thea took that to mean Kira was excited. "I don't know, but I was hoping you'd allow me to change my shape. There's no reason I can't try otherwise."

"Go on then," Thea prodded. "Show us what you can do."

What followed was a struggle and a weird phenomenon happening around them as Kira took a different shape. The cloud ebbed and flowed, the light fading until a form came into focus. Something of a human person, a female, stood before them. She was pale and slightly deformed as well as naked.

Thea and Mia gawked. While they were both fascinated, they were also creeped out. "Could you possibly become something that doesn't look like me?" Thea asked, seeing Kira had copied her looks with hardly anything else to go on.

"Or me," Mia inserted. "By the way, most humans walk around wearing clothes." She pointed out her skirt as an example.

"I'll try again," Kira offered. "There's another shape I've wanted to try."

A few minutes later, the human form became smaller. Shadows pooled around it until a new shape appeared.

Thea and Mia smiled at the cat before them. A beautiful, sleek, gray creature with wide, bright eyes. "That's much better." Thea had to laugh at the clothes Kira had manifested for her cat form. "I've never seen a cat in jeans and a button-up before. The same rules don't apply to animals."

"Good," Kira noted, still speaking like a human in cat form. "They don't feel good on this body anyway."

"As glad as I am not to have to interpret meowing, most

people will be freaked out to hear a cat using human language. Only speak like that when it's us around you," Mia instructed.

"Oh, that won't be a problem," Kira assured them, hopping onto the back of Thea's green sofa. "I can communicate telepathically with other magic users anyway." A pause, then Thea heard in her mind, *See?*

Can you hear me? she thought back.

Yes.

Mia glanced between the two. "This is wild shit."

"There's one other problem," Thea pointed out a moment later. "If my landlady ever finds out I have a cat, she's going to fucking kill me."

Kira's cat eyes sparkled. "I'll turn into something else then. She'll never know what hit her."

Indeed, Thea wasn't sure what had hit any of them. She smiled at her new friend. "So, when can we start using our magic together?"

CHAPTER FIFTEEN

"Few Extra-Dimensional Entities have been recorded as coming through the Veil into the human world. Most of these creatures either died quickly upon entrance or were banished by magic users. Only a few Entities have taken up residence in the human world and been studied by various people throughout the years. The last report of one is over a century old and tells of how these Dimensional creatures' primary method of communication is telepathy. Only those with magical abilities can communicate with a Dimensional creature through this method."

—*Richard Knight,* On Creatures Beyond the Veil

The evening of AID's operation arrived, and Brandon was more nervous than a long-tailed cat in a roomful of rocking chairs. It wasn't about seeing ghosts or running into spirits in a cemetery. It was about whatever was out there, prowling for people to snatch. From the pattern they'd picked up on so far, each snatching had been planned and intentional, with the people being sick shortly before they went missing. Brandon felt an itch in his throat, then became paranoid that he was getting sick.

Don't go there, he told himself. *You're not sick.*

It was also his first full operation for AID since moving to New Orleans. He couldn't fuck this up. He had to not only prove himself but also demonstrate that Thea had trained enough and was ready. If things went to hell because of her, the responsibility fell on him. Then there was the added pressure of ensuring she stayed alive lest they risk more wrath from the coven leadership than ever.

In the car on the way to Lafayette Cemetery, where they would meet Thea and the junior agents, Brandon did his best to hide his nervousness. He thought he was doing a good job until Jax glared at him. "Stop fiddling with the radio, Cole. Switching the station every five seconds isn't going to change a damn thing. The mission will go fine."

Brandon wished he had that much confidence. He was glad to realize he wasn't acting as cool as he thought before Thea showed up. He'd been playing back everything Claire said about displaying leadership. If he looked like he was about to lose his shit, Thea would have no reason to trust him. *Trust is the name of the game,* he reminded himself.

They arrived to find the junior AID agents already setting up around the cemetery, working alongside local law enforcement to keep things clear and prevent anyone from interfering. Brandon checked his watch. The sun had set three hours ago, and it would be another hour before midnight. He and Jax had decided to send agents earlier to prevent more sunset snatchings and familiarize themselves with the area before the witching hour.

"Do you know why they call it the witching hour?" Jax asked as they got out of the car.

Brandon nodded. "It's actually hours, not only one. It's the time of day when witches and other supernatural beings are said to be at their strongest. Something about the pull of the heavenly bodies, I believe."

Jax frowned. "Sounds like a load of malarkey."

Brandon shrugged. "Thea seemed to think it meant something." He approached the three networking vans set up outside the cemetery. "Make sure all three vans stay in contact with us. One with me, one with Jax, and one with Miss Blackwood." When it came to ghosts and spirits, AID knew from experience that electronic communication could get dicey.

Jax followed Brandon around, noting how flustered he became. "Everything's going to be fine, Agent Cole." Brandon didn't reply. He didn't tell Jax about how, when the big man thought no one was looking, he'd seen him cross himself and kiss a small wooden cross before quickly tucking it back under his shirt. They were both nervous, it seemed. Somehow, it made Brandon feel better.

Twenty minutes later, another car pulled up, a simple silver sedan with several bumper stickers on the back. Thea emerged with a large satchel slung across her body. She looked around, frowning at all the agents and vans. As soon as she caught sight of Brandon and Jax, she ambled over, not looking nervous in the least. "A lot going on, huh? I thought it would only be us three."

"Only us three going into the cemetery," Brandon clarified. "The surveillance teams will be outside in case something happens."

Thea raised a brow as if to say, *You're overthinking this.* Maybe he was, but Brandon was a better-safe-than-sorry sort of guy.

It was a wonder she was so cool and calm, though he concluded she could be good at hiding wariness. After reviewing their plan, Brandon remarked, "We'll wait a while longer, then go in." He checked his watch. Thirty minutes until midnight.

When the time came, Brandon led Jax and Thea to the gate. He noticed movement to his left and turned to see Thea struggling to hold something down in her satchel. He frowned.

"It's nothing," she insisted. "Something I need for the ritual." She didn't bother elaborating, and Brandon was about to demand an explanation when he remembered what Claire had said about extending trust to earn trust.

"Let's go," he called instead. They moved through the gate and down a broken and cracked sidewalk filled with vines and weeds. The cemetery's upkeep had not been good in the last several years. Above them, the moon was almost full, giving them enough light to see by. The cemetery was eerie and quiet, only a soft wind brushing through the treetops.

"There," Thea whispered a few minutes later, stopping short. She pointed ahead to where three wispy white figures floated. Brandon could not make out much of their features. He wasn't sure if they had faces. It amazed him how much more open such things became over time.

Once, seeing a ghost would have been a rare experience, one many people did not believe. Now, if you came to the right place at the right time, you could see many.

Brandon wondered if what they saw now had anything to do with having a witch in their presence. Had the ghosts come out after sensing a magic user among them?

Studies over the years confirmed the whole thing. Even without those studies, over the years, the world had grown a lot less shy about supernatural beings. Some could point out their favorite haunts. "They're not paying much attention to us," came Jax's low voice. Only one had looked their way, giving them a vacant stare, then drifting into the shadows past huge gravestones and disappearing.

Brandon and Jax stared after them with wide eyes, struck halfway between amazement and fear. Thea smiled. "It's been a long time since I've seen a ghost. I should have come here sooner."

Brandon tried not to shiver at the thought of coming here alone at this hour. Or any hour, for that matter. Thea started through the cemetery again, trailing after the ghosts. What she planned to do, Brandon did not know, but he followed her anyway. They came closer to the spirits. By this time, he made out faces. The echoes of lives past.

He wondered which bodies buried beneath the copious headstones belonged to these ghosts. They all had names and years of life attributed to them. The more they walked, the more the ghosts took notice of them. A few turned, trying to shout something, but the gulf between the spirits and the living world was distant enough that anything they tried to say became distorted. The words emerged as faint whispering or wailing. The ghosts soon decided trying to communicate wasn't worth it.

Thea would scry eventually. Brandon realized she was

trying to decide where to do it. At that moment, Jax hissed from behind Brandon. "Shit! Go on! Get away!" he whisper-shouted. Brandon turned to see a ghost who appeared offended at Jax's presence and rushed at him. For the first time, Jax revealed he was on edge by bearing down on the spirit.

"It can't hurt you," Brandon reminded him. "At least not that sort." He gestured at the translucent being. The ghost glared in his direction, then turned and made off through the stones.

Jax began to breathe easier and muttered, "You never know."

Thea's voice carried over to them. "Brandon's right. They won't hurt us. Not these ghosts, anyway. They're only echoes of past lives. The most they can do is startle or scare." Well, they had already done that to the toughest of the three of them.

"Wraiths or specters are a different story," Thea explained. "Those spirits can manifest enough to interact with the physical world on some level. They're the real threat because if they've taken the time to connect to the physical world and maintain that energy, they're probably pissed off or scared."

"Which makes them dangerous," Brandon added.

Thea nodded. She had spoken these words in a matter-of-fact tone, not once looking afraid they would encounter such a spirit.

"I know all this," Jax replied, almost growling. "Determining which is which has always been overly academic to me."

Brandon and Thea shared a look, both suppressing

smiles. Brandon had experienced a few wraiths and specters while dealing with supernatural creatures. "Don't worry about that. You'll know the difference when the bad thing pops up."

Thea met his eyes, and Brandon could have sworn they were bonding for a second. She glanced away, stating, "Let's go farther in. I can sense the right spot is close." Brandon realized she had been searching with her magical awareness the whole time, looking for the right spot to gather a few ghosts. "If we find a place at the center of the cemetery, I'll get the most coverage for my spell."

It made sense to Brandon.

A few moments later, Thea found an area that seemed suitable. She bent beneath an oak tree. The branches fanned out far and wide. Thea set down her satchel and opened it, drawing out something that made Brandon's eyes bulge. Jax crossed his arms, giving the cat a rueful look. "Is that for a sacrifice? I didn't think ghosts required that sort of thing."

Brandon and Thea glanced at Jax, then at one another.

Brandon didn't give Thea time to answer. "You brought your cat?"

"Emotional support." Thea smiled.

Brandon had a feeling she was holding back her true reason.

Jax shrugged. "This is why you don't count on me for the magical know-how."

As Thea rifled around in her bag for other materials, the cat ambled its way to Brandon and began rubbing against his leg, looking up at him with green eyes. The animal released a low purr, and Brandon could not help but think, *Is this cat flirting with me?*

Brandon shook off the thought as Thea scooped the animal up, muttering, "Behave, Kira. Don't embarrass me."

Thea had a cat named Kira. Brandon scratched his head. He had expected odd things to happen tonight, but not this.

Thea prepared the ritual circle, drawing lines of magic in the dirt. The cat moved with her, seeming to nod each time Thea empowered one of the lines. Brandon could almost feel the air thrumming around the pair. Thea stood a moment later, looking somewhat strained.

"I'll admit I'm impressed," Brandon commented. "I've only seen this sort of thing done before with witches acting in a coterie or Sabbat. To see one witch and her…uh, pet doing this is a sign you have real power." Perhaps more than he had ever seen in one witch. He didn't tell her this last part, though. He wanted to encourage her without giving her too much of an ego boost.

Thea remained serious, seeming unfazed by his comments. "You two can keep an eye out while I summon the ghosts. I'll have to see which ones are interested in talking." She stood in the middle of the circle where her lines were drawn, the cat remaining close to her, though it kept stealing glances at Brandon.

Thea uttered a few words Brandon did not understand. A ripple came into the air. Brandon watched as the cemetery became the quietest it had ever been. The wind stopped. The trees stilled. The buzzing of insects ceased.

"Did something go wrong?" Jax asked after a few silent beats.

Thea did not answer. A figure had appeared across from them. At first, he looked like a workman in overalls. He was an older fellow with wispy white hair and a beard to match. He held a shovel over the ground and made the right motions without actually digging. He was less translucent than the ghosts they had already seen but faded enough in appearance for Brandon to know he was a spirit.

"A specter," Thea whispered. She remained in her circle but spoke to him. "Hello there. Can you see me?"

The specter turned, seeming unsurprised to find her there. His gaze roamed to the cat, then his eyes narrowed as if he sensed something about it. They lifted again to meet Thea's gaze but did not go to either of the two men. Brandon wondered if the specter could see them. "You're in danger," the specter intoned, his voice low and husky. "You need to come and stand beside me if you want to be safe."

He stepped toward her, taking no notice of either Brandon or Jax, and grabbed her arm.

Brandon moved to intervene, but Thea stated, "I think I'll be okay." At that moment, she began sinking into the ground as if it was quicksand.

"Thea!" Brandon shouted. He tried to grab her, but a shield of magic had gone up around her, and he could not make contact. However, the cat jumped onto her shoulder. Thea, the cat, and the workman specter disappeared beneath the ground, leaving Brandon and Jax in shocked silence.

After a few beats, Jax cursed. He knelt to feel along the ground, but it seemed as solid as ever. Brandon shouted into his radio. "Thea? Are you there? Thea, talk to me!"

No answer.

Brandon was on the edge of panic, wondering if he had gotten a third witch liaison killed, when the workman's face emerged from the ground like he was surfacing from water. His body remained beneath it. "The nice lady says you should run. She'll catch up to you when she's finished down here."

"What happened to her?" Brandon demanded.

The specter didn't seem to hear or see them. Brandon concluded that Thea had sent him back to the top with the message, though the specter did not know they were there. The ghost started sinking into the ground but added, "I'd run fast if I were you. The Lancer doesn't like being disturbed."

"The what?" Jax demanded.

The workman vanished.

Brandon's whole body went cold. He looked up to see a ghostly figure on a horse made of pale blue flame hefting a lance of pure shadow. He was several yards off but had fixed them with a heated stare. The workman specter might not have been able to see them, but this creature sure as hell could. Brandon's heart hammered. *Shit.*

He scrambled for the shotgun at his side, loaded with a special silver and salt mixture. Jax's eyes went to where Brandon's had gone, and he cursed again.

"That right there is a wraith!" Brandon exclaimed.

CHAPTER SIXTEEN

"But evil things, in robes of sorrow,
Assailed the monarch's high estate;
(Ah, let us mourn!—for never morrow
Shall dawn upon him, desolate!)
And round about his home the glory
That blushed and bloomed
Is but a dim-remembered story
Of the old time entombed."

—*From the poem* The Haunted Palace *by*
Edgar Allan Poe

Thea went down into the darkness. Slipping underground like sinking into water had not been what she'd expected, but the specter had assured her she would be all right. "Go easy now," he told her. "Stay here till the old Lancer is put off. Then you'll go right back up to the top."

Why the workman thought she should avoid the wraith but not her friends, she did not understand. Then she realized he had not been able to see Brandon or Jax because they weren't magic. That was when she pleaded for him to return to the surface and tell them to run.

She was alone now, waiting for the specter to return in a tunnel lit only by the glowing walls. The light took fantastic shapes, whorls in the stone that the specter who'd brought her here created to bring her to this ephemeral side of space. *This means I'm in the realm of ghosts. More or less.*

She had never been to a place like this before but had heard what it was like from her professor and from Mia, the former of which had been many times and the latter only once. Both had warned her that, if she were ever to find herself in this realm, she could not stay long. The knowledge of where she was going had allowed her total calm as the workman specter pulled her through the ground.

Distantly, Thea heard Brandon's alarmed cries and cringed. At least she had sent the specter back up to tell them to run. The Lancer could be a real piece of shit if what Thea had heard from Mia was true.

Many a hedge witch had dealt with the old bastard before. Not only did he roam cemeteries late at night, but he enjoyed riding through farms and gardens, taking whatever the hell he wanted. In recent years, the hedge witches had put wards up around their places to keep him out. This meant he spent more and more time around the dead.

Thea followed the tunnel until she entered a large rock cave where the same glowing whorls shone all around her, casting the area in a pulsing blue shimmer. She knew she'd be all right for now, but if she stayed too long, there was a real chance she'd get stuck down here. She could lose her connection to her soul, then to her magic. There would be no escape after that. In short order, she'd become a real ghost.

I'm not ready for that, she decided, looking around at the shapes forming on the stone. *I have to be quick about this.* About what, exactly, she did not know. She'd done her job in summoning a spirit, and now that spirit had brought her here. As soon as he came back, she'd ask questions.

She stared around in wonder, waiting. Kira, still on her shoulder, seemed to have only wonder, too. No fear of where they had ended up. Kira's voice purred into Thea's mind. *Why'd we have to come down here? I miss those handsome males.*

Thea remembered leaving Brandon and Jax to face what she had sensed as an angry old wraith. A creature quite put out with finding two human men prowling in his cemetery so late at night. The Lancer was not a death sentence for the two competent AID operatives, but Thea still couldn't help feeling guilty for leaving them to figure it out. *But they brought me here to find answers, so shouldn't I have come where the answers are?*

She was glad for the entity on her shoulder. If she needed to tap the Lake for more power in order to get out, she could.

Thea sensed rather than heard the workman specter returning as he came up behind her. She turned. "Thank you for telling my friends to run. They'll have a chance now." The specter seemed nervous. He wrung his hands and around as if they were about to be caught at any moment. Thea wondered if she should even be down here.

"You're one of the Fearful, aren't you?" she asked. Such specters were called this because fear and anxiety drove them. Something else she had learned from Mia.

"My name is Whitney," the specter replied. "I am the keeper of this cemetery. Please don't be angry with me for how things have gotten out of hand. There is only so much I can do. And when you summoned me, well…" He trailed off, shaking his head. "It's a load of shit what's been going on."

"That's all right. I'm not angry." Thea showed concern on her face and in her voice. "I hope you can help me. Are you babbling on about the wraith? What's he called again? The Lancer?"

"No, no, no," Whitney countered. "Leonar—sorry, the Lancer. He likes to be called the Lancer. He's nothing but a cranky old bat, that's all, mostly scarin' folks or lookin' to rough 'em up. You riled him up somethin' good, girl. He don't like feelin' witches 'round him. Still, your friends will be fine." He swallowed. "At least, I hope so. He ain't the problem, though. Ain't why I'm so dreadfully nervous."

Whitney's description of the Lancer reminded Thea of Sabbat leader Fouche. Maybe when she died, she'd become friends with the cranky Lancer. "If it's not the Lancer bothering you, what is it?"

Whitney kept his gaze on the ground. "Never mind that. Let's move along. We can't be down here long."

"I thought you said coming here was the only thing to keep me safe."

He breezed past her to the entrance of another tunnel winding down into the earth. "It will, but not for long."

Uh-oh, came Kira's voice in her mind. *Don't you humans add "spaghetti-o" to the end of that sometimes? I don't get it.*

Thea didn't reply, merely followed Whitney. The tunnels remained lit by the glowing substance in the walls, though the path narrowed, and Thea had trouble breathing. The specter seemed familiar with his surroundings and led her through passages resembling a honeycomb. Instead of dripping with honey, the patterned walls glistened with the same glowing, bluish substance she'd seen all along. It looked sticky enough to the touch that Thea did not reach out.

There were many twisting passages, and Whitney wove through all of them, setting a nervous pace. From time to time, he would go right through the floor, down into another tunnel. The cartoonish sight might have been amusing to Thea if not for how distraught Whitney kept getting.

"What's wrong?" Thea asked as she trailed him down into another tunnel. "If you can tell me what's going on, maybe I can help you fix it."

Whitney turned to her with wide eyes. "Really, can you? Do you think so? It'd be awful nice if you could do something." He moaned. "Oh, but I don't think anyone can help now!"

"I'll certainly try, but you need to tell me what's happening first."

Whitney lowered his voice to a hoarse whisper. "It's the Pale Stranger. He's come again."

"The what?" Thea had never heard of such a creature before.

"That's right. Look, I wasn't always the keeper of this

place. Only been here 'bout the past fifty years or so. Soon as I died, they put me in charge. Honestly, though, when you're dead, you stop tracking the years. I could be wrong 'bout how long I've been here."

"Right," Thea returned. "And was this Pale Stranger around when you became the keeper?"

"Yes and no." Whitney continued through the tunnels, his voice becoming squeakier as he went on. "The Pale Stranger was put into the cemetery long before I came here, but I don't know when he first arrived. All I know is he's been around at least since the Stranger's Disease."

Thea looked puzzled.

"Yella fever, that is."

"What?"

"Yell-oh fever."

"Oh, yellow. I see." That had been a long time ago. The epidemic started in the early 1800s and lasted for nearly a century if Thea remembered history correctly. All thanks to those damn mosquitos. What did that have to do with anything, though?

"He disappeared for a long time. Some of the ghosts 'round here said he never left, was just hidin.' From what, we don't know. He mighta left, too. No one knows. He's worse than the Lancer or any wraith that has ever been around the cemetery. He doesn't only attack those who come in here, you see. His goals are always bigger. He's always lookin' to attack the wider world."

Well, at least we know who the snatcher is now, Thea thought. "Why such lofty goals?" she asked aloud.

"He says it's to make everybody pay."

Thea frowned. "Pay for what?"

"I don't have a damn clue."

Thea's mind buzzed with other questions, but she refrained from asking them as Whitney continued. "He makes folks pay by bringin' up big trouble. Natural disasters, plagues, and the like. He don't cause 'em, you see, but he makes what's already happenin' worse. A lot less folks woulda died if he didn't come around."

A centuries-old ghost making everyone sick. Great. Thea had been hoping for a rogue mage up to some ritual shit. Not this.

"Did he do that with the Yellow Fever?" she asked. "Make everything worse?"

"It's the first time he did it, far as anybody in this cemetery knows. The whole ordeal inspired a bunch of priests and other religious types who were in on the supernatural side of things to find the Pale Stranger and bind him so he couldn't spread death and destruction anymore. I'm glad they did it, too. Though things ain't good now, they ain't as bad as they used to be, at least from what I've heard."

Thea concluded there could be plenty of spirits in this cemetery who had been alive when the Pale Stranger first began his tirade. Many of them might have died of the yellow fever.

She thought of something. "Were you a groundskeeper here at the cemetery before you died?"

Whitney turned, seeming surprised, then nodded. "How'd you know?"

"You're still wearing a uniform." She gestured at the jumpsuit and nametag, noting they both looked at least seventy years old. She wondered if he had had family. If anyone had known him well before he died. However, now was not the time for friendly conversation or getting to know one another.

"Right," Whitney remarked.

"Do you know what brought the Pale Stranger back?" she asked. Obviously, the binding had not worked. Perhaps the creature had broken it and was again loose in its old haunt.

"I don't know for sure," Whitney replied. "There's been a lot of different folks 'round here lately. They move 'round the cemetery doin' who the hell knows what."

"Humans?"

"Yes. Some with magic."

Thea found this very interesting. As far as she knew, AID had not started investigating the cemetery itself until tonight. Who else had been here?

"That ain't all," Whitney went on. "Even the free-ranging spirits, that is, ones that ain't bound to one cemetery or another, have brought news from other places where the same thing is happening. Maybe it's got to do with that."

Thea decided to mention this to Brandon and Jax when she saw them next. She started to ask how the hell any ghost could have the power to enhance plagues or natural disasters. Then she remembered all the abducted people. *He's using them like batteries, collecting them to charge up his efforts. Gross.*

With no huge event outside the abductions, it suggested their life force had not yet been expended. Maybe there was hope for saving them. Thea remembered all the reports of the missing people being sick before they were snatched. Was something like a plague coming again?

Furthermore, the stolen people would have to be kept nearby where the spirit could draw on them. *They must be somewhere in this cemetery.*

"Where do you suppose the people he's taken could be? Are there crypts somewhere in these tunnels?"

"I don't know where," Whitney replied. "There ain't no tunnels or crypts. If he's put 'em underground, he's buried 'em another way. Then, of course, there's all the tombs aboveground."

Thea was getting exasperated. "Well, we can open all the tombs and search them."

Whitney turned, horror written on his face. It was as though she had suggested the most insane thing in the world. He might as well have had the spectral version of a heart attack. "We can't do that! No, no! The ghosts are all worked up with so many odd comings and goings. It's one thing to interrogate spirits. It's another matter to disturb their resting places!"

Thea could understand that, at least.

"You'll be a lucky girl not to create an army of wraiths many times more pissed off than the Lancer. You'd have them goin' on a wild ride all through town, and God have mercy on anyone caught in their path."

"Right," Thea replied. "No breaking into tombs. Got it. Then we'll have to figure something else out."

Another voice joined them, though it was in Thea's head, not out loud. Kira spoke in a light, curious tone. "I can see your bones, Thea. Is that normal?"

"Shit. I've been here too long." Soon, she'd be as much of a ghost as the one standing before her. She faced Whitney again. "I need to get out." Coming down here had been a fool's errand. She had learned who the snatcher was, but with so little information, she didn't have a damn clue how to deal with him.

This only made Whitney panic. "The sun is coming up soon. Yes, we need to get you back before the dawn drives me to my rest. I can get you most of the way up, but with the dawn coming, I can't go to the top. You'll have to push yourselves the rest of the way."

"Is that possible?" Thea asked, wide-eyed.

"I'm sure a smart girl like yourself will find a way."

Thea wasn't sure she felt complimented. "Fine. Take us as far as you can."

CHAPTER SEVENTEEN

"The Arcane Investigation Division has thirteen offices across all of North America. Its tenth office, located in New Orleans, is called the Gulf Coast Office and oversees all of Louisiana and southern parts of Alabama and Mississippi. This location is known for its unique Cajun and Creole culture, as well as its coastal cities and oil industry."
—From an online article detailing the offices of AID across the United States by journalist Brock Stanton

Brandon aimed and fired. The silver and salt blasted from the end of his shotgun directly at the wraith perched on the horse. Even the saddle seemed to simmer with blue flames, doing nothing to hurt the wraith. The Lancer veered his horse left, out of Brandon's fire, as if he had expected it.

"Shit," the agent muttered, aiming again. The Lancer veered right, then left. He evaded the fourth shot from Jax while moving forward. Almost as if he had done this before. Brandon wasn't sure it was common for an AID agent to encounter a wraith in this cemetery. Or anywhere, for that matter. If this was the case, no one had bothered to tell him about it. Brandon had always been an accurate shot. Why the hell couldn't he make it count now?

"We have to run, Cole," Jax growled, already turning away to sprint back through the cemetery, hoping the wraith would not follow them beyond the stone walls and wrought iron fences. Jax had shot a few more times in quick succession. His last blast had gone directly toward the Lancer, but the wraith had batted it away with his weapon.

Jax wasn't the sort of man who ran. He stood his ground until he was out of options. Until now, he had never run out.

Brandon didn't want to flee. Not when that thing galloping toward them on a horse could easily outrun them. Then they'd be out of breath with nothing to defend themselves. The shotgun with silver and salt wasn't doing a damn thing. Perhaps it only worked against magical creatures that were *alive*, not made of pure blue flame, prancing through a graveyard in the middle of the night.

Fine. They'd run.

Jax was already sprinting away. Brandon took off after him, the end of the cemetery coming into sight. The gate was closed. Why? They had left it open behind them when they entered. Perhaps the spirits had shut it so as not to let any more disturbances inside. The sky was beginning to lighten. Brandon hoped that by dawn, the wraith would retreat to his resting place and leave them the hell alone.

His head swam with other thoughts. Where the hell was Thea? Was she in danger? Better the Lancer chase them than her, he supposed, though he wished he had someone with magic around right about now. Someone who could send that bastard back where he came from.

A shrill scream rang out behind them. Brandon's first thought was Thea being captured and harmed. It was only the Lancer letting them know their presence was not wanted. "Cranky bastard," Jax muttered, breathing hard as they took toward the closed gate. "We came into his cemetery, and he ain't happy about it."

No shit, Brandon thought. He glanced over his shoulder to find the horse had slowed down, but not for a reason favorable to them. It gave the wraith sitting on it a better distance to throw his lance.

"Down!" Brandon cried, grabbing Jax's shoulders as the wraith released his swift-moving weapon. They dropped to the ground, sprawling on their fronts as the lance whizzed directly over their heads, hot and sharp. If that had entered either one of them...

Brandon didn't want to think about it. He started to stand, but Jax called out, "Stay down!" The lance wasn't an ordinary throwing weapon. As soon as it was out of range, it turned, flying back into the hand it belonged to like a boomerang.

That was when Brandon felt like he had to run for his life. He and Jax sprang to their feet, taking off like their lives depended on it. And it might have. "We won't make it out in time!" Jax called to his companion. "We need to stop the damn bastard!"

But how?

Brandon didn't have a spare moment to think. The Lancer was on their heels, then driving space between them.

Brandon could hardly see Jax beyond the form of blue fire between them. The Lancer pulled ahead, and Brandon wondered if it was still chasing them anymore when it halted and turned, stopping them in their tracks. Loose dirt sprayed around Brandon's boots as he skidded. Either they could turn and run deeper into the graveyard where they would be trapped, or they dealt with this being here and now.

Jax fired once more. A blast of silver and salt almost hit the Lancer. The wraith released another piercing sound, batting away the salt with his lance like it was nothing. "We'll leave you alone!" Brandon called, hoping he could make the Lancer hear him. "Just let us leave!"

The Lancer either didn't hear or didn't care. He pushed toward them. Brandon and Jax stumbled back. Jax glanced behind his shoulder, seeming to sense something, then back at Brandon. The latter saw the meaning in Jax's eyes and nodded. It could work. It was a long shot, but it was either try it or get melted by the lance's blue flame.

There were other spirits at work in this cemetery.

Jax turned first and took off the way they came toward the center of the cemetery as the sky slowly brightened. The stars faded as the AID agents made their way to the center, leading the Lancer along. How Jax had sensed a greater spirit emerging from the graveyard, Brandon did not know. It wasn't magic, that was for sure.

Furthermore, running into a second spirit might not accomplish what they wanted. It might trap them instead of the Lancer.

Worth a try, Brandon kept reminding himself.

A cloud of yellow smoke seeped up from the ground,

growing until it began to take shape. A figure stood behind it, so obscured that Brandon could not quite make it out. He and Jax separated, going around the smoke and into the darker parts of the cemetery.

Brandon leaped behind a tree and watched what happened next. As he and Jax hoped, the Lancer brought his horse to a screeching halt. Both horse and wraith released piercing sounds of alarm as the yellow-gray smoke welled up, consuming them whole. Then, in a flash, it was all gone. Vanished. Any sign of the Lancer disappeared except for one thing.

Jax stepped out from behind a tall headstone, chuckling. "Guess that fella can't fight us anymore without that." He pointed to the lance lying on the ground, its flames extinguished. The weapon was black as night and singing with a foreign energy. Magic, no doubt. It must have been strong magic for Brandon to feel it, as someone who did not use the world's raw powers.

He and Jax stood there for a moment, panting. Brandon looked his companion over, noting they were both exhausted, sore, and dirty from the commotion. His shirt had torn, perhaps on a branch. He didn't know.

"Brandon," Jax pointed at the younger agent's shoulder. Brandon peered at the rip in his shirt and found blood pooling on his skin.

"Shit, I didn't notice." He'd felt pain sometime after he hit the ground but had not realized he'd been cut. Had the lance touched him, or had the fall been enough? He ripped off part of his shirt and staunched the area before having Jax tie it for him.

"You can deal with that when we're out of here," Jax insisted. "Right now, we need to find the girl."

Thoughts swarmed Brandon's head. What the hell was that thing in the yellow smoke? Was the Lancer or something else responsible for the snatchings? Most importantly, had he failed AID and Thea by losing another witch liaison? *All on my first fucking mission,* he thought.

They'd reprimand him much more than Jax, especially since he was the leader of this operation. They would strip his title and job, and his superiors at AID would make sure he never worked in this industry again. Not after the debacle that had brought him to AID in the first place and his failure to keep Theadora Blackwood alive for one fucking night. Panic threatened to well up, but his years of training and experience allowed him to stamp it down. They hadn't lost her yet.

"The girl knows what she's doing," Jax's calm voice stated. He must have read the distress on Brandon's face. "She knew what she was doing when she went underground with that…thing. She might not be a good team player, but she won't be taken out by a specter or wraith if anything I know about her is true."

She would go down fighting, Brandon knew. He merely had to listen to Jax and find her. A little difficult, he thought, since the last place they'd seen her was going into the ground. It wasn't like they could dig her up, and they didn't have a damn clue how far she'd gone or if she was still in the cemetery.

They returned to the tree where Thea had disappeared and found many of the lingering spirits heading back to their resting places. They drifted into the dark shadows of the cemetery, disappearing into stones, trees, or walls. Soon, only the two men stood there. Brandon shivered, noting the dew across the grass and the stars still fading from the sky. Dawn would soon be upon them.

Still, no sign of Thea.

Brandon rubbed his eyes, hoping to ease the exhaustion pressing into him. It didn't help one bit. It had been a long time since he'd pulled an all-nighter, and he'd never spent most of his night evading a cranky wraith with an ancient lance. "Should we take that thing with us?" Jax asked, gesturing to the lance on the ground. Brandon was half inclined to do so, but the thought of that creature coming back for his favorite weapon sent a chill down his spine.

"Not a chance I'm taking anything but Thea out of his cemetery."

"She might have already left," Jax suggested. "Think about it. Maybe she came out of the ground, saw what we were dealing with, and decided to step out."

Brandon bristled at the thought of Thea leaving them to fight the Lancer instead of helping them. He shook his head. "She might not be much of a team player, but I don't think she's an asshole."

"All I'm saying is she's not here anymore." Jax checked his watch. "It's almost sunrise. She knows when she's supposed to be back. Nobody alive can stay down there without losing air after the sun is up."

Jax had a point. Again, Brandon was in a position where he needed to trust the girl. God, he hated it. "She said she'd meet up with us later, didn't she?" Jax questioned. "Maybe she didn't mean in here." He gestured at their general surroundings. Brandon liked the sound of that. It meant they no longer had a reason to idle here. Though it was unlikely they'd see another spirit with the sun coming up, he didn't want to risk it.

"Let's hope Thea found something out about the snatcher," he commented as he and Jax headed for the cemetery's entrance.

Outside the cemetery, the vans waited. Several AID agents approached them with wide eyes, wondering what had happened when they heard piercing screams and gunfire coming. "We'll explain when we're at headquarters," Brandon told them, dreading the need to explain anything. "Pack up the vans and head back. Jax and I will finish tying up loose ends."

The agents' wary looks told him they had all noted who wasn't with them. Word would soon get around AID headquarters that the witch liaison was missing. Shit. Claire couldn't get Brandon out of this.

"We'll find her," Jax assured him as he laid a firm hand on Brandon's shoulder. The other AID agents had dispersed, muttering about what had happened. Brandon would deal with that later.

"You think Thea might have gone back to headquarters?" he asked Jax, turning.

Jax shook his head. "Not a chance. Not after the night she's had. If anything, she probably went to her place to sleep."

Her apartment. Brandon could find out where it was in her paperwork. He didn't like the idea of showing up at her place at the crack of dawn, but he had to make sure she was safe. So, grumpy and grimy, the men climbed into Brandon's car and headed across town.

When Thea emerged from the ground, she found the cemetery empty. Not a sign of a single spirit was around. Judging by the gray tint in the sky, she assumed they had gone back to their resting places before the sun rose. There was no sign of Brandon or Jax, either. A lump formed in her throat at the thought of the Lancer yanking them underground. Or something worse. However, something told her they were not here. No signs of AID agents beyond the cemetery, either. Someone had told them to pack up and go home. That's what Thea wanted to do, too.

They must have thought I left already, she thought. *Or Brandon is pissing himself because he thinks his witch liaison is dead.* It had been a close call. Even with Whitney's help, crawling through the ground had been no easy task. Thea certainly looked like she'd come from a hole in the cemetery. Mud caked her hair, and her face, arms, and hands were grimy with dirt. *It's going to take forever to get this shit out of my fingernails,* she moaned inwardly to Kira. *At least I thought to wear clothes I don't mind ruining.*

Well. I, for one, think you still look spectacular, Kira replied.

Thea gave the animal on her shoulder a wry grin. *Maybe the extra-dimensional world knew I needed someone like you around for an ego boost.*

Thea reached for her phone to call Brandon. Dead. "Shit."

Feeling tired to the bone and with her stomach growling, she thought it best to return to her apartment, get her phone charged, and call Brandon from there. She plodded through the cemetery, only stopping when she spotted something long, dark, and menacing lying on the ground. She frowned and approached it.

"What the hell is this? Something a knight would use?" A lance, she determined. From the wraith Whitney had mentioned. By the looks of it, Brandon and Jax had evaded the creature's fury. The question now was why had the wraith left his weapon behind?

Thea shivered, and it wasn't only because of the morning chill. Something was still around. She felt like she was being watched, and a strange odor hung in the air. She sniffed, wrinkling her nose. The scent hadn't been here before she went underground. *Maybe it's me,* she thought. *I'm sure I don't smell spectacular right now.*

Everything Whitney said about the Pale Stranger played in her mind. Was the creature here right now? She shivered again. *We're not waiting around to find out.*

I'm hungry, Kira's voice announced in her mind.

Ow! Thea hissed. *Your claws are digging into my skin.*

Sorry about that. I got scared. After everything that workman said about the Pale Stranger... The cat shivered. *No, thank you.*

You're going to have to work on that, Thea told her as she headed out of the cemetery. *One day, you and I might have to face that thing, and we'll need to be ready. Besides, a lot of people are much more afraid of an extra-dimensional being like you than a wraith.*

Are we going back to your place now? Kira asked.

Thea nodded as she walked to where she had parked her car, out of everyone else's sight. *I know a shortcut or two to get there faster.*

CHAPTER EIGHTEEN

"For night's swift dragons cut the clouds full fast,
  And yonder shines Aurora's harbinger;
  At whose approach, ghosts, wandering here and there,
  Troop home to churchyards: damned spirits all,
  That in crossways and floods have burial,
  Already to their wormy beds are gone."
  —William Shakespeare, A Midsummer Night's Dream

By the time Brandon and Jax reached the main road, the early morning traffic had piled up. *How long are we going to have to sit through this shit?* Brandon wondered. They both tried calling Thea a few times now that they had service, but they couldn't reach her. Their calls went straight to voicemail.

Brandon hoped Thea's phone was dead, not that she was ignoring them. Maybe after the ordeal in the cemetery, she had decided she never wanted to see them again. He didn't blame her. Still, he had a responsibility to make sure she was safe.

Twenty minutes later, he had wound through the traffic to Thea's apartment building and stood outside with Jax, ringing the buzzer. When no one came down to open it or answered, he tried the door and found it unlocked. After sharing a glance with Jax and shrugging, Brandon went inside. He found Thea's apartment unit and raised his fist to knock, his heart beating faster than it had a minute before. What if she wasn't here? What was he supposed to do then?

He knocked. At first, there was silence. He knocked again, holding out hope that she was home.

"Coming!" a voice announced from the other side.

Brandon's chest would have filled with relief if the voice belonged to Thea.

The door eased open, and a dark-skinned girl with wide, pretty eyes at least a foot shorter than him stood there. She took in the mussed-up, dirty AID agents with surprise, then wariness. Her gaze rested longer on Brandon than on Jax, as if she had heard more about him. "Who are you?" she demanded, but the way her eyes swept over their tactical gear bearing the AID symbol suggested she already knew.

"Agents Ajax Maddison and Brandon Cole," Jax answered in a friendly tone despite being dead tired and wanting to be anywhere but here. "We're looking for the young woman who lives here. Is she home?"

The girl frowned. "I don't have to talk to you if I don't want to."

Jax's face softened. "Of course you don't. We want to make sure your friend is safe."

The girl blinked. "Safe? Thea's not with you?" The

alarm cleared her eyes, and Brandon noted they weren't brown. More like a dark honey color. He couldn't help but feel mesmerized.

Brandon noted other things about her appearance. Her long, hand-sewn skirt, the crystal she wore around her neck, the pentagram tattoo on her forearm. This girl was a magic user like Thea. Perhaps a hedge witch, by the looks of her earth-toned clothing and the heavy scent of lavender around her. Coven witches didn't have such style. He tried a gentler approach. "Are you a friend of Thea's?"

The girl's eyes narrowed, her hand tightening on the doorknob like she might slam it shut any second.

"That's right. We know Thea," Brandon added. "And we know she hates being called Theadora."

"Ah, so you must be the guy who chased her across Tulane and forced her to join your organization," the girl remarked. "Bryce, is it?"

He stiffened but tried not to sound displeased. "Brandon, actually." What other unfavorable things had Thea shared with this girl?

The girl didn't seem to care what his name was, and Brandon wondered if she had gotten it wrong on purpose.

"What's your name?" Jax asked.

"Mia," she answered curtly. "Why are you looking for Thea here? I thought she was on the mission with you tonight."

Brandon rubbed the back of his neck. "We got separated. Long story. We were hoping she came back here."

Mia's face fell, telling Brandon the truth he dreaded. Thea wasn't home.

Mia's face hardened, and her voice shook when she

spoke. "You'd better not have gotten my best friend lost or hurt. How dare you think..." She trailed off, tears coming into her eyes. Apparently, she was well aware of the witch liaisons who had gone missing.

Her voice rose, still shaking. "I don't know why she went in the first place! I told her throwing her power around like that would only lead to disastrous results. And you, both of you, were supposed to protect her!"

Brandon hated hearing the girl yell, especially so early in the morning, but he couldn't blame her. He also didn't have the heart to tell her that protection went both ways. Witch liaisons were supposed to have the backs of the AID agents they worked with. Thea hadn't done that. Still, Brandon couldn't put all the blame on her. He was the team leader and had lost her.

He realized Mia had been expecting Thea to show up this morning, not two dirty AID agents saying they'd lost her to a specter in the middle of the night in one of the sketchiest places around. Jax spoke up next. "Maybe Thea is on her way here. If it's all right with you, Mia, we'd like to come in and wait."

Mia hesitated, then sniffed, half because the two men smelled and half to keep herself from crying. She didn't seem too comfortable with the idea, but she eased the door open enough to let them in. "Sorry about the smell," Jax told her. "We've been in a cemetery all night dealing with wraiths and the like." He mentioned this as casually as one would state the weather conditions.

Mia's eyes widened, but she simply went to the kitchen and began preparing something to drink. Brandon doubted it had anything to do with hospitality. The poor girl was probably trying to keep herself busy. In the meantime, Brandon surveyed Thea's living room.

The plush green sofa looked thrifted but comfortable. A desk littered with papers, photographs, and little pieces of stone stood in one corner with a rug folded over as if she'd moved the desk in here recently. A TV was on but paused, showing Mia had been up all night waiting for her friend. Brandon's heart twinged at the thought. Thea may have been an orphan, but she still had people who loved her. It was more than he had in New Orleans.

Brandon approached a wall where a few framed pictures hung. One was a map print of New Orleans, another was a band poster, and a few more showed pictures of people Brandon recognized as Thea's parents. One was old, featuring the pair as a young couple. Another was more recent, with elementary school-aged Thea sitting between her parents. Even as a child, she wore a winning smile and sparkling charm in her eyes. That fierce, rebellious streak showed up in her young face.

Footsteps made Brandon turn to see Mia entering the room, holding mugs of coffee. Though she handed one to each man, her expression remained stern. "So what the hell happened? I told Thea not to go, especially with that…cat of hers."

"Ah, yes, the cat," Jax drawled with a small smile. "What is that thing anyhow?"

Mia took on a startled look.

Brandon stepped forward. "You're a hedge witch, aren't you? You know what that thing Thea had was, right?"

Mia stepped back, her expression hard. "It doesn't matter what I am, and I'm beginning to think the two of you should go. If Thea turns up, and you better hope she does, I'll make sure she calls you." She gestured at the door.

Brandon was half inclined to leave and let the girl alone. She was clearly upset and had every right to be. Their presence, especially if she was a hedge witch, was not welcome.

He'd blown it by bringing it up. That and the cat, whatever it was. They didn't need to make Mia more uncomfortable. As a hedge witch with no coven to lobby on her behalf, she had often been under worse scrutiny from AID agents. *It won't be like that with me,* Brandon decided. Not when she was a friend of Thea's. A close friend, if the ferocity in her eyes and voice told him anything.

"All right, we'll go," Brandon relented.

Jax glanced at him in surprise before downing his coffee and handing the cup back to the girl. "Thank you, Miss. That might have been the best coffee I've ever had. We appreciate anything you can do regarding Thea. We want to make sure she's safe."

Mia's eyes glinted as if to say, *Sure. I don't believe that for a second.*

Brandon hoped they could prove her wrong. He turned to the front door to find Mia had never closed it when letting them in. She must have forgotten in her distracted state. As the men headed for the door, it opened a fraction farther, and a figure sauntered in.

The cat's gray and white fur was matted and dirty, covered in mud from the cemetery. The creature did not seem to mind the state of her appearance. It didn't stop her from batting her wide eyes and long eyelashes. Brandon had never seen a cat with such mesmerizing eyes. The cat blinked at him, and he could have sworn she smiled. She came directly to Brandon, rubbing along his leg to get the mud out of her fur. A low purr reverberated from her.

Mia's eyes widened at the sight of the cat, but she didn't say anything.

Brandon hissed. "Get off me, will ya? I don't want to get dirtier than I already am."

The cat ignored him.

Mia stepped forward and shooed the animal away. The cat loped into the kitchen, seeming to understand from Mia that she'd find something to eat there.

Jax chuckled despite the situation. "Where that little one is, the other should not be far behind, right?"

He was right. A moment later, the door opened wider. Thea appeared at long last, looking like she'd crawled out of a hole. Brandon presumed that definitely could have been the case.

Thea stopped short at the three faces, directing an *explain yourself, young lady* look at her. Slowly, she smiled and gave a little wave. "Hey there. I didn't know I was coming back to a party at my place." The stern looks from Mia, Brandon, and Jax wiped away her amusement.

"You need to tell us what happened to you," Mia demanded. "Especially since you've come home looking like that." She gestured at Thea's disheveled appearance.

"There's more to tell than whatever happened in the cemetery." Jax's eyes glinting. "I also want to know why you have an extra-dimensional entity disguised as a cat roaming your apartment."

At that moment, the cat appeared in the living room.

She hadn't walked in but simply materialized at the sound of Thea's voice. It seemed they had not yet discussed that cats didn't appear out of thin air. Thea, Mia, and the cat froze.

Jax smiled. "I sensed it the second I saw her. We have technology to do that, you know. I also know you are aware that extra-dimensional entities are an absolute no-no for witches or anyone working for AID."

Thea cringed, and her gaze slid to Brandon. He had not sensed it, hadn't thought to question why Thea might bring a cat along with her. However, Jax had thought further once again. *I feel fucking stupid,* Brandon thought. He hoped Thea didn't see it. He hardened his expression and crossed his arms, giving Thea a look that asked, *Well, what do you have to say for yourself?*

Thea faltered for a good thirty seconds, trying to come up with excuses and exclamations, none of which she could ever seem to word. Finally, she sighed. "I'll tell you everything, including how I'm about to save all our asses with the information I got from Whitney."

"Who?" Mia asked.

"The worker in the graveyard."

Brandon's heart skipped a beat. Had Thea found out who the snatcher was? Did it have anything to do with the cloud of yellow smoke he and Jax had seen?

Mia shook her head. "I think I'll need more context than these two." She gestured at the men standing in Thea's living room.

"The least you all can do is let me grab a shower and clean the dirt from my ears before you yell at me for hours," Thea remarked, turning down the hall.

Mia scooped up the cat. "I'll get this one cleaned up."

Thea glanced over her shoulder at Brandon and Jax before disappearing into her bathroom. "Maybe you two should get your dirty boots off my rug." She shook her head, *tsking*. "Sometimes you men have no manners."

CHAPTER NINETEEN

"Most witch groups form a coven but can break up into smaller groups for situations that do not require large amounts of power. These groups are called sabbats or coteries. The coven hierarchy is in place for the sole purpose of ensuring that power is distributed according to the skill of the individual witch. When acting independently, most witches can only do very rudimentary magic. Independent magic is frowned upon by coven members due to the risk of a witch injuring themselves and others, staunching their magic for good.

"The 'independent magic,' they say, should be left to the menial skill of hedge witches. Overreaching with magic alone can become explosive in nature. A witch who taps into the Lake of Power alone is at risk, if they survive, of a lifetime of crippling agony."

—*From* The History of Covens and Their Adjacent Societies *by Orlena Gorbana*

Finally, a moment alone to get herself clean. Thea's shower had always had shitty water pressure, and it only stayed hot for about fifteen minutes. It was enough time to get clean on days when she didn't have to scrub every inch of her body because it was covered in mud.

Thea didn't want a "get clean" shower. If it were up to her, she'd stay under the water forever, letting her thoughts roam while Brandon, Jax, Mia, and Kira remained in her living room. She'd scrub every layer of dirt from her body and pretend she hadn't spent most of her night underground learning about a spirit who'd been draining the life from people for centuries.

Why do I have to deal with this? she wondered. Why couldn't the coven know about this and be concerned? Furthermore, she had a lot of explaining to do about Kira. *How am I going to tell them I've dragged an extra-dimensional entity into our world, befriended it, and brought it on my first AID mission? Without getting kicked out of both AID and the coven, that is?*

It seemed impossible, but so had tapping into the Lake of Power. She'd done that. *I can convince them not to tell anyone about Kira,* Thea decided as she worked shampoo into her hair. The dirt caked there slowly loosened, and she felt bad for a heartbeat that Brandon and Jax hadn't had a chance to shower.

They'd come here to find her. Their cross expressions told her she was in hot water. Then, Jax had somehow figured out what Kira was. Thea groaned, half in dread for what she would have to tell them and half because the hot water running into a cut along her leg burned. She had not realized coming out of the ground would result in a minor injury. Even so, Brandon had gotten a worse blow. She'd seen the bloodied shirt on his shoulder. They had a story to tell her, too.

From her bathroom, Thea heard the distant voices of her friend and the two AID agents, along with Kira's occasional loud purring. "Here, let me help with that," Mia offered. Undoubtedly, she had seen Brandon's wound and wanted to help with her magic and knowledge of herbs.

Thea had to apologize for the AID men showing up while Mia was around. Her hedge witch best friend wasn't having a great morning, that was for sure. Even so, Mia was a kind-hearted soul who helped even people she didn't align with. Wounds were wounds, and everybody bled red. Mia had said those words a few times since she and Thea became friends.

Well, not everyone bleeds red, Thea mused. Some otherworldly creatures, those with dark magic in their veins pumping from hearts of stone, bled other colors. Or so her father had told her in stories he'd shared while she was growing up.

What would they think about all this? Thea wondered, her mind going to her parents. What would Irene and Peter think of their only child going into a cemetery in the middle of the night to speak to spirits while leaving two AID agents to fend for themselves against a wraith?

Her father might have chuckled but told her she wasn't much of a team player. Her mother would have had firmer words but, in the end, might have praised Thea for being brave enough to follow a specter below ground.

They had always taught her finding out the truth was of utmost importance. It was why, years after their deaths, she still sought to find out what had actually happened to them. What did Ambrosius and his books have to do with anything? Furthermore, what was she going to do with the truth when she got it? None of that would matter until she dealt with the Pale Stranger. Until her neighbors stopped disappearing.

Maybe it had been a bad idea to leave Brandon and Jax alone, Thea decided. Still, she'd done what she'd gone to the cemetery to do. She had found out what the hell was taking people when the sun was setting or rising. *We have to move quickly to catch the damn thing before it takes another person,* she thought, hurrying through her shower with a new sense of urgency.

Thea heard more voices, then the front door closing. Silence followed. She turned off the water and dried her body, listening intently. Brandon and Jax had left. All she heard was the soft padding of Mia's bare feet and Kira's paws into the kitchen. Seconds later, the coffee machine was back on.

Thea didn't want to think about waking up more. She wanted to roll into bed and sleep for days. Who knew contacting ghosts could make one so tired?

When Thea at last emerged wearing a bathrobe, Mia gave her a tired smile. "I convinced those two to go home. Clearly, they needed rest and freshening up. I figured they could lecture you better after a good sleep." She gave Thea a wry grin as if to say, *And I think you might deserve it.* Out loud, she added, "You look much cleaner but also more tired."

"My head is pounding like someone hit me with a brick." Thea managed a grin despite herself.

"I told them you would call when you were awake and

let them know what's going on. It didn't take much convincing to make them leave. I think they heard you turn the shower on and got FOMO."

"Thank you, Mia. You're wonderful, and not only for making them leave." She squeezed her friend tight. For staying up all night waiting for her, for helping her prepare for a night in the cemetery. For offering to bathe Kira's feline form. Thea eyed the cat. "You and I will talk later about how Jax noticed what you were. I have a feeling you weren't being so secret about it."

Kira batted her cat eyes and swished her tail as if to say, *I don't know what you're talking about.*

"I'll go get dressed now." Thea turned from the kitchen into the hallway leading to her bedroom.

"Don't think because I got them to leave, and I'm relieved you aren't dead in a ditch somewhere that I'm letting this go," Mia called after her. She followed Thea to her bedroom and stood outside her closed door as Thea changed into her softest pajamas. "I'm sure you have your own side of the story or some shit, but those guys made it clear you left them high and dry. Not much of a team player, Thea?"

Thea's heart sank. *I guess I'm not,* she thought. Not if she was trying to break free from a coven and become a witch mage. She had been the only one who could find out from Whitney what was going on. A long silence passed between the girls in which Thea's thoughts swirled.

Mia sighed, then asked in a gentler tone, "Are you all right, Thea?"

Thea opened the door. "Maybe I'm supposed to do everything on my own."

Mia frowned. "Bullshit. I can remind you of several instances where my help saved your ass." She nodded to the cat sitting in the middle of the hall. "I'm guessing this one helped you tap into the Lake tonight."

Thea gave a subtle nod. "I don't mean to be ungrateful. I just…" She trailed off and buried her head in her hands.

Mia shuffled closer to hug her friend. "I know what you mean, Iz. It's not easy feeling like an outsider."

Thea paused. Mia had always felt like that, hadn't she? She'd barely had a community growing up. As far as Thea knew, not many people outside their friendship understood what it was like to live with magic and not be able to use its full potential. "I'm sorry, Mia. For making you worried and for what you had to tell Brandon and Jax."

Mia's lips twitched as she held back a smile. "He's actually kind of cute, you know. That Brandon guy. I got a better look at him while I stitched up his shoulder. Of course, he didn't smell too good."

Thea grinned. "He smells much better when he hasn't been chased by a wraith called the Lancer all night."

Mia's eyes widened a fraction. "Now you have to tell me everything."

They curled up together on Thea's bed. Mia lit a candle while Thea recounted the night's events. From arriving at the cemetery and meeting Whitney to going underground and hearing about the Lancer and the Pale Stranger. From coming back up and not seeing anyone left to finally arriving home with Kira. The longer Thea spoke, the harder it became to recount details. She was so damn tired, but Mia wasn't done asking questions.

"I'm assuming you used your power with Kira for the first time, right? How did that go?"

Thea glanced at the cat as Kira spoke into her mind. Kira chose to speak only to Thea, not Mia, so Thea turned to her friend and relayed, "Kira says it went splendidly and sings both her praise and mine. I wouldn't go as far as to say any of that, but at least it didn't go badly."

Mia glanced at Kira with a raised brow. "Modesty must not be a trait extra-dimensional beings possess."

Thea chuckled, but her amusement quickly faded as she remembered all Whitney had shared with her. "I'm stumped about what he said. I don't know what kind of spirit we're dealing with regarding the Pale Stranger. I'm pretty limited on my knowledge of spirits as it's never been my field of interest."

Mia considered this, then tilted her head. "Do you still have the last gift I gave you for your birthday?"

Thea's eyes widened, and she sat up enough to glance about her room. "You mean the tome of supernatural critters and how to deal with them?"

Mia nodded, smiling. "That's the one. Though I wish you wouldn't call them 'critters.' Real critters are delightful creatures. We're talking about vengeful spirits and ancient practitioners of dark magic."

"My favorites," Thea returned dryly. "I know it's on one of the shelves in here, only not which one."

Mia searched Thea's cluttered shelves, rifling through makeup, tissue boxes, empty perfume bottles, picture frames, and other trinkets before finding the book she was looking for. Meanwhile, Thea's attention drifted to Kira, who was no longer in cat form.

The extra-dimensional entity stood before the floor-length mirror Thea had propped against one wall, utterly naked. She moved her body to check herself out from various angles. Thea couldn't help but stare. No longer did Kira look like a half-formed person, lopsided and not quite put together. She was the total opposite. She was probably the most beautiful person Thea had ever seen.

Waves of golden hair hung down her back, brushing against every perfect curve. Her skin was glowing and clear, her eyes bright like sapphires. "Are you always going to look like that when you're in human form?" Thea asked, a spark of envy igniting in her chest.

Kira turned with a bright smile. "Do you like it? I can turn into other forms, too." Slowly, her features changed until she was a dark-haired beauty with gleaming green eyes and tan skin.

"Mia, are you seeing this?" Thea demanded.

Mia did not turn away from the bookshelf but replied, "Oh, yes. Instead of letting me give her a bath in cat form, she showed me her new skills. Remember what I said about modesty? Extra-dimensional entities don't care for it. Not this one, anyway."

Thea returned her attention to Kira and found her wearing a shimmering light blue dress. She hadn't gotten it out of Thea's closet. She must have made it appear out of nowhere with magic. Another spark of envy. Thea wished her magic allowed her free clothes so she didn't have to spend money shopping. "And where do you think you're going in that?" she demanded.

Kira's bright smile did not falter. "I'm getting ready to

meet the handsome males. We're going to tell them sorry, aren't we?"

Mia turned slightly from where she was searching and shared a look with Thea. It took Thea a second to understand what Kira meant, and she laughed softly, shaking her head. "You will only be going around 'handsome males' in your cat form. Maybe a bird would work, but not like that. Not if we're going to figure out what is going on."

"Why not?" Kira sounded coy, but her expression was total innocence. She looked sexy as hell but seemed to have no concept of her appeal.

"Because you'll be too distracting," Mia remarked. "Every male who sees you and a few females will want to sleep with you."

"Sleep with me? Why?"

Thea sighed. "Mia doesn't mean literally sleeping next to you. Anyway, it doesn't matter right now. We can talk about this later."

Kira didn't take it too badly. Instead of looking disappointed, she shrugged, then reverted to cat form, hopping onto Thea's bed as if she had been doing this all her life.

"Here, I found it," Mia announced from the bookshelf as she opened the tome she'd been looking for. She returned to Thea's bed and began to flip through the pages.

"What is using this book going to help me with exactly?" Thea asked.

"If you can give Brandon more concise information about what you learned during the night, he might be more willing to hear you out about Kira."

Kira lifted her head and quietly meowed.

Thea propped her chin on one hand. "At least they

didn't take her with them. That means I'm not in super big trouble, right?"

"I don't know what it means." Mia sighed. "I found the section on ghosts. You can read it and maybe find out more about what you're dealing with." She met her friend's eyes and, seeing the exhaustion there, added, "Go to bed for now. You're dead tired. I can see that." Weariness etched Mia's face, too.

Thea squeezed her hand. "Thanks for everything."

Mia stood. "You will have to apologize to Jax and Brandon too. They were worried about you."

"I'm not so sure about that. I think they were more worried about getting their asses whipped for losing another liaison."

Mia shrugged. "That might have been part of it, but I saw the relief on their faces when you turned up. It wasn't only because you're a liaison. They care for you as a person."

Thea paused. Mia was seldom wrong about such things. It made everything worse. She'd put Brandon and Jax through it, apparently. Thea sank into her pillows. "As soon as I'm awake, I'll arrange a meeting to apologize."

"No tricks?"

"No tricks."

Thea eyed the cat curled at the end of her bed, fast asleep, and grinned. "Though I can't promise anything about that one."

CHAPTER TWENTY

"The Onryō are best known in Japanese culture as vengeful spirits returning to harm those in the living world for what was done to them before their deaths. Three of the most well-known Onryō are Japan's past rulers and politicians. These are Emperor Sutoku, samurai Taira no Masakado, and poet Sugawara no Michizane."
—Orlena Gorbana, Collections of Ancient Spirits

Thea drew a deep breath before dialing Brandon's number. She tried to make her voice sound cheerful. Best they get back on the right foot. His answer on the other end wasn't as formal as she expected. A simple, groggy "hello" reached her ears.

"No 'Agent Cole' at your service?" Thea quipped.

"Oh, hey, Thea. Sorry, you woke me." He hadn't realized it was her calling, it seemed. Thea glanced out her window at the sunlight streamed through the trees lining the street. It was late afternoon, and she had been awake for about an hour, gathering her courage to call Brandon and fucking apologize already.

"Sorry about that. I didn't know you were asleep." She should have guessed. Maybe texted him first. He had had a long night, too. Maybe longer than hers, what with being chased by a wraith on a phantom horse, hurling a lance and all. He was also the operation's leader and probably had to report their findings to AID. He must have found an excuse to go home and sleep first. Plus, he still had to find out from Thea what was going on.

"We should meet up," she suggested at last.

He paused. "Yes. We should." Maybe it was because he'd just woken up, but he didn't sound delighted with her idea.

"Do you know Laura's Candies on Chartres Street?" Thea asked.

"I've heard of it."

Thea smiled. "Not only do they have my favorite chocolates, but I've heard they have great glazed and flavored pecans. I've noticed you dipping into mixed nut packs a few times during training. Might be a good pick-me-up, right?"

She tried to sound light-hearted, but he did not share her bemusement. "This isn't you trying to butter me up before we talk about more serious matters, is it?"

Thea paused, then answered lightly, "Of course not."

"Fine. Laura's Candies it is."

"Good. Meet me in twenty?"

"Give me thirty."

"Take however long you need." As Thea said this, she tapped her foot impatiently on the floor. She stole a glance at the book lying on her couch, dying to tell someone about what she and Mia had learned that morning.

"Should I bring Jax?" Brandon asked.

"No, I'll talk to him later. For now, I want it to be only us." Thea glanced over her shoulder to ensure neither Mia nor Kira had heard her, afraid teasing about her wanting to go out with Brandon would ensue. Both were still asleep in Thea's room.

"See you soon." Brandon hung up. The dullness in his voice could have been from lack of sleep, but Thea sensed he'd changed his demeanor toward her for a reason. He had his guard up.

And no wonder, she thought as her eyes strayed to her bedroom, where the extra-dimensional entity curled on one of her pillows. She would not bring Kira to this meeting, that was for sure.

Thea picked through a pile of clothes she'd left in the bathroom so she wouldn't disturb her sleeping friends in the bedroom. After pulling on denim shorts and a light sweater for the cool evening air, she brushed her hair and put on makeup. She jotted a quick note for Mia before leaving, detailing where she was going and when she expected to be back.

Out on the street, the French Quarter grew busy as evening encroached. Laura's Candies was only a few blocks away, so Thea decided to walk instead of taking her car. Even walking, she arrived a few minutes before Brandon, who pulled up in his car across the street and got out. Thea took a second to appreciate the simple street clothes he had donned, a nice break from the tactical gear and suits. This was official AID work, but Thea hoped the ease of their street clothes and meeting in public would make it feel less serious.

Though this is pretty fucking serious, she admitted.

Brandon spotted her from across the street and approached after the walk sign turned. He did not greet her with anything more than a subtle nod. Thea led him inside, promising him the best treat of his life. She showed him the array of chocolates, pointing her favorites out.

The old man behind the counter recognized her as she stepped inside, teasing her for coming so late in the day when he was used to seeing her bright and early every morning. "Who might this young fella with ya be?" he asked, regarding Brandon with curious eyes.

"A co-worker," Thea answered quickly. "Thought I'd show him my favorite place in town."

The older man, Samuel Henderson, merely nodded, giving Brandon a pleased smile. "Thea here is my best customer, so anyone she brings in will surely become one too. Tell me, Thea, how's your friend Mia doing?" The two chatted briefly while Brandon surveyed the glazed pecan selection. Finally, he ordered some to appear polite to Thea's friend. After they had their orders, Thea led them back out to the street, her cheeks glowing with warmth. "Mr. Samuel has been one of my best friends since I moved here. I don't know where I would be without him."

"Has he…helped you in any way?" Brandon asked.

"You mean besides making sure I don't go ballistic because I don't have my favorite chocolate on hand?" Thea sounded serious, but amusement glinted in her eyes. "Come on." She tugged his sleeve. "We can sit outside at a café down the street and talk things over."

She chose Café Fleur De Lis, where a balcony overlooking the street was open with a few tables. Brandon ordered an appetizer while Thea got herself a drink, prepping herself for however this conversation went. Brandon remained quiet and reserved. She couldn't blame him, but she had always been good at breaking other people's walls down. *Getting them to like me*, she thought. *Well, I've done a good job getting people to hate me too.*

It had been a few weeks since she'd heard from anyone in her coven. Mother Folsom seemed more than happy to send her off to AID and get her out of the way, even if her sneaky assistant Arthur had taken to following Thea around. Well, at least she hadn't seen him recently.

Thea tried to relax, but the thought of more people disliking her, especially those she had befriended at AID, made that impossible. Suddenly, she could not bear the thought of Brandon Cole hating her. Not because he was her brand-new boss or because sometimes she found him semi-attractive. He was a good person and one of the few in an organization like AID who gave a shit about a person like her. Plus, he hadn't taken her cat away.

"I'm sorry for what happened," she told him, her expression earnest. "Everything happened so fast, and I didn't think. I should have had Whitney slow down or taken you two with us. I should have stayed and dealt with the Lancer first. Then we all could have had a chance to talk to Whitney after the coast was clear."

Brandon raised a brow. "Whitney?"

"Oh, yes. He's the groundskeeper you saw." Hurriedly, Thea brought Brandon up to speed on who Whitney was, how long ago he had died, and how he had remained in Lafayette Cemetery since.

When she finished, Brandon leaned forward. "I understand that making decisions like this so quickly can be hard to adjust to." He paused and glanced gratefully at the pecans he'd been munching on. "Especially if a person is used to working alone and not being accountable or depended on by others."

Thea stiffened, remembering what she had said to Mia early that morning. *Maybe I'm supposed to do everything on my own.*

She banished the thought when Brandon spotted the change in her expression and added, "Maybe 'depend on' rubs you the wrong way, but I assure you, learning how and who to trust is vital in the work we're doing. Whether a person is a witch, an AID agent, or someone who doesn't want to be alone all the time."

Thea nodded slowly. "I'm not as alone as I seem sometimes. I have Mia and Kira. Mr. Samuel and my professor. A few other friends here and there." She sighed. "Even with them, sometimes I feel like the loneliest person in the world." She thought of her parents but did not mention them.

She thought about how every day she wanted to call them, how she had their phone numbers memorized and had not deleted their text threads from her phone. How sometimes she texted them anyway and watched the messages not deliver. How it broke her every time. How being in a cemetery the night before had been hard for reasons having nothing to do with ghosts. *Sometimes, I wish my parents were ghosts,* she thought. *At least then, I'd have a chance to talk to them.*

Brandon must have read that she was thinking through some things because his voice lowered, becoming gentler. His face became softer and more open. "We can stop with all the back-and-forth apologies. I dragged you into this mess. How about you tell me what Whitney said while you were underground? I can tell you're bursting with information."

Thea glanced around them to make sure no special attention was upon them. Passersby might think they were a couple on a date, nothing else. Thea preferred that despite it being nowhere near the truth. Better for strangers to think they were going out together than to know they were discussing ancient spirits who snatched people out of nowhere and took them...

Well, Thea didn't know where, and she dreaded finding out. *But I have to.* Learning the truth, as her parents had taught her, was of the utmost importance.

So she told Brandon everything Whitney said and some of the conclusions she had drawn before returning aboveground. After that, Brandon gave a short description of all they had dealt with regarding the Lancer, including the cloud of yellow smoke that welled up to take the Lancer in the end. His face blanched, and he leaned forward, lowering his voice. "You don't think that smoke thing was the Pale Stranger, do you?"

Thea swallowed. "Could be. Actually, I'm pretty positive it is." To Brandon's surprise, she pulled out an old-looking, leather-bound book from the satchel sitting at her feet. At least it was a better surprise than the cat she had pulled out last night. She laid the volume on the table. Brandon read the title. *Collections of Ancient Spirits* by Orlena Gorbana.

Thea turned to a page she had marked before rotating it to show Brandon the words and images. He frowned. "What's this got to do with anything?"

Thea pointed. "That's the Pale Stranger. I'm sure of it. Well, not him exactly, but the type of creature he is. Nothing else in this book describes it more accurately." Brandon raised a brow that asked if she had spent all day looking through it. In truth, Thea had used a touch of magic to help in her search. The art was an old Japanese style depicting a strange, grotesquely proportioned apparition.

"What we're dealing with is a vengeful spirit the Japanese people call an onryō." Thea pointed out several passages, reciting information she had gleaned earlier in the day. "Such spirits are sometimes called wraiths. Other times, they're simply ghosts. It doesn't matter what they are, only that they're capable of harming living people they consider enemies."

"Or causing natural disasters such as plagues," Brandon added. "You don't think this onryō calling himself the Pale Stranger is Japanese, do you?"

"No, I don't. They can come from all over the world. Onryō is the word the Japanese use for this sort of being." She paused, brows drawing together. "Injuring and killing isn't all they do to their enemies. They can 'snatch' spirits from their dying bodies. Most onryō are depicted as wronged women, as seen here." Again, Thea indicated the grotesque image on the page. "That doesn't necessarily mean the Pale Stranger will look the same. You didn't get a good look at it in that smoke, did you?"

Brandon shook his head. "I'm afraid not."

Thea closed the book and slid it off the table, into her satchel as if leaving it open would direct too much attention their way. "Regardless of what this thing is called officially, the same basic principles exist. We're dealing with a spirit obsessed with vengeance that, when 'fed' properly, can have a hand in natural disasters."

Brandon's face paled further. "Fucking hell." He paused, then asked, "How were these things dealt with in the past?"

"In the East, a man of faith could pin them down by performing a ritual," Thea told him. "In most Japanese tales, it's a Buddhist or a Shinto priest. I've already looked around New Orleans, and the closest thing we've got is a Catholic priest. If we can convince one to help us, we can bind the thing while also saving the captive people. We have to hope they haven't been…used yet."

Killed and drained of life was what Thea didn't say aloud.

Brandon had lost interest in eating by this point, but Thea was inclined to finish her drink. The slight buzz and warmth flowing in her veins somewhat eased the horror of their topic of conversation.

"Let me worry about the man of faith part," Brandon stated, leaning back and crossing his arms as he considered the gravity of their situation. "If this onryō has been using his power to keep the captives alive, the sudden shock of them coming out of his magic could be serious. We need to be ready with medical attention right away." He leaned forward again. "Where do you think the captives are?"

"I don't know for sure. Maybe in the tombs around the

cemetery. I'll need to look around." At the sight of the pull of his brows, she added, "And I'll need Kira's help to do that."

"I'm assuming Kira is that *thing* you have holed away in your apartment." There went Brandon's guard again, right back up. Thea didn't blame him, but she'd have to explain before he made any wild assumptions.

Even though the story is wild, she thought.

Thea lowered her voice further and gave Brandon the quick version of how she had met Kira, first by going to the Lake of Power, then by containing her in a binding box only to be opened a week later after her training. She left out everything about getting possessed.

Brandon's eyes looked like they might bulge from his head. "Are you insane?" he hissed. "Even I know tapping into the Lake of Power alone is a big no-no. Does your coven know about this?"

Thea's face hardened. "No, and they're not going to find out about it if I can prevent it. I'll be Fleeced if they hear about it."

Brandon considered her words, then sighed deeply and shook his head. "Fine. I won't say a word. Not to your coven Mother, at least."

"What about your higher-ups?" Thea asked. "Are you going to tell them your brand new witch liaison has an extra-dimensional entity tagging along?"

Brandon weighed her question. She could see him thinking about what to do. He had to tell someone, even if it was Claire. Yet doing so would mean no more Thea helping them. No more witch liaison tracking down the Pale Stranger. And by God, they needed her, especially now with that thing on the loose. Brandon released a long, controlled breath. "I won't. For now. We'll see if my mind changes after we deal with the onryō."

Thea didn't smile, but relief and gratitude filled her eyes. "I promise it'll be worth it. Besides, we have binding rituals on her. Kira has proven herself trustworthy." *Though she might have strange tastes in men,* Thea added silently. They could deal with that little problem later.

"That doesn't change the fact that you don't know how to handle an entity like this," Brandon reminded her. "According to the rules, I'm at least supposed to report you if not have you banished." He drew a deep breath. "I don't want to do either of those things."

Banished. From more than the coven. AID could have Thea moved anywhere they wanted to. She'd have to go on the run, saying goodbye to the life she'd built in New Orleans. It wasn't much, but goddamn it, it was hers. Brandon must have seen the emotions swimming in her eyes because he added, "Again, we can talk about it after we deal with the onryō. I'll be in bigger trouble if more people get snatched than if I let my new witch liaison keep her pet."

"What about Jax?" Thea asked.

"Jax won't tell anyone. Not until the matter of the Pale Stranger is resolved."

"Because he obeys you?"

"It's not so much because I'm team leader," Brandon clarified. "If anything, Jax is on your side about this."

Thea's eyebrows lifted in surprise. "Really?"

"He must see something in you that reminds you of himself. Probably that whole 'have to do everything on my own' attitude. From what he tells me, he used to be the same. He changed in the Marines."

Thea nodded.

"Now, explain to me how the hell Kira is going to help us."

"Well, for one, she can shapeshift. She's the only one of us who can turn into something small enough to get into the tombs and out again without being noticed. That way, we don't have to open each tomb and coffin and check it. Mia and I will rig up obfuscation charms to help her. Kira will tell us which tombs have captives, and we can rescue them in one fell swoop, hopefully without setting off the ghost bomb situation Whitney was talking about. Or giving him a heart attack."

"Ghosts can't have heart attacks."

"Well, whatever the version of that is for ghosts, Whitney will have it."

Brandon thought over her plan while Thea held her breath. Finally, he nodded. "That might work."

Thea smiled. "You see, Kira isn't only useful and fun. She's important to me in what I'm trying to do with becoming a mage."

"Right," Brandon drawled. "Blowing yourself apart by touching the Lake of Power."

Thea's winning smile did not vanish with his words. "I'm being careful." Her face sobered. "It might not seem like I have a lot to lose, but I do. Kira is part of that now."

Brandon's guard dropped. His face softened. "I get that part at least." He stood when she did. "Thank you for trusting me with this information. It's helping me trust you in return." He dragged a hand through his hair, huffing out a laugh. "Damn it, Claire might have been right about that."

Thea arched a brow. "About what exactly?"

"Never mind. It's not important. I'll get this information to Jax, and we can make a solid plan. I'll hunt around for the right priest."

Thea grabbed her satchel, and they headed out of the café back onto the street. By now, the sun had set, and the street glowed with light pouring from buildings, cars, and street lamps. The cool air on Thea's skin provided the right touch of relief from a hot day.

"I'll keep Kira off the record for now," Brandon reminded Thea before walking across the street to his car. "That all depends on if you can keep the damn thing under control."

CHAPTER TWENTY-ONE

"Although covens work on their own, in the face of dire circumstances, there have been recorded instances where multiple covens come together, or the senior members of covens will gather for the purpose of some great magnitude of magic usage. Though the rumors of sacrifice and darker practices are often associated with these events, they are not necessarily the reason.

"These senior members are referred to as the Arch-Coterie or Sabbat, depending on the level of skill and how many members there are. These gatherings have only happened when the threat of evil is against all witches around the world. Only three instances of this kind have been recorded in the history of covens."

—From The History of Covens and Their Adjacent Societies *by Orlena Gorbana*

Back at her apartment, Thea found Kira fast asleep and a note from Mia telling her she'd gone home for the night but would check in the next day. Thea tried to rest, first by lying on the couch with the TV on, then by climbing into bed. She remained awake all night, tossing and turning. She considered all she and Brandon had talked about, and thoughts of her parents and Ambrosius' books flitted through her mind. Finally, as dawn approached, she got up.

Where are you going? Kira asked, stretching her feline body at the end of the bed.

To pay someone a visit, Thea silently answered as she slipped a hoodie over her head and grabbed her keys. This visit required a long drive.

Can I come with you? Kira asked.

As much as Thea wanted Kira to come along, she couldn't risk bringing her. She answered aloud. "Not this time. Stay here. I'll be back in a few hours."

Thea was halfway to the coven estate when she considered whether she actually wanted to go. *I'm already on my way,* she thought. *Might as well.* She was determined to find out if Mother Folsom knew anything about the Pale Stranger. If so, why the hell wasn't the coven doing anything about it?

One of the things Thea remembered her parents not liking about the coven was they often did not care for the needs of others. This included defenseless humans. Thea gripped the wheel, thinking about the words she'd use to give Mother Folsom a piece of her mind.

When Thea arrived at the estate, the sun had only been up for about an hour. The grounds were quiet, with most of the coven members still inside, some of them not awake for the day. Thea's boots crunched over the gravel drive as she headed to the front door. No one was in the hall, so she went upstairs to Mother Folsom's office. She knocked on the door. No answer came, so she let herself inside. The office was empty, and Thea took her time ambling around, observing the things Mother Folsom had on display.

Behind a glass case was a necklace made of crystals. A conjuring necklace, Thea assumed. One Mother Folsom had for many years but perhaps had not used in a long time. Along one shelf was a row of framed photographs, many so old that the people in them were black and white.

One color image showed a group of witches, a Sabbat Thea's mother had once belonged to. She knew this because she recognized her mother right away. Irene stood on the end between two other young women. She wore a broad smile, her dark curls falling in waves around her shoulders as wild and untamed as Thea usually had her hair. Even in the hazy image, Thea saw the brightness in her mother's eyes.

Standing in the middle of the group was a younger-looking version of Mother Folsom herself. This had been the state of the coven before Thea was born. Before things went to hell for several years, ending with the death of her parents.

The sound of the door opening and a startled noise from someone's lips had Thea turning, wearing a wry smile to greet Mother Folsom. The coven Mother's startled reaction fled, and she frowned. "Theadora. What a surprise."

Thea found she had done a lot of that throughout her life. Surprising people, and not often in ways they liked. "I figured, after you haven't been answering my calls, I'd pay you a visit," she quipped lightly to her superior.

Mother Folsom ignored Thea's comment and came farther into the room, moving to stand behind her desk.

She swept Thea with a sharp gaze, noting the casual outfit the girl had chosen to wear. "AID doesn't give you a proper uniform for your work?"

Thea tried not to snap at Mother Folsom, but her voice wasn't exactly warm when she answered. "I'm not here on behalf of AID. Just because I'm their witch liaison doesn't mean I can't come here on my own business."

Mother Folsom sat behind her desk, already dressed for the day with hair and makeup done to perfection. She folded her hands. "Well then, what business have you come to conduct, Ms. Blackwood?" The formal use of her name took Thea aback. Mother Folsom had never called her Thea, but at least Theadora sounded like they had familiarity with one another. Ms. Blackwood put distance between them. *Fine. Be that way then*, Thea thought.

She doesn't want me around, does she? Thea plopped into the seat opposite the coven Mother. "I've come to ask you about the Pale Stranger. Have you heard of him?"

Mother Folsom's expression changed. First to surprise, then suspicion. "Of course I have. Everyone has. He's a pesky spirit who can't stay in his grave. He roams all over the place but has never done anything beyond waking other spirits and starting fights between ghosts."

"Yet he's been responsible for about a dozen missing persons cases in New Orleans," Thea corrected, her tone cold.

Mother Folsom leaned back, wearing a satisfied smile. "So, you have come to conduct business on behalf of AID? I heard about a little operation that went on in a cemetery. A witch going missing underground, and two men chased by a wraith."

Thea shifted. "I'm here because no matter what AID is doing, the Pale Stranger is up to no good. Any coven that knew about it and hasn't done a damn thing should be ashamed of itself."

Mother Folsom *tsk*ed. "How funny this is. Theadora Blackwood joins AID, thinks she's all that, and suddenly she's lecturing *me* about using magic."

Thea's eyes darkened. "At least I'm trying to help people." If she ever got out of this damn coven, if she ever became a mage like she wanted, she'd use her power to help others. Not sit behind a pretty desk and order witches around to do…what, exactly? Thea wondered. *That's right. Nothing. This coven does fucking nothing.*

Mother Folsom must have read the ire in Thea's eyes because she sighed. "The coven cannot involve itself in such small junctures. That work is for AID and AID alone."

"But people are *dying* or will very soon," Thea argued, her voice rising.

"Then their blood will be on AID's hands. Now, I suppose, yours as well." Mother Folsom gave Thea a smile that made her squirm. "I also happen to know of your efforts to tap into the Lake of Power on your own. After everything that happened with your parents, I would have thought you'd know better."

Thea froze in her seat, but only for half a second. She schooled her features, not wanting to let on that she had *already* tapped into the Lake, let alone brought something from the dimension out with her. It was obviously no use denying her efforts to Mother Folsom. How she knew about it, Thea wasn't quite sure. Higher witches had the ability to find things out in ways a less skilled witch could not. Sometimes, it hit Thea how much more powerful her coven Mother was.

Mother Folsom stood and approached big windows overlooking the estate grounds. "I'm not going to stop you, Theadora, simply because I don't think there is anything I can do. I could have you undergo the Fleecing, and your power would be cut off from you. but..." She turned slowly. "Then I'd have to offer one of my more obedient witches to AID."

Thea felt like she couldn't breathe. She didn't care what Mother Folsom thought about AID or the lake. The words about her parents had rattled her. "What do you mean after everything that happened with my parents?"

Mother Folsom tilted her head, her voice light as she answered. "Don't you know, Theadora? Your parents tried to tap into the Lake of Power without sanction from a coven, without the aid of those who were on their side."

Thea's heart hammered. Why? Her parents wouldn't have done such a thing unless they felt threatened. By who?

Mother Folsom went on. "It's the reason they're—"

Thea cut her off before she could say the word. "I don't want to hear it." Her voice was somewhere between a growl and a snarl, firm enough for Mother Folsom to snap her mouth shut.

A look of regret came over her face. "I'm sorry, Theadora. I know it's still hard for you."

It would always be hard, especially as long as Thea was in the dark about what had truly happened. Her voice shook as she stated, "What about the fire? That's got nothing to do with tapping into the Lake." If her parents had tapped more power than they could handle, it would have left them in torment. The fire had resulted from something else entirely.

Sorrow entered Mother Folsom's eyes. "Oh, Theadora. Don't you see? They were the ones who started it."

Thea felt like there was no more air in the room. Her voice rose, still shaking but angered. "Was it their fault, or were they punished for something?" Tapping into the Lake would have been a punishable offense, but not by death. Fleecing would have been as far as the coven could go. Her heart hammered. *What the hell happened?*

Mother Folsom did not answer, only stared at Thea as if the weight of the world lay on her shoulders. True sadness filled her eyes, but still, Thea could not help feeling the truth had been held from her.

Thea stood. "Fine. I'll leave you to do whatever it is the hell you do here while I fix real problems." She left Mother Folsom's office before the coven Mother uttered another word. She didn't bother to see if anyone was awake and watching her as she marched from the estate house and back to her car.

As she pulled onto the road, she thought, *Find the truth. No matter what it takes.* The Lake of Power, on the other hand? She would prove she was capable by dealing with the Pale Stranger.

Brandon had to force himself to AID headquarters the morning following his conversation with Thea. For one, he had to make an official report of what happened at Lafayette Cemetery and their findings. For another, he couldn't hole up in his apartment and pretend none of it was happening. On the way, he considered how much to tell Claire. He hated lying, especially to his superiors. Especially to someone who had been as generous to him as Claire had.

It won't be a straight-up lie, he told himself. *Only holding back information for a few more days.* It sounded better than dropping a bomb on her like, "Oh yeah, I lost our new witch liaison. But it's okay because her extra-dimensional entity, who may or may not be a demon, was with her and helped her out." He shook the invasive thoughts from his mind as he entered the headquarters parking lot.

Claire was waiting for him when he arrived. "I trust you rested well yesterday? Jax came in last night saying you both needed time at home."

For a second, Brandon wondered if Jax had spilled any beans.

Claire sighed and added, "When I asked Jax to give an official report, he refused, saying that was the job of the 'operation leader.' He's right, of course, but we've been waiting."

"I'm sorry," Brandon told her and meant it. "I was tying up loose ends."

Claire raised a brow in question.

"Thea got the information. I spoke with her last night to hear everything."

Claire motioned for him to take a seat, which he did. Brandon reported what had happened, not bothering to leave out the part where Thea went missing, and they left the operation site without her. Claire was displeased, but the moment she heard Thea's findings, she relented.

"Losing track of the witch liaison this soon into her work is unacceptable, but given how much help the girl has been already, I will let this one go. I won't be so willing next time."

The firmness in her voice made Brandon nod and promise, "It won't happen again." For a fleeting moment, Brandon considered telling Claire about Kira but decided against it. *Only a few more days. Until we find out how that thing can help us with the Pale Stranger.*

"So, what is your plan for dealing with this thing?" Claire asked after jotting down a few notes.

Brandon laid out the plan he and Thea had put together. Claire seemed impressed with how much input Thea had given, and Brandon had accepted. He left out the part where Thea would have an extra-dimensional being turn into something small enough to creep into tombs. "Sounds to me like you and Ms. Blackwood are working together well," Claire noted. "If we ignore the part where she left you and Jax to a wraith, that is."

"She apologized profusely for that."

"Do you think she's genuine?"

"I do. She's still getting her footing." It might take time, but if Thea kept helping them out the way she was now, he'd allow her grace.

"And what sort of man of faith do you have in mind for this plan of yours?" Claire asked. Brandon was glad she didn't need to know the details of how they would get into the closed tombs.

Brandon grinned. "I know the right guy. He doesn't have to hold an official office in a religious order, mind you. Not based on what Thea and her friend Mia said."

Claire raised a brow. "There's another witch involved?"

"A hedge witch. She's Thea's friend."

Claire considered this. "Be careful, Brandon. If AID puts a hedge witch in danger, we could be in hot water." The hedge witches were protected in some cases, especially in recent years, since violence against them from both coven witches and AID agents had been reported.

"I will," he promised.

Claire shook her head in disbelief and chuckled. "This is the part where I'm supposed to trust you, Brandon Cole." She rose, her expression solemn once more. "Don't let me down."

CHAPTER TWENTY-TWO

"I have gone out, a possessed witch,
haunting the black air, braver at night;
dreaming evil, I have done my hitch
over the plain houses, light by light:
lonely thing, twelve-fingered, out of mind.
A woman like that is not a woman, quite.
I have been her kind."

From the poem Her Kind *by Anne Sexton*

"Round two," Thea murmured as she stepped from her car and stared across the street at the wall surrounding Lafayette Cemetery.

"Bit of a run-down place, isn't it?" Mia climbed from the passenger seat, holding Kira in cat form in her arms. Kira dozed, having slept on and off all day in preparation for tonight. Or maybe she was truly taking to her cat form by napping all day and getting the zoomies at night.

Mia looked the same as ever, wearing a long skirt and knit cardigan. When she got nervous about what they were doing, she toyed with the pink crystal hanging around her neck. She looked much different than Thea, who had shown up in her AID tactical gear. Sleek black pants, form-fitting shirt and vest, and an array of weapons Brandon insisted she bring with her.

Thea had finally admitted to never having faced a wraith before. Growing up, she had seen many spirits drifting across the Blackwood family estate at night, but she had never gone out to greet the unfriendly kind. She had only befriended one ghost, a housekeeper who had died centuries earlier.

Thea only wished the Pale Stranger was as welcoming as the ghosts she knew at her old home. She surveyed the exterior of the cemetery like it was the first time she'd been here. "Somehow, the more I look at it, the more rundown it seems."

"You're noticing more about it," Mia suggested. She pointed out cracks in the walls, potholes in the sidewalk and road, and chipped paint on the front gate. She shivered. "Certainly seems like the sort of place ghosts would haunt."

"The sun isn't quite down yet, either. It was dark when I got here last time." Thea gestured toward the horizon where the sun dipped low, glowing red but not yet out of sight. She was supposed to meet Brandon, Jax, and whatever team they brought with them after dusk, but she, Mia, and Kira had come early.

I don't see why I couldn't come as a girl like you two, Kira bemoaned into Thea's mind as their eyes met.

"Don't complain about the fact that you can't shapeshift," Mia spoke up. "We don't need the guys dropping their jaws on the pavement before the mission." The bigger reason was that although Kira could turn herself into a realistic, dazzling woman, she could not hold the form for long. It took too much of her magic and energy. She'd have to build up to it over time. For now, smaller creatures were in her wheelhouse. That was exactly what they needed tonight.

Thea led them to the cemetery entrance, hoping to slip inside and reach the middle before anyone else showed up, especially the spirits that would come out at night. The ghosts would probably not start appearing until close to midnight, giving Kira plenty of time to slip into the tombs in mouse form. The tombs had enough holes and cracks for her to find her way in. That was precisely why they had come early, so Kira could figure out how to shapeshift into something smaller before Brandon and Jax arrived.

Mia shivered as she walked beside Thea, still holding Kira. "I don't like this one bit."

Thea smiled at her. "I'm glad you came all the same."

Brandon and Jax would bring paramedics for when they found the captives. Thea was holding out hope they were still alive. They might also need some magical healing, hence why Thea brought Mia along. That and no one in the world could give Thea better moral support than her best friend. *I'm going to need a lot of that,* Thea thought as they approached the center of the cemetery.

Mia took her spot, watching the area for any weird activity while Thea set Kira on the ground and began to coach her into changing. "Go slow if you need to, a little bit at a time. You've got this."

Kira tried to turn into a mouse but became something halfway between a hamster and a cat. Thea tried not to look away from the deformed animal. "Shapeshifting isn't as pretty as you sometimes make it seem, I guess."

I take that to mean I don't look like a mouse?

Try again.

Another minute later, Thea had to say, *No, not that. You're a cockroach now. Somehow grosser. I don't know where you've seen one of those to know what it looks like.*

I quite like this form, actually. I think it could work.

It would work, but you also might get crushed by someone up here when you come back out.

Kira tried once more and finally changed into mouse form. Now, the trick was staying there and getting used to how she was supposed to move.

Inside each tomb, you're not looking for a spirit. You're looking for human bodies that aren't dead yet. Thea swallowed. *Hopefully.* She imagined the people in there only surviving because a dark spirit was vegetating on their energy. She tried not to shudder. "Run around the cemetery for a while," Thea coaxed Kira. "Get used to it." She watched Kira dart into the shadows, then turned back to Mia. "Anything?"

"Nothing, thank goodness."

Thea further considered her reasons for coming early. No AID agents should be here watching an extra-dimensional entity work. If this went haywire, they could blame Thea, not Brandon. "He doesn't need to lose his job because of me." Thea did not realize she'd spoken her thoughts aloud until Mia eyed her and grinned.

"There you go again, Iz. Caring about people other than yourself."

"I *always* care."

"Most of the time."

They laughed, then a skittering at their feet caught their eye. A white mouse landed on Thea's foot. Normally, she would have yelped, but she knew it was Kira. Slowly, she turned back into a cat, blinking at Thea as she said, *They're here. They're coming.*

Men wearing black tactical gear entered the cemetery from the gate, with Brandon at the front and Jax bringing up the rear. They wore far more armor than they had last time and carried an array of guns loaded with silver and salt pellets.

Thea was glad to have something other than her magic to deal with whatever came at them tonight. She and Kira had been practicing using the Lake of Power, but sometimes, it wouldn't come to Thea. She felt like a dried-up well. *I don't know what's wrong with me,* she'd told Kira. *It's like the connection is wide open sometimes, and other times, it's closed off like a clogged pipe or something.*

Mia had concluded the connection was not strong because Kira and Thea hadn't had much practice together. It didn't help that Kira still had to focus most of her energy on shapeshifting and could not give Thea as much help as she needed. However, Thea hoped everything would go to plan tonight. Brandon approached a few seconds later, brows furrowed with confusion about why she was already there.

"We came to make last-minute preparations," Thea told him with a smile, hoping he caught her drift about Kira without having to say around the other agents that the extra-dimensional was ready to explore the tombs.

She glanced past Brandon to Jax and the others, her brows furrowing. "You said you would take care of the man of the faith. Where is he?"

Brandon beckoned Jax forward, who fished a small wooden cross on a chain around his neck from the inside of his shirt and dangled it in front of Thea's eyes. "Still can't say why I'm needed, though. As a former Marine and AID agent? Sure. As a practicing Methodist who's ordained in the faith, I'm not so sure."

Brandon answered while Thea stood there with her mouth hanging open. "Historically, a man of faith accesses good spiritual energy and can enhance the efforts of the witch or magical person doing the binding. Or something like that. There used to be rituals involved."

"We'll make this as simple as possible," Thea added after she got over her surprise.

Brandon spoke up again. "We've had our team clear the area around here as much as possible." He gestured at Jax. "Soon, we'll see about drawing the Pale Stranger out to try to attack Jax. Maybe the spirit will have something against men of faith."

"A lot of people do," Jax drawled.

Thea continued. "When it does appear, Jax and I will bind it while you—"

"Get into the tombs where the captives are," Brandon finished. "As long as your…little friend marks the right ones."

"Let's find out," Thea replied. She whistled for Kira, and the entity scurried out from under a hedge in mouse form.

Brandon gave the creature a raised brow. "Well, that might actually work."

Thea scooped Kira into her hands and walked to a large piece of stone that led into one of the tombs, helping Kira find a small opening.

"Once you're in there, you should have room to see," Thea instructed.

The mouse squeaked to tell Thea she understood, then skittered into the darkness. Thea watched her go, holding her breath. *Now, we hope for the best.*

The time ticked down. The sun touched the horizon and vanished, leaving the dusk sky a soft pink meeting darkness. "How long do you think this will take?" Brandon asked, checking his watch after twenty minutes.

Thea shrugged. "Couldn't tell you. It's a lot of work for Kira to shift, then find her way back out here." She hoped her nervousness didn't show up in her voice. She was more worried about Kira not being able to find her way out than about the Pale Stranger showing up before they found out which tombs held captives.

Mia waited behind them, twisting her skirt in her hands. Jax, calm as ever, stood beside Brandon with his big arms folded. Finally, when the sky was completely dark, Thea sighed in relief. Kira scampered from the dark opening. She took cat form again, meeting Thea's eyes to tell her *I found them all.*

How many?

Kira answered, and Thea turned to Brandon. "She says

there's thirteen. Do you think you and your team can get them out?"

Brandon nodded. "I'll call them in now."

They had sent Kira into the hole to go unnoticed. Unfortunately, Brandon and his team could not do the same. It helped because Kira could slip into the tombs in her mouse form and see the bodies of those captured. *Are they still alive?* Thea asked the entity.

Yes.

Thea thought of her neighbor, relieved. He'd have one hell of a story to tell, that was for sure.

Mia scooped Kira up, then moved under a large tree to wait. Kira would be close enough for Thea to call on if her magic ran out. She hoped the magic Kira had given her earlier in the day to prepare for this would be enough.

"Showtime," Thea told Brandon and Jax after Brandon's team was in the cemetery. None of them seemed to know about the extra-dimensional entity, though a few cast puzzled glances in Mia's direction, wondering what a hedge witch and her cat were doing here.

Brandon signaled his team to follow him while Thea and Jax watched them go. Thea checked her watch. The spirits would be coming out for the night soon. "Do you think the Pale Stranger will come for us, or should we go looking for him?" Thea asked Jax.

The former Marine scanned the cemetery. "If he's been out tonight snatching, he'll be around. Wouldn't hurt for us to look for him. He might be at the other end where the second gate is."

"We won't go too far," Thea promised. She gestured at Mia and Kira. "Wouldn't want to leave them alone."

Jax nodded in understanding. They wandered past the center of the cemetery through a row of tall headstones so cracked and overgrown with ivy that Thea thought they might crumble any second. "How long has this place been around anyhow?" she wondered out loud.

"A long time," Jax answered. "Almost three hundred years."

"It looks that way. I don't see how anyone would want to be buried here now." Thea pointed out the symbol of a broken flower on several headstones. "That marks the end of life."

"How do you know that?" Jax asked.

Thea swallowed. "Because it's on my parents' headstones. They requested it in writing before they died." Her voice had sobered. Jax fell silent beside her, not because he was uncomfortable about the turn in the conversation but because it felt more respectful not to say anything. He was quiet for a long moment before he added, "I've lost people too. My brother died when I was a teenager, and my wife died giving birth to our son many years ago."

Thea glanced at him. "I'm sorry."

"The child went with her."

Heavy grief hung between them.

Jax gestured at the stones with the broken flower symbols. "For my son, we put a broken rose stem with the flower not yet in full bloom."

Thea felt her heart aching. She could not imagine such sorrow. "How long ago?"

"Ten years." Jax gave her a sad smile. "I do this work for them, you know. I want to help people, no matter who they are." He paused, then stated, "I haven't told many people that. Not even Brandon."

"I won't say a word."

Jax looked like he was about to respond. Instead, he stopped short at a sight a few yards off.

Thea gasped. The being approaching them did not look like the other ghosts or wraiths. He looked as human and tangible as they were. She knew at once the person approaching them was a spirit because he wore the ragged clothes of a poor Irish immigrant. Not only were they dirty and torn, but they looked a few hundred years old. Thea was sure this was the Pale Stranger.

The man came toward them, silent as most spirits were when they moved. He lifted his head, his dark, empty eyes staring at them from under a tattered hat. He raised a filthy hand to tilt it back. Finally, he halted before them, only a few feet away.

Thea and Jax stared. At last, the Pale Stranger chuckled. "I see someone has finally come to visit me. You're too late."

"Who are you?" Thea demanded.

The spirit eyed her and growled. "They call me many names. The Soul Snatcher. The Plague Maker. The White Thief." He had long, ivory fingers perfect for a pickpocket or lock picker. His voice was low and whispery. "The Pale Stranger."

"Who *were* you?" Jax prodded. He gestured at the spirit's ragged clothes. "Before misfortune found you."

"Ah, just a poor man coming from a far-off island in search of a better place. They called this the land of opportunity, but all I found was pain and misery. They did not welcome me because I was Irish. They did not let me have a job because I was not acclimated to Yellow Fever.

"I went and got the illness for myself, hoping I might gain natural immunity. Instead, I died and was cast into a grave with three other corpses. No one knew but the dirty men who'd done it. Those men who ran their factories and didn't give a damn about anyone else. Those men who drank and cheated and whored."

Thea guessed by the weight of his voice that he wasn't only angry for the injustice of not being given a job and buried with three others. Many cruel things had happened to him. *But the people he's snatched don't deserve what he's doing to them. They shouldn't have to pay*, Thea thought.

The Pale Stranger spoke once more in his low, whispery voice. "I am going to make the whole world pay for what was done to me."

"It won't be that easy," Thea responded.

Jax fished the wooden cross from his shirt and held it up toward the Pale Stranger. Thea summoned magic into her palms, orbs of glowing white light. The spirit seemed to understand what they intended to do, but instead of showing fear, he laughed. "You can try to take me, humans, but it won't work. As for your friend who ventures into the darkness...well, he'll have a little surprise waiting for him."

Thea found it hard to breathe. "What are you talking about?"

"I've sent a few of my new friends. Wraiths, I think you call them, to meet the others. After I saw your little mouse friend going in, I knew it would not be long before humans followed."

Shit.

The Pale Stranger laughed again. "If my wraiths don't kill them first, the darkness and lack of air will."

Jax moved fast as lightning, mostly because he didn't want to hear the damn thing talk anymore. He drew his pistol, aimed, and fired. Before it hit the Pale Stranger, the creature vanished into the night air.

CHAPTER TWENTY-THREE

*"I have walked a great while over the snow,
And I am not tall nor strong.
My clothes are wet, and my teeth are set,
And the way was hard and long.
I have wandered over the fruitful earth,
But I never came here before.
Oh, lift me over the threshold, and let me
    in at the door!"*

—*From the poem* The Witch *by Mary
    Elizabeth Coleridge*

Damn, it was dark in here. The light on Brandon's helmet was bright, yet it didn't seem to penetrate the darkness in the first tomb. This was a deep, long-standing darkness. No one had been down here in...well, centuries. Not anyone alive and conscious, anyway. They had gotten into the tomb from the back, where parts of the stone were so crumbled they could break it apart.

Brandon hated venturing into the resting place of long-dead individuals, but it wasn't like they were here anyway. The Pale Stranger had taken their bodies elsewhere, replacing them with his captives.

He tried not to shiver. It was cold in here as well as dark. The shallow breathing of his team behind him kept him company, and the lights on their helmets danced along the walls. This first tomb was huge, and several coffins lay inside. It must have once belonged to a family.

"I see them, sir," came a voice. One of the junior AID agents had spotted a row of stone coffins along a wall, sealed shut with age. Cracks along the coffins showed how long they had been down here. At least a century, maybe longer. Brandon stopped short, casting his light over the room. All was still and unbothered. He wondered if the people inside the coffins knew what had happened to them. Or had they been unconscious since getting snatched?

He turned to his men. "Open these coffins. After you have the person out, get them on a stretcher and out of here." Brandon hoped he wouldn't have to explain how he knew which coffins they had to open.

The men fanned out, searching stone coffin after stone coffin. Voices came back to Brandon. "One here, sir." "Another over here." "Found one over here." They worked on removing the stone lids. They were heavy and had not been moved by human hands in a long time, not since their original dead were placed inside.

Brandon hoped Thea and Jax were far from these tombs in another part of the cemetery, doing what they needed to. "Move quickly," he reminded the men. The sooner they got out of here, the better, no matter what Thea and Jax were up to.

Brandon headed for a narrow doorway leading into another part of the tomb. Thirteen coffins, Kira had said. It made sense the Pale Stranger put them all in one place. He hoped they wouldn't have to stay down here long.

This hope was banished from his thoughts when a cry of alarm from one of his agents rang out behind him, followed by a horrendous shrieking that could only belong to a wraith. He whirled to see two oversized skeletal figures, glowing white and wearing loose strands of tattered clothing, headed directly for his men.

"Shit." He drew both pistols, aimed, and fired without a second thought, careful to avoid hitting his men.

The tomb descended into chaos. While some men were busy opening coffins, others had turned to face the wraiths. The spirits went down quickly, for they did not have enough room to avoid the silver and salt pellets that blasted them apart on contact.

It would have been fine if not for the other wraiths coming through the walls. So many of them. A dozen by the time Brandon gathered his wits.

He'd have to fight off every last one of them while the others freed the captives from the coffins and got them out of here without the wraiths dragging them away. A cry rang out from another agent. Brandon turned to see a wraith pulling his agent into a coffin, intent on shutting him inside, smothering him. "Stop!" he shouted, firing his pistol. The wraith went down as another grabbed Brandon's shirt collar and yanked him back.

This would not be like fighting people, where he could

grapple, punch, and get injured. He swung his arm back, firing into the wraith's face. The silver and salt burst apart the grotesque shape of the eyes, nose, and mouth. Another agent blew the head off another phantom, and its headless form lunged toward a third. The spirits collided. The headless one went down. The other met the end of an agent's blade imbued with salt and silver.

Brandon counted quickly. Five of his men had joined the fight. At least ten more wraiths had come through the walls. The others were prying the lids off the coffins.

His heart thundered. The wraiths were there to slow them down. Kill them if they could. All to give the Pale Stranger more time. "Hurry!" Brandon shouted to the men rescuing the captives as he drew a salt-imbued blade and spun, sinking it into one wraith, then another. The crunching, slicing, and slashing sounds of blades could not be heard over the wraiths' shrieks. Their sounds were the worst of all. Brandon's ears rang. He knew he'd be hearing those screams in his sleep for months after this was over.

Before he understood what was happening, five wraiths slipped through the stone wall, coming directly at him. He was about to be overrun. Overwhelmed. He couldn't fend them all off at once.

Another shrieking cry joined them, and a horse of blue flame galloped down the tunnel Brandon had peered into only a few minutes before. Riding atop it was the Lancer, and with him, another figure he recognized. *That must be Whitney.*

"I can see you now that you're underground!" the groundskeeper shouted. Brandon realized the Lancer was on their side now. The horse-riding wraith cut the others apart with his lance, swinging and screeching with rage. How Whitney had gotten the Lancer to come to them, Brandon did not know. Perhaps the Lancer was pissed off with the Pale Stranger for coming into his territory. *Fine with me,* he thought.

Whitney leaped down from the horse, wielding a shovel that he swung back and forth, sending wraiths back into the walls from which they had come.

Thea stood still as a statue for a beat before she exclaimed, "Where the hell did he go?"

"I don't know, but we've got trouble coming for us," Jax growled.

Thea was about to snort and say, "No shit," but then she saw what Jax was referring to. The six or seven wraiths emerging from the ground a few hundred feet from them.

"Shit."

They were tall, skeletal figures, almost like trees, with grotesque shapes and dark, empty eyes of swirling blackness. Each wielded a heavy blade of searing blue fire. Jax didn't waste any time. He leaped toward them, shotgun out and firing. Silver and salt pellets flew. While a few wraiths fell before they could step more than a few feet toward them, more were emerging from the ground, the piercing sounds of their screams filling the air.

Thea summoned an orb of blazing magic and tossed it toward Jax, turning it into a bubble of shielding light before it could harm him. A wraith lashed out with its fiery sword, hitting Jax's shield but not breaking through.

Thea felt the hit in her magic, her blood. It sang with energy. She summoned a white-hot shield for herself, encasing her body in its protection before leaping forward. Pistols out, she fired one shot after another. The silver and salt exploded the wraiths, sending their swords to the ground, where they melted into the earth.

The spirits' decrepit appearance told her they might be people who had also died of yellow fever all those years ago and were tossed into the ground as if they were nothing. Part of Thea could not stand the thought of fighting them. *It doesn't matter,* she reminded herself. *It's not like they're alive anyway.*

Jax seemed to have no inhibitions. He swung and spun, never missing his shots. After his shotgun was empty and seven wraiths lay scattered on the ground, their pale, distorted limbs fading, he unsheathed twin blades and cut through more like water.

Thea strode forward, her body quick and strong, taking one out after another. She was slower than Jax, but had an equivalent ability to duck, dodge, and strike. She went through the motions Jax had taught her, pretending this was merely another training lesson. The magic Kira had helped her tap into blazed white and bright in her body. Her skin began to glow with it. *Slow down,* she told herself. *If I use too much of it, I blow myself up.*

Though she did not slow her movements, she reduced the flow of her magic, giving a little here and there to her weapons. As they struck, sliced, or slashed into her attackers, they seared the wraiths, who went down. A second strike to each made sure they would not get up again. After her pistols were empty, the blades in her hands felt like extensions of her arms. It was as though her magic and blood pumped into the knives, too.

Jax whirled, dancing more than fighting. He became a blur to Thea as she continued to fight. Bodies fell around them until they were both panting hard for breath.

A low laugh skittered across the ground and reached them. Thea's blood ran cold at the sound of that laugh. "I see you've done well bringing down my distractions, but there are so many more where they came from."

Thea gasped. Several more wraiths lifted from the ground in a mass of milky white, translucent light. More than several, actually. Closer to twenty, maybe fifty. "Holy fucking shit," she gasped. How long would this go on for? Did the Pale Stranger have this small army here with him all along, or had he simply turned the spirits who already lived here to his will?

She didn't have another second to consider the possibilities.

A cold hand clasped around her neck with a grip hard as iron. A colder breath brushed her ear as the Pale Stranger spoke. "I have you now, little witch. You are what I need to come back with a cold, hard vengeance. I hadn't counted on someone with magic being able to help me. Yet, just as I hoped, you've come to me."

The groundskeeper of Lafayette Cemetery was more badass than Brandon could have ever guessed. Who knew a ghost with a shovel could be so deadly?

Well, maybe deadly wasn't the word since the creatures Whitney struck down were already unalive. Brandon thought about this for half a second before he went to the men opening the coffins, leaving the five fighting to assist Whitney and the Lancer. With the fiery blue horse and its two riders, the tide had turned in their favor. Thank God, since they were finally getting the coffins open and people onto stretchers. He stopped short in horror at the sight of them. Their skin was pale, deadly white or deep blue.

"Get them aboveground now!" he called out. "Get them to the EMTs!"

The men moved quickly, now only having to avoid the falling wraith bodies instead of moving attackers. Brandon counted ten bodies and ten open, empty coffins. This meant three more were farther in. He signaled for a few men to follow. "This way!" He delved deeper into the darkness, leaving the furious sounds of the Lancer finishing off the unwelcome wraiths behind.

Finally, more coffins came into sight. Three more. Kira had counted right. Not for the first time, Brandon was glad Thea had brought her along.

It turned out trusting Theadora Blackwood had been the right move. He hoped she was pulling through at the other end of the cemetery.

Thea did not take any time to think. The Pale Stranger had her by the back of the neck, which was only slightly better than having her by the throat. She sure as hell wasn't going to let him drag her underground. Jax might have noticed.

She wasn't sure. He lunged toward the wraiths with a fortitude she wished she had time to admire.

Thea lifted her knife and struck back into the center of the Pale Stranger. He loosened his grip on her neck, staggering back a step, but he did not explode. *Shit. The salt must have worn off.*

She had time to whirl, slinging her magic like a net over the creature. "Jax!" she shouted. The grunts and commotion of his fight with the wraiths joined the horrendous screams that filled the air.

Thea used her magic to pin the Pale Stranger to the ground. The strain was enormous, and she wasn't sure she could keep him down for long. Not without her magic bursting out and consuming her whole.

It glowed bright and white, almost searing inside her. Thea ground her teeth together, fighting through the pain. Perhaps she had taken too much power from the Lake. It began to cloud her mind, her vision. *For fuck's sake, work with me here!* she commanded her magic.

The Pale Stranger thrashed, screaming. "You can't keep me below! You can't banish me until my work is done!" His screams were awful, more than the strain of Thea's magic in her body.

"Jax!" she cried again.

The wraiths continued to fall behind her, heavy thuds following terrible screams. Finally, he was at her side, panting heavily. He bent beside the Pale Stranger, a knife out and against his throat. The salt sang against the magical energy radiating off the dark spirit. "Say goodbye to the places you haunt, you old Irish bastard."

Thea sensed more spirits coming at them from behind.

If she could bind the Pale Stranger and get rid of him, they would vanish. Or so she hoped. This ordeal was stealing the last of her magic. She'd be a dried-up well without a drop left when she was done.

Thea released a strained cry and pushed the rest of her light into the bindings. The Pale Stranger arched, screaming as her magic cut into his flesh, guided by Jax's voice. Thea hit him with one more blast, wishing her coven was here to see her working as a lone witch.

Then, he was gone.

CHAPTER TWENTY-FOUR

"Of the thirteen regions of AID offices around the country, the NOLA office is known to have the most work on its hands given the exorbitant number of magical practitioners in the area. Many surveys have shown the New Orleans area has more practitioners than any other region due to its high number of hedge witches—that is, magical practitioners who do not belong to a coven.

"Though most AID offices do not consider hedge witches a threat, crime rates among magic users are rampant in this area due to the high number of former coven members converting to the mage lifestyle. The coven numbers are lesser but still on par with numbers around the country. Though most of the other districts are larger in size, the population of magic users has increased over the years in the NOLA area."

—From an online article detailing the offices of AID across the United States by journalist Brock Stanton

"Don't call me crazy, but I might be able to do more than one month with AID," Thea announced from where she lay on her green sofa, surrounded by chocolate bar wrappers.

Mia poked her head into the living room from the kitchen, her brows arched. "Theadora Blackwood, notorious for her obsession with becoming a witch mage, wants to stay with the organization that hunts down and imprisons witch mages? You might be a tad crazy."

Kira, in cat form, lifted her head from where she sat at the end of the sofa, curled at Thea's feet. Thea sat up. "They don't hunt down and imprison witch mages, per se. Only criminals."

"I can tell you a few cases where the captives were innocent."

Mia was right.

"All the more reason for me to stay with them," Thea added. "Someone has to be on the inside making sure those boys behave themselves."

This earned her a small smile. It had been three days since their night in the cemetery, and both were still exhausted. Thea from using every ounce of her magic to bind and send away the Pale Stranger and Mia from helping to heal the thirteen captives brought from the tomb. All were on the mend now, though some were recovering slower than others. Thea's neighbor, for instance, would not be returning home for a few weeks.

Thea liked that Mia had been around for several reasons. The moral support had been nice, but Mia's aid meant higher-ups at AID would hear about a talented hedge witch who had helped save the day. Thea guessed it wouldn't be Mia's last time to shine, either.

"Sooo," Mia drawled as she entered the living room with a cup of tea cradled between her palms. "Does this mean you're going to work with AID for the full thirty-six months?"

"I think it's the best option. Brandon and Jax will be better to work with than anyone in my coven."

She hoped Mother Folsom heard what she'd done. Accessed the Lake of Power and used it to defeat a vengeful wraith, all while not blowing herself apart or putting herself into spiritual torment for the rest of her life. Still, Thea thought about what the coven Mother said about her parents. It lurked in the back of her mind, haunting her. She banished the thoughts, not ready to talk about it, even with Mia.

Her friend sat beside Thea on the couch, tucking her knees to her chin. Reality TV played in the background. "You might be right about that," Mia commented at last. "Thirty-six months is a long time. You'll be busy, assuming you have missions all the time."

Thea squeezed Mia's arm. "But I will always make time for the two ladies who mean the most to me." The cat glanced at her. "Yes, that means you too, Kira. We're roomies now."

"You'll have to come up with a story for her when she starts turning into a human on a regular basis," Mia remarked.

Thea nodded. "I'll tell everyone she's my insanely hot cousin from...somewhere."

"Anywhere that isn't an extra-dimensional reality."

Kira met Thea's gaze and, through silent communication, told her she was quite pleased with the things they were saying.

Mia brought the subject back to AID. "What happens after the three years are up?"

Thea chuckled. "You know I don't think that far in advance, Mia. I have to make sure AID keeps me alive first."

Mia smiled. "You might kill Brandon by stressing him out."

Thea's eyes glittered, but that went away when she realized she was out of chocolate. She moaned. "I'll have to get more candy here soon."

"All you have eaten for two straight days is chocolate!" Mia exclaimed.

Thea gave her a wan smile. "That must be why my stomach hurts."

"No shit. You need a proper meal. I'll make you some —"

Thea's ringing phone cut Mia off.

Thea sighed. "AID calls. They must need my help if they're calling me on a Saturday evening."

"Brandon?" Mia asked.

"Jax, actually." She answered in a sing-song voice. "Hello?"

"Thea, it's Jax."

"I know that."

"Do you look as grumpy as you sound right now?" Jax lowered his voice. "Come over to Brandon's apartment. He's...partying. Well, his version of partying."

Thea's brow rose. Mia gave her a questioning look. Thea asked, "What's that supposed to mean?" Jax didn't respond right away because someone in the background started shouting.

"It's the TV."

"The TV is shouting?"

"No, Brandon is shouting at the TV. Something about a draft. I forgot the man is from Pittsburgh. Something to do with that."

Thea chuckled. "I've had one too many Tinder dates with guys who are wayyy too into football. I think I'll pass."

Jax sighed. "Look, we're a team now, right?"

"Right?" Thea wasn't sure where this was going.

"If I have to suffer through this, so do you. We're Brandon's only real friends. The ones who live away from his home, that is."

Thea sighed. "Fine. Send me the address." Her phone dinged immediately after, as if Jax already had it typed in.

"Thanks, kid." He hung up, and Thea laughed. She had apologized to Jax for the first incident at Lafayette after the second incident was over and included a big thank you for saving her ass. The least she could do was save him from enduring a football draft alone.

"Going out tonight?" Mia questioned.

"Apparently." Thea stood. "My first social engagement in a while that has nothing to do with mage business. You should come along."

Mia waved a dismissive hand. "I'm going to a poetry reading tonight, but I'll see you in a few days." She stood to gather her things, then gave Thea a tight hug goodbye. "Have fun with the boys." She grinned. "Text me when you get home later so I know you've survived them."

After Mia left and the apartment felt empty and cold

without her, Thea got ready. She changed out of her pajamas, finding she had melted chocolate on one of her sleeves. A quick dash of makeup and brushing her hair, and she was ready.

Kira hopped down from the sofa, purring loudly.

"Fine," Thea told her. "You can come with me as long as you promise to stay in cat form the whole time we're out."

I'll behave like an angel, Kira replied.

Thea chuckled as she scooped her up. *Funny because a lot of people seem to think your kind are demons. They would be wrong, wouldn't they?* She smiled more to herself than to Kira. *People have been wrong about me a lot, too.*

Kira snuggled into her and purred in response.

When someone knocked at the door, Brandon turned to glare at Jax. "Who did you invite over?"

Jax shrugged, playing dumb, but he didn't offer a verbal denial. Brandon went to the door and opened it quickly. Then he stopped short at the sight of Thea standing in the hall, dressed in flared black jeans and a short-sleeved flannel top. The grin she wore and the cat in her arms paused him the most. "H-hi, Thea." He raked a hand through his hair, suddenly embarrassed she was seeing him in his head-to-toe Pittsburgh Steelers fan gear.

She'd never seen him in anything but AID uniforms except those two times they ate out. Thea looked him over, one dark brow arching and a small smile curving her lips. "I can see now why Jax called me to come and save his ass."

Brandon flushed and glanced back into his apartment

at Jax, who shrugged again. He gave the older man a look. *I'll deal with you later.* His apartment's appearance further embarrassed him. It wasn't exactly dirty. He always kept it clean. However, it wasn't in the sort of condition he wanted when having a lady over. Two ladies, he corrected himself, glancing at Kira the cat once more.

"Well?" Thea prompted. "Are you going to let us in or what?"

"Y-yes, sorry. I wasn't expecting you." Brandon opened the door wider, and Kira hopped down from Thea's arms, going to explore the apartment as if it were her home. Brandon watched her nervously for half a second before closing the door. He ushered Thea into the living room, where Jax occupied a couch with an open bag of salt and vinegar chips on his lap. Several beer cans lay open and emptied.

Thea grinned. "You wouldn't happen to have wine here, would you?"

Brandon shook his head, flushing further. "I'm sorry. Usually, I—"

"That's all right. I brought my own just in case." Thea toted her stupidly large satchel. She reached in and withdrew a full bottle of white wine.

Brandon cleared his throat. "Let me get you a glass and ice for that."

She trailed him into the kitchen. Brandon busied himself with finding a glass. He didn't have wine glasses, so he settled on a mason jar. He glanced into the living room to find Kira curling up beside Jax. The older man gave the cat a rueful glance, but when the animal purred and rubbed her head on his knee, he smiled. By the time Brandon and

Thea returned, Jax had taken to scratching Kira behind the ears and petting her glossy fur.

Brandon wondered how that would look if Kira took the shape of a woman and not a cat. He banished the thought. *Let's not make things weirder than they already are.*

To his relief, Thea made herself at home, sitting between Jax and Brandon like they were her best friends and she had been coming here for years. Brandon redirected his attention to the draft on the TV. "Here," Thea commented after several minutes. "You look like you need something to help you relax."

"It's just that this draft is really important. We get the seventh pick this year, and…" Brandon trailed off as he watched Jax and Thea share a look. Thea fished something out of her bag and handed it to him. It was a plastic sack of those glazed pecans he'd eaten from Laura's Candies. Truthfully, he'd been craving them since that night. He thanked her, then started munching.

"I'm sure you boys don't want to talk about work tonight, but I came over here to tell you something," Thea remarked after a while longer.

She smiled when she had their attention. "I've decided, when my one-month trial is up, which is in…err, two days, I'd like to stay with AID. I'll do the thirty-five months."

Jax's and Brandon's faces broke into smiles. "I'm glad to hear that, kid." Jax thumped her on the back.

Brandon grinned, glanced at his pecans, and inquired, "Will you be getting me more of these?"

Thea swatted his arm, laughing.

Jax grew serious. "We have to shape up more. Act like a

team. Things worked out last time, but we've got kinks to work out."

Thea put her arms around both of them. "All in good time. I think, eventually, we'll be able to do incredible stuff."

Brandon met Jax's gaze and felt his chest glowing. He hadn't expected this. If anything, he thought Thea might decide to hell with AID forever after what she had to do with the Pale Stranger. They still had a ton of unanswered questions. They didn't know how a spirit like the Pale Stranger had been capable of making existing plagues more severe. They had bound him and sent him away without questioning him. More spirits like him could exist. It might not be the last time they dealt with such a creature.

As for Thea, her reaction to the ordeal had been the opposite of what he expected.

Maybe Michelle Folsom wanted to get rid of Thea because she found her unpredictable and impulsive. Whatever spirit made Thea like that had been exactly what they needed for AID. Excitement raced in his veins. He'd have good news for Claire on Monday. He would keep working with Thea and Jax. Maybe the higher-ups would let him expand their team.

He told himself to think about it later. Brandon sank back into the sofa and nudged Thea with his elbow. "You've surprised me, Theadora Blackwood. More than you will ever know."

She flashed him a charming, white smile. "I tend to surprise a lot of people. Just you wait. There's a lot more where that came from."

Brandon wasn't sure what that meant. It made him a bit nervous, but also…

Thea might turn my life around and get me back on track, he thought. He had a feeling, deep down, that he might do the same for her.

THE STORY CONTINUES

The story continues with book two, *The Witch-Mage Awakens*, available at Amazon.

Claim your copy today!

NOTE FROM ISABEL

NOVEMBER 20, 2023

Thank you for taking a chance on the first book of my new series! For those who didn't catch my last series, *The Magic Academy of Paris*, I have included a bit about me below. For those who read my previous author notes, you can skip that part.

I was born in York and grew up in England. I lived with my maternal aunt and uncle while I was in uni (that's college to my American readers!). Being with them for more than an odd week here and there in the summer made me connect deeply with my Scottish side, and I realized that Scotland was the home of my heart.

I miss wandering the Yorkshire Moors, but the Highlands more than make up for not getting back to York as much as I should! Currently, I live in a wee Borders town with my schnoodle (schnauzer-poodle) Emma. I write to the music of the seagulls since I live right on the harbour in a homely flat by the sea. I quite love my town. It's peaceful and hectic by turns. I have a quiet life here with Emma unless the American contingent is in town. Renée Jagger,

NOTE FROM ISABEL

the LMBPN author who brought me on board, often visits, and then we go on adventures. At those times, life is not quiet.

I almost visited the States and would have discovered cheesecake there!

I almost went over to visit Renée this month when our mutual friend Nat, who lives in my town, did, but I had finishing touches to put on this series, so I couldn't wag (play hooky for the Yanks). Kelly O from LMBPN also visited her. While they were there, Renée and her American friends cooked up an early Thanksgiving dinner, and Nat raved about the Basque cheesecake Renée made. If you haven't tried it, you'll fancy it if you like cream cheese at all.

In the UK, "cheesecake" is whipped cream cheese (sometimes flavored with chocolate or caramel) spread on a biscuit base, with chopped fruit on top. I have discovered that Yanks bake the cream cheese in a batter with eggs and other flavorings. I had to try it, so I looked up the recipe for the Basque version, went to Marks and Sparks to get the proper ingredients, and spent the afternoon baking.

By heck! It is an entirely different experience! I consulted with a chef friend, and Jai was surprised that I had never had a baked version. Apparently, the New York variety of American cheesecake is most popular over here. I'm not sure how I missed it, but I will be on the lookout from now on. Maybe I can get the wonderful lady at our local coffee haven to make some, so I don't always have to cook it (and eat it!) myself. Renée suggested that I try something called Philadelphia cheesecake with lemon zest and sour cream baked on top.

That's next. Stay tuned.

What else is happening?

It's cold and rainy. That's not new. It's autumn in the northern part of the United Kingdom. We did see the Northern Lights for a few days earlier this month, which is somehow becoming more common. I was up one night when the clouds cleared, and Emma and I wandered down to the beach to see them. They were stunning!

I hope you enjoyed meeting Thea and some of the members of the coven as much as I enjoyed telling the first part of their story. If you have a moment, leaving a review would be very helpful for me (as it is for any writer).

I always have to thank LMBPN's staff for making my journey to publication as painless as they could. From the beta team who suggested improvements to the series to Kelly O (who does everything) to the editor who smoothed my prose to the just-in-time team who caught last-minute errors, it has been a joy working with you!

I look forward to catching up with you in the next book.

Izzie Campbell

BOOKS FROM ISABEL

The Chronicles of the WitchBorn
(with Michael Anderle)
The First Witch-Mage (Book 1)
The Witch-Mage Awakens (Book 2)

Le Paris Magic Académie
(with Michael Anderle)
The Forbidden Incantations (Book 1)
The Treacherous Alchemy (Book 2)
The Cursed Enchantments (Book 3)
The Perilous Secrets (Book 4)
The Sinister Onslaught (Book 5)
A Resilient Requiem (Book 6)

BOOKS BY MICHAEL ANDERLE

Sign up for the LMBPN email list to be notified of new releases and special deals!

https://lmbpn.com/email/

For a complete list of books by Michael Anderle, please visit:

www.lmbpn.com/ma-books/

CONNECT WITH THE AUTHORS

Connect with Isabel Campbell

Facebook: https://www.facebook.com/IsabelCampbell.author

Website: http://isabelcampbellauthor.com/

Connect with Michael Anderle

Website: http://lmbpn.com

Email List: https://michael.beehiiv.com/

https://www.facebook.com/LMBPNPublishing

https://twitter.com/MichaelAnderle

https://www.instagram.com/lmbpn_publishing/

https://www.bookbub.com/authors/michael-anderle

www.ingramcontent.com/pod-product-compliance
Lightning Source LLC
LaVergne TN
LVHW091717070526
838199LV00050B/2437